A Long Way
to Fall

What Reviewers Say About Elle Spencer's Work

Give In to Me

"As always, Spencer writes great banter. It's natural. It's not so perfect where you think, "Nobody is that witty all the time." …Spencer nails the locales, the beach vibe, and the behind-the-scenes movie drama Southern California is known for. The entire atmosphere of the book feels right which in turn helps make Whitney and Gabriela feel authentic. There's an easiness to this romance that left me content and gratified."—*Lesbian Review*

The Holiday Treatment

"If you are looking for the perfect Christmas read, *The Holiday Treatment* should be top of your list for Santa. Light-hearted, laugh-out-loud funny with all the right ingredients for a perfect Christmas rom-com, it would make the ideal screenplay for a Netflix special. …It's well written, well-paced and brings welcome relief after a difficult year. Perfect reading for the holiday season and a great stocking filler for your friends."—*Curve Magazine*

"The whole book is funny. Holly our main character is a hot mess. She is adorable, witty, and keeps you in stitches. Meredith is 100 percent taken with her and the chemistry is palatable. The push-pull of their love story keeps you engaged the whole time. At times it is so sweet and the other times, well it is super sexy. Great read, highly recommend. If you need a book to escape, this is it. You will love this adorable read that gives you a ton of fun."—*Romantic Reader Blog*

30 Dates in 30 Days

"Spencer is adept at dropping an emotional bombshell at just the right time for maximum impact. She adds her own brand of flair, making the romance formula feel new and fresh."
—*Lesbian Review*

"I'm an Elle Spencer fan. I want to say that this was surprisingly good, but I guess I shouldn't really be that surprised. She generally delivers on everything I love about reading romance. Feelings, chemistry, conflict, angst, tears, and happiness. The characters were likable. Fun situations. Great chemistry. A slow burn romance that satisfies in the end."—*Bookvark*

"As usual with Spencer, the characters are wonderfully layered and flawed, [and] the chemistry is out of this world..."—*Jude in the Stars*

"Spencer imbues the story with some great humour and witty banter that brings the characters to life and the romance works wonderfully. I really enjoyed this one—it hit all the right notes for me and left me with a bit of an aw, shucks smile on my face when I finished."—*C-Spot Reviews*

Private Equity—*Novella in* Hot Ice

"This story had a lot of heart and quite a bit of depth for so little time. This was the strongest among the three novellas."—*Bookvark*

The Road to Madison

"The story had me hooked from its powerful opening scene, and it only got better and better. I feel like Spencer tailored this book just for me. For anyone who has read my reviews, it's no secret that I love romances that include lots of angst and *The Road to Madison* hit the bull's-eye."—*Lesbian Review*

"Elle Spencer is fast becoming one of my favourite authors. She transports me into the story and I feel like I'm living vicariously through the characters."—*Les Rêveur*

Unforgettable

"Across both novellas, Elle Spencer delivers four distinct, compelling leads, as well as interesting supporting casts that round out their stories. If you like angsty romances, this is the book for you! Both stories pack a punch, with so much "will they or won't they" that I kind of wondered how they'd turn out (yes, even though it's marketed as romance!)"—*Lesbian Review*

"I was stunned at how Elle Spencer manages to make the reader feel so much and we end up really caring for the women in her novels. ...This book is perfect for those times you want to wallow in romance, intense feelings and love. Elle Spencer does it so well."—*Kitty Kat's Book Review Blog*

Casting Lacey

"This is a very good debut novel that combines the fake girlfriend trope with celebrity lifestyle. ...The characters are well portrayed

and have off the charts chemistry. The story is full of humour, wit and saucy dialogues but also has angst and drama. I think that the book is at its best in the humorous parts which are really well written. ...An entertaining and enjoyable read."
—*Lez Review Books*

"This is the romance I've been recommending to everyone and her mother since I read it, because it's basically everything I've been dying to find in an f/f romance—funny voices I click with, off-the-charts chemistry, a later-in-life coming out, and a host of fun tropes from fake dating to costars."—*Frolic*

"In *Casting Lacey*, Elle Spencer gives us a hilarious new take on a classic storyline, complete with nosy mothers, fawning assistants, and two beautiful actresses who might learn about true love. If they don't kill each other first."—*BlackstoneLibrary.com*

By the Author

Casting Lacey

Unforgettable

The Road to Madison

30 Dates in 30 Days

Waiting for You

The Holiday Treatment

Give in to Me

A Long Way to Fall

A LONG WAY
TO FALL

by

Elle Spencer

2022

Credits
Editor: Barbara Ann Wright
Production Design: Susan Ramundo
Cover Design By Tammy Seidick

Acknowledgments

Huge thanks as always to Rad, Sandy, and everyone at Bold Strokes Books who does the behind-the-scenes heavy lifting so well and makes my author life so easy. A special thanks for all you've done during these challenging times to virtually keep us authors and our books in front of readers.

To my editor and friend, Barbara Ann Wright, thank you for once again getting me, and my writing, and for keeping me laughing during edits. I wouldn't want to do it without you.

Thanks to my other BSB friends, who I haven't seen for far too long, for the support and laughs from afar: Carsen, Kris, Melissa, Georgia, Ruth. Can't wait to see you in person again.

Thanks to the "Poodles" for making Covid isolation more bearable. Also, FU for never reading my books, haha!

To my BFF…you are a BFD! How did I get so lucky? When I snap, you'll be second to last to go. #rideordieuntilisnap

To my incredible wife, Nikki…I still swoon every day. Multiple times a day. In fact, just call me Swoony McSwoonerson. You and me, baby. Forevs.

Last, but never least, thank you to the readers who continue to read my books. I appreciate every comment, review and email. Hope you enjoy Bridget and Kennedy's story.

Dedication

This one is for Sue and Jerry (who is much more charming than the "Jerry" in this book). Thank you, for all of the love and support.

Chapter One

*C*lunk. *Clunk. Clunk.* The sounds of early morning skiers trudging awkwardly down the hallway in their heavy ski boots crept under Bridget's door.

Normally, she'd be on the slopes with them for the first hour, then hard at work the rest of the day in the lodge. Especially after the kind of snowstorm they fondly referred to as an "overnight dump" had added six inches of fresh powder to what was already a decent snowpack for early December. There was nothing quite like being the first one to carve a path through fresh snow, but being a Friday, she'd opted to rest up for what was sure to be a busy weekend. There would be no complaining, though, since a heavy snowstorm was what the entire resort had been praying for. A deep snowpack meant that the lodge's clientele wouldn't go elsewhere to ski during the Christmas break, which was only a few weeks away. The last thing Bridget needed was a half-empty lodge during what should be their busiest time of year.

She opened the curtains and sat back in her chair so she wouldn't be seen while she sipped coffee in her thermal underwear. From that window, she could see everything going on in front of the lodge, not that much was happening just yet. It was barely seven a.m.

That early, the real action happened at the back of the ski-in, ski-out lodge. Her employees would be busy helping guests with their gear, serving hot cocoa or a cup of their famous dark roast. They spent more time than they probably wanted to looking out for underdressed skiers. Bridget would never understand how someone could show up on one of Utah's biting-cold days thinking they could navigate the slopes without a jacket. The staff would try to convince them to add a few more layers, and if they wanted to lose those layers once the sun came out, the staff would be there to take their coats and return them to their rooms so they didn't have to interrupt their day on the slopes. Happy skiers spent more money, ate more food, and gave better tips, so if the staff could keep them from getting frostbite, it was good for everyone.

Of course, no amount of staff attention could help the person—and there had been more than one—who insisted on skiing in a swimsuit. As one particularly memorable guest put it, "Hypothermia is a small price to pay for a viral post." The entire staff had bets on how long TikTok Tiffany would last in her skikini. When she came skulking back about forty-five seconds later, the schadenfreude was palpable. She spent the rest of the weekend après skiing without actually skiing. Bridget suspected that particular TikTokking guest had influenced exactly no one.

Fortunately, the majority of their guests were there to ski. And then ski again. Sure, they were well-off and sometimes had unreasonably high expectations. *Oh, you'd like fresh orchids delivered daily? At the top of a mountain in January? Let me get right on that.* But, hey, at least they knew how the zipper on their two-thousand-dollar Gucci ski jacket worked.

Bridget chalked her cynical thoughts up to being a big bag of nerves. She'd always loved their guests, most of whom she knew personally. At least, that was how she felt before she'd been so abruptly put in charge of absolutely everything. Unfortunately, those carefree days were over. But again, she couldn't, or rather shouldn't, complain.

The Boden Berg Lodge was one of only a few ski-in ski-out hotels near the summit of Elk Mountain. That alone made it exclusive. Add in the cachet of it being owned and named after a famous Olympic downhill skier who regularly mixed with his guests, and you had a recipe for success. At least, that was how it had been before Boden's unexpected death almost a year ago.

Bridget set her coffee aside and doubled over with her face in her hands. The weight of it all, along with the grief that never seemed to subside, felt overwhelming at times. She wasn't her dad. She wasn't the legendary storyteller who'd stop by the Peak, the lodge's fireside bar, to charm his guests. Men were always greeted by her father with a hearty slap on the back and an offer to share a drink. Women often got a kiss on each cheek. It was the "European way," Boden would say. They either didn't notice or didn't care that while his parents were Swedish, he'd been born and raised in Utah.

Boden Berg was a national hero who'd brought home gold—twice—in the downhill. Guests paid a premium to wear themselves out on the slopes all day and then stay up all night to hear skiing tips, gossip about well-known Olympians, and exaggerated tales of mischief in the Olympic Village. Bridget felt confident a famed Russian ice dancer did not, in fact, make vodka out of nothing but glacier water and his partner's brassiere, but the guests never doubted him. It was all part of Boden Berg's charm. And it was why the high season was usually sold out by regulars more than a year in advance.

With her dad gone, Bridget worried how she'd ever be able to honor his legacy. She knew people came for the world-class skiing, but Boden Berg the man was what set the lodge apart. Sometimes, she thought she should just look for a buyer while the travel sites still listed the lodge as an exclusive getaway for the wealthy. She knew she never would, though. It would break her heart to sell the place, as if it wasn't already broken after losing the most important person in her life. No, her only choice was to do everything she could to keep it up and running.

Was she up to the task? She asked herself that question constantly. She'd soon find out since the first big weekend of the season was upon them. But the truth was, she didn't have a clue how she'd restore the Boden Berg magic. In so many ways, her father was irreplaceable, and she considered herself a poor substitute for such a special man who managed to make everyone he met feel important and cared for.

A part of her wanted to get back in bed and hide under the covers the way she used to when she was scared as a kid. She tried to remember the last time that had happened. She wasn't sure, but she could still see her dad leaning against the doorway in his jeans and boots, telling her it was safe to come out. He wasn't there to do that this time.

He wasn't there. Those words had brought her to her knees more than once. Not only because of the heavy load that now rested solely on her shoulders. She'd also lost her best friend. Her confidant. Her teacher. Her ski buddy. He wasn't just Dad to her. He was also Boden.

It never bothered him that she sometimes called him by his first name. Then again, Boden was a free spirit who didn't let much in life bother him. If he felt agitated, he'd go ski the moguls for an hour and come back with a smile on his face. Everyone loved Boden, but no one more than Bridget.

It startled her when she heard laughter in the hallway. She lifted her head and wiped away a few tears. It wasn't as if the guests knew which room was hers and could come knocking if they needed something. It was more that she didn't want the employees to witness her sadness. Even when she didn't feel strong, she felt like it was her duty to at least give an air of strength. For the lodge. For her dad. For everyone who was counting on her.

As the sound of laughter faded down the hallway, the familiar roar of the county snowplow working its way up the road got louder and louder. Bridget stood and peered out the window in hope she'd see the food delivery truck following behind the snowplow. They were high enough up the mountain that they needed to stock up on supplies and liquor when heavy snowfall was in the forecast. The county kept the road plowed, but if it was bad enough, the lodge's vendors could decide not to deliver until the weather cleared up.

The guests wouldn't be happy if their favorite wine or whiskey wasn't available, but it was nothing compared to the fit Chef Lawrence would throw if he didn't have the right supplies.

She ignored the soft knock on the door. Whoever it was could wait a few more seconds. The snowplow's flashing lights came into view, but she couldn't make out if anyone was behind it.

Another knock. "Bridge? I come bearing a gift from Chef."

"Hold on!" Bridget needed the plow to make it to the slight curve in the road so she could see what was behind it, and sure enough, the truck she'd been looking for was there. "Thank God," she whispered. And then she shouted, "Coming."

Normally, she'd ask her employee to leave her breakfast outside the door, but since it was Harriet, the lodge's longtime manager and her father's right-hand woman, Bridget went to the door and looked through the peephole. "Are you alone?"

Harriet looked to her left, then her right and nodded. "All clear."

Bridget opened the door. "I asked because I'm still in my pajamas."

"Who did you think I'd have with me, the mayor of Elk Mountain?"

Bridget pulled her into the room. "No, but a guest could've been walking by."

"That wouldn't be a problem if you'd stayed where you were," Harriet said. "I still don't understand why you insist on being in this tiny room when you have your dad's penthouse suite. It isn't right, Bridge. He wouldn't like where you are now. And neither would your mom."

It didn't make sense for Bridget to stay in her dad's suite during the ski season. Not when she could rent it out at a hefty price. It hadn't ever been done before, but unlike her father, she didn't need a large suite for entertaining VIP guests. Or even friends, for that matter. So why not rent it out?

"I don't need that much space," she said. "Besides, it's a piece of history. People will fall all over themselves to stay in Dad's suite once the renovation is finished."

Bridget told herself she didn't have the luxury of sentimentality, and the guest room was plenty big enough for her, even if the view out her window wasn't quite as stunning. Besides, she'd rather watch the traffic out front than sit in that huge suite surrounded by memories.

"You're probably right about that," Harriet said. "It's a good business decision. Tell your mom that next time you talk to her."

Bridget's mom, Ingrid, hadn't lasted on the mountain. It was too isolated for her. Too far away from her family back in New York. She was a city girl through and through.

When Ingrid had left the mountain, Bridget was only ten years old, but her mom had given her what she still considered to be the best gift she could've ever received: to choose who she wanted to live with for most of the year. Bridget had chosen her dad. She'd chosen Elk Mountain. It was home, and she had no interest in city life. She'd always be grateful to her mom for not dragging her away out of a sense of motherly duty.

It was for the best that Bridget had stayed on the mountain because her mom had gone through two more marriages and was most likely working on a third. Her dad had stayed single, which was also for the best since women loved him, and he loved them right back. Bridget often teased him about being a chick magnet, and when she came out to him at twenty-one, he said, "Well, look who's going to be the chick magnet now."

He wasn't off base. In the last ten years, Bridget had been in a few relationships. None with any sort of staying power due to her hectic training and travel schedule as a competitive skier. That was what she blamed it on anyway. The truth was more complicated, but admitting to anyone that she feared commitment because of her parents' divorce would surely seem like a cop-out. It was easier to blame it on her quest for Olympic Gold. And now she could blame it on her dad for dying and giving her the lodge that, for the most part, took up all her time and energy. There. Problem solved.

"Mom's too busy with future husband number four to worry about me," Bridget said. "I always tell her everything is fine and not to worry about me, and I expect you to do the same." She raised an eyebrow and waited for a response from Harriet, who suddenly seemed to find the ceiling of great interest.

Every time they talked, Bridget's mom seemed to know more than Bridget had told her, so she'd assumed the information was coming from Harriet, who'd taken it upon herself to play a surrogate parent role in Bridget's life since her dad's death. She loved Harriet for it, but sometimes it felt intrusive. They hadn't found that fine line between friend and employee, but she had faith that they would eventually.

She gave Harriet a quick once over. "What's different? Did you change your hair?"

"I had no choice. My regular hairdresser left town, and the new one told me he wouldn't let me stay stuck in the eighties. He cut my bangs so I can't curl them in what he called a 'sausage roll' anymore. She patted her hair. "I kinda like the way it turned out."

Her style had always been a short bob with bangs with the same bottled shade of reddish brown. Now the bangs fell more naturally over her eyebrows, giving her a softer look. "I like it too," Bridget said. "Now, about that gift from the chef." She lifted the plate to her nose and inhaled the sweet scent of cinnamon. "Sorry, Harriet. You'll have to order your own because this one is all mine."

Bridget had given up one of the lodge's top floor rooms for the entire season so she could hire an onsite chef. But not just any chef. Chef Lawrence was known for his decadent breakfasts, social-media-worthy sack lunches, and an inventive dinner menu. She'd lured him up the mountain with the promise of autonomy and creative control. The menu was his creation. The kitchen staff were his selection, and as far as Bridget was concerned, it helped that Chef was a non-skier. It meant he *wasn't* working on the mountain because he loved to ski. He was there because he loved his work, and that spelled success for everyone.

Bridget was especially fond of his homemade English muffins served with a delicious cinnamon crème schmear, but her dessert-for-breakfast euphoria was interrupted by the sound of a helicopter. She set the plate down. "VIP?"

Harriet moved to the window. "Not that I'm aware of. We didn't book anything from the airport, and no one else has requested authorization to land."

Bridget joined her at the window. Harriet's answer could only mean one thing. Most skiing accidents were minor enough that the skier could be taken down the mountain on a sled. But every once in a while, they would hear the Life Flight helicopter, and everyone would hold their breath while they watched the sky.

Bridget opened the sliding glass door and stepped onto the small balcony. A sleek helicopter with a large cabin made almost entirely of windows came into view. It wasn't Life Flight. It was the second worst-case scenario, right after a life-threatening injury.

"It's him," Bridget announced. She might have inherited a one-of-a-kind resort lodge, but she was also the heiress to a years-long fight over property lines with their obnoxious neighbor, Jerry Fleming, better known in Bridget's head as JJ, for Jackass Jerry.

Harriet stepped up next to her and gripped the balcony. "He hasn't shown his face since early last season, and God knows we're not ready for his idiotic shenanigans. Not with Boden out of the picture."

Bridget hoped he wouldn't show up until after Christmas, but here he was on their first big weekend. Jackass. "I guess he's mine to deal with now."

"Kill him for me, would ya?" Harriet gave Bridget a side glance. "You think I'm kidding, but I'm not. I always told your father he went too easy on Jerry." She put her hands on Bridget's shoulders. "This is your chance to set the tone. Let him know up front that you won't tolerate his disruptive pettiness. I'll back you up, and so will everyone down mountain. There isn't a soul in town who likes the man. Now, come back inside. We want hypothermia to get him, not us."

As far as Bridget knew, Harriet didn't have a mean bone in her body, so her suggestions came as a surprise. Especially the part about killing him. Bridget wasn't willing to go to prison for the jerk. She refused to give him that kind of satisfaction. Even so, Harriet was the only other person at the lodge who'd had a front-row seat to the crazy neighbor sideshow. Sure, everyone knew he was caustic and mean, but only Harriet had been privy to the full scope of his batshittery. She slid the door closed. "Warn the employees. Same rule as always: if he approaches, call for backup. Oh, and tell Seth to make sure the warning signs along the trail haven't been covered in snow. And for God's sake, make sure nothing is blocking the entrance to the man's driveway."

"The only thing blocking that steep driveway is three feet of snow," Harriet said. "He usually has it plowed before he gets here. I can only assume the plow guys have finally declined the pleasure of serving him."

Bridget pushed her chin out and folded her arms. Harriet was right. She'd need to take a tougher stance than her father ever did. Zero tolerance. "His driveway is not our problem."

"Oh, honey," Harriet said. "He'll make it our problem. In fact, he'll probably pay off some new snowplow company to dump it all in our parking lot again."

Bridget's eyes widened. "Dad never told me about that."

"Oh, it's been five years now. I shouldn't have mentioned it. Forget I said anything. Your job is to handle him in the future, not worry about the past."

The feud had been going on for a long time, but in the last few years before her father's death, Bridget hadn't been at the lodge for more than a few days at a time during the ski season. Not long enough to catch up on all the latest gossip. "What did my dad do about it?"

Harriet's expression softened. "Most of the time, Boden's easygoing attitude played in my favor. He let me do most things my way, but he insisted on handling Jerry all on his own, and let's just say, there were times when I wished he'd been more inclined to lay down the law."

Bridget hadn't inherited her dad's easy demeanor. She worried about everything, had a quick temper, and a sharp tongue, as her mother would say. The confusing part was that her dad had raised her to not take crap from anyone. So why had he taken JJ's crap for so long?

It was a question she might never get an answer to, but Harriet didn't need to worry about Bridget's backbone. She stood and went back to the window. "Why is the pilot hovering? Can't they just land already?"

Harriet patted her shoulder. "It's Jerry's thing, honey. If he can find a way to disturb our guests, he'll do it. See you downstairs."

Harriet left, but Bridget watched the helicopter hover over the incoming guests. She knew he couldn't see her, but she refused to look away. Enough of hiding in the shadows. She stepped back out so the petulant little prick could get a good look at her. Turning the other cheek, rising above the pettiness...those were no longer viable options. Her dad might have grown weary of the fight, but Bridget was just getting started.

❖

Helicopters were not Kennedy's favorite mode of transportation. She adjusted her headset and shouted, "Can you just land already?" Why in the world did they have to hover twenty feet when there was literally nothing but snow for miles around?

"Sorry, Ms. Fleming. Mr. Fleming preferred it if I hovered. In fact, he tipped extra if I circled for a few minutes. Should I circle, ma'am?"

"Just land before I throw up all over your back seat." She took off the headset and tossed it on the seat next to her. After a five-hour flight from Miami, an hour delay in the Salt Lake City airport while they looked for but never found two pieces of her luggage, and then a rough helicopter ride, she had no patience left. "Please," she added much too late, especially since she'd already removed her headset.

It looked cold outside. Bitter cold. If she was lucky, she'd be done and out of there in a few days. Once the blades stopped and she had both feet on the ground, she scanned the area. She stopped short when she noticed a woman standing on the balcony of a building, her red hair blowing in the wind. "And who might you be?" she muttered.

The pilot appeared out of nowhere with her carry-on bag. "Oh, that's Bridget Berg. She runs her dad's lodge now. Nice girl."

Kennedy didn't realize she'd said it loud enough for him to hear. She continued to scan the area, but there really wasn't much to see. "Where's the town? I thought Elk Mountain was a town or a village or whatever."

"Technically, yes. But we're at the top of the mountain. You'll have to ski or drive back down to town."

She hadn't noticed the elevation when she'd looked up the address of her dad's cabin on a map. And Michael certainly hadn't mentioned that it was at the top of the mountain. He probably left that minor detail out on purpose when he'd begged her to fly to Utah in the dead of winter. And then she remembered another not-so-minor detail. "Are you sure the airline can get my lost luggage to me up here?"

"Your guess is as good as mine," he said. "But here's the good news. You have your gear, so what else do you need?"

He took her ski and boot bags out of the helicopter and set them by her feet. She'd only brought them to pass the time until she went to the meeting she'd been sent here for. And what else could she possibly need up there? Oh, maybe every single thing she'd packed in her luggage. Warm pajamas, clean underwear, clothes, makeup. She didn't consider herself to be high maintenance, but she liked to look and smell good, unlike the pilot, who apparently thought she'd be fine to ski in street clothes. The thought made Kennedy cringe. In related news, she wished she'd thought to buy a toothbrush at the airport.

A gust of wind reminded her how she'd too easily acquiesced to her stylist's burning desire to give her a shorter hairstyle the day before. Oh, and he was so damned proud of himself after he'd styled it too. She had to admit that the textured pixie suited her angular face, but announcing to the entire salon that he'd just created the next big trend for dark hair seemed like overkill. Besides, she could've really used those extra seven inches of hair to keep her warm right about now.

The pilot handed her a business card. "Call this number to schedule a return flight to the airport." They stood awkwardly for a moment before he turned back toward his "rig," as he called it.

"Clint?" She pulled up the collar on her wool coat.

He turned around. "Yes, Ms. Fleming?"

"I'm sorry I haven't been great company. I've had a pretty rotten day, but I had no business taking it out on you."

"I appreciate you saying that, ma'am. Don't give it another thought. I know you've lost a lot more than your luggage."

"Thanks, Clint. And enough of this ma'am business. Call me Kennedy." She took a hundred-dollar bill from her wallet and handed it to him. "Just one other thing. Did my brother happen to schedule a car to take me to our father's cabin?"

"You won't need one." Clint pointed just to the side of the lodge. "It's right there."

Kennedy looked in the direction he'd pointed to. The cabin didn't look at all familiar to her. Michael said that she'd been there when she was a child, but she had no memory of it. And surely, she'd remember such an atrocity.

He'd also said that their mother hated the place, but their dad went to Elk Mountain quite a bit on his own to work on the cabin in the summer and ski in the winter. Thinking back on it, Kennedy had always assumed that her parents divorced because her dad was a workaholic. She wasn't close enough to her mom to call and ask if she'd been wrong all these years and maybe find out that it had really been because he spent too much time in this place, of all places on earth.

Their relationship was complicated, and Kennedy didn't have time to ask a question and then argue for two hours about why she didn't visit her mom more often. That call would have to wait for a time when she wasn't standing on a helipad in the dead of winter, ten thousand feet above sea level. That was an altitude estimate that she'd have to corroborate later over a hot cup of coffee.

Kennedy told herself it would be fine. Really. She'd be fine. She was practically sure of it. Like Clint said, she had her gear, and she could ski down the mountain if she needed to. It had been a few years since she'd clicked into a pair of skis, but it was just like riding a bike, right? The kind of bike that had no brakes and she could easily wrap herself around a tree on. Sure. Everything would be fine.

The helipad was well-sanded and thoroughly plowed, but that was the end of the easy terrain. Kennedy slung her ski bag over her shoulder and picked up her carry-on and boot bag. She took a step off the helipad and realized her suede ankle boots weren't the best choice, considering where she was. The last thing she needed to do was break an ankle and get frostbite on her extremities before someone found her. Since birth, she'd grown rather fond of her fingers and toes. Evidently, she'd also developed a fear of freezing to death alone when she was maybe a football field away from the valet entrance of...what the hell was that place called?

She carefully navigated each step. After a good distance—approximately six feet—she looked up to see a short, snow-packed trail with a wooden arrow-shaped sign that pointed to the Boden Berg Lodge. Her dad's house was in the other direction with no trail leading to it. Just snow. Deep snow. At least it was slightly downhill from the helipad. If only she had snowshoes.

She damned the airlines for losing her luggage. Not that she had snowshoes in them, but still. *Damn them.* Maybe she could ski to it. Her skis and boots were the only checked luggage that had made it from Miami. It'd be a hell of a lot better than trudging in suede boots. God, she loved these boots. So fine, she'd be in street clothes, but it'd be such a short trip, who would even see her? And who even cared?

She bent down and unzipped the ski bag. "Hello, pretty skis. I know, I know. It's been a while, but could you do me a solid and get me from here to that house down there?" She set them on the ground and unzipped the boot bag. "You too, boots. The sooner we get to that house, the sooner we can all sit in front of a nice fire and warm up. What do you say?" She was almost certain she heard the boots respond. So she answered, "Fine. Yes, I said, 'do me a solid.' Yes, I know that's, like, from the year two-thousand-nothing, and no one says that anymore. Sue me. Could you please just keep me from breaking a bone? Any bone? Thank you."

She figured if she put both poles in one hand and her carry-on in the other, she'd have enough balance to ski the short distance. Since her carry-on was the slick, hard-sided kind, she could extend the handle and pull it behind her. Easy peasy.

She buckled up the boots and clicked into her skis. "Okay, we got this. Right, skis? We've so got this." She eased off the snowpack and sunk into the deep stuff. What she thought was light, powdery snow turned out to be so thick and heavy, she couldn't maneuver her skis left or right. "Oh, God," she shouted as she picked up speed. She had no choice but to let go of her carry-on bag and try to maintain some sort of balance. It careened down the hill in front of her on the top layer of ice that her knees were cutting a path through. She also careened down the hill, completely out of control and screaming at the top of her lungs.

Her left ski caught on something and threw her into a sideways summersault. She tumbled and tumbled, and in the span of a few seconds, she had plenty of time to assess the situation. *This is it. The end.*

But it wasn't truly the end. She was alive, face-up in the snow, and crying like a little baby. Not because she'd been badly injured. Her fingers and toes still worked. It was that what she'd just experienced happened to be the ten scariest seconds of her life so far. Well, maybe not as scary as being chased by the neighbor's German Shepard while pedaling her little five-year-old heart out on her brand-new bike and crashing into a tree. That had been pretty scary too.

Kennedy lifted her head to assess the situation after the *second* scariest ten seconds of her life. All her limbs seemed to be facing in the right direction. She winced as she sat up. No doubt there would be some bruising from doing summersaults with her skis and poles, but overall, she seemed to be okay. And she'd gotten to where she needed to be. With a sigh of relief, she said, "Hello, ugly cabin, house, military quarters, whatever you are. I'm going to have to find out who designed you and send them a nasty letter."

She'd forgotten about Clint until she heard the engine start up. Had he watched her little skiing disaster from start to finish? She threw an arm over her eyes, not only to block the wind his rig kicked up, but also so she didn't have to think about anyone seeing her ridiculous display. It seemed like the entire neighborhood had witnessed the bike meets tree incident. Maybe she'd lucked out on this one, and no one had seen or heard a thing. And who cared, anyway? It wasn't as if she'd have to grow up with these people and have them remind her on every birthday by saying things like, "Try not to crash this one into a tree, okay?"

Kennedy tilted her head and said, "Oh, my fucking God." Because after all these years, she finally put two and two together and realized that the reason she got a new bike every year for her birthday was just so her dad could say those words to her and then have a good old laugh about it with her brother. "They fucking reminisced," she said. "Every year, they reminisced about the worst moment of my life."

The epiphany angered her so much that she got up and threw her poles toward the house. And then one ski, followed by the other, each with a guttural yell.

She trudged through the snow and sat on the edge of a wooden deck on the back of the house. She wasn't there for more than a few seconds when a gust of wind caused a deep shiver to course through her body. The anger she felt for her dad and brother made her forget for a moment how cold she was, but she knew she needed to get inside ASAP and warm up, so she unzipped her purse and pulled out her phone. She had the four-digit code that would unlock the door, if only she could remember where she'd stored it. Another gust of wind caused her body to shudder enough that she dropped the phone in the snow. She managed to fish it out and also grab her carry-on bag, which had landed close by, but by the time she got to the door, her hands were so cold she could barely move her fingers.

"Come on," she whispered. "Where are you, code?" She eventually found it in her brother's text messages, and after a few tries at inputting the code, the door opened.

Once inside, she had to find light switches, the thermostat, and a bathroom because wow, did she need to pee. But first, she needed to warm up her frozen fingers. She went to the kitchen sink and turned on the water, the sound of which had her squeezing her legs together. "Nope. Bathroom first."

She shrugged off her coat and opened the first door she came to. With half-frozen fingers, she managed to get her pants unzipped only to sit on what was surely the coldest toilet seat she'd ever experienced. After a loud gasp, she breathed a huge sigh of relief, as one did when one had too many cups of coffee on a plane, then got in a helicopter, and followed it up with an ill-advised attempt to ski to their father's vacation home, if one could call it that.

Thankfully, the water from the tap heated up after a few seconds. There wasn't any hand soap on the small vanity, so she opened a drawer and found a men's comb and a very old hair brush. She knew it was old because her dad hadn't needed a hairbrush in years or probably ever in his life. He had very fine, thin hair, what was left of it.

In the next drawer down, she found some individually wrapped bars of hotel soap, which begged the question, when did her dad get so cheap? He'd made good money in commercial real estate. He always took his two kids on nice holiday trips. He lived in a nice house in Miami. This place didn't fit with the man she knew.

Her phone rang, so she skipped the soap and wiped her hands on a towel. As much as she wanted to rip her brother a new one for sending her to this place, she certainly wasn't going to admit what had just happened. She had too much pride for that, so she picked up her phone and tried for an only slightly angry tone. "The helicopter was a nice touch."

"I thought I owed you that since this trip was so last-minute."

"You owe me a lot more than that, Michael. When was the last time you saw this place?"

"When you did, I guess. I don't know, we were kids."

"Okay, but you were an older kid by six years, so surely you remember more than I do."

"Not really. It's a cabin on a hill. That's all I remember."

"Don't you mean, on top of a freaking mountain? Like, a big-ass mountain in the Rocky Mountains. And it's not exactly the well-appointed mountain home I expected. It's more like awkward add-on hell. Zero curb appeal. Or mountainside appeal. Whatever you call it."

"I definitely don't remember any add-ons, and I swear I'll make it up to you."

"Damn right, you will. In fact, I insist on being my unborn niece's godmother. Screw anyone else who has dibs."

"She'd be lucky to have you," Michael said.

"Yeah, yeah. You're just being nice because you know how high up on the mountain this place is. How am I supposed to get my lost luggage up here? I seriously doubt the airline will send that pilot back up here with it."

"Lost luggage?"

Kennedy sighed. "My skis and boots made it, but my suitcase did not. Go figure."

"You mean, the skis you bought when you were at Middlebury because you had a crush on the instructor?"

"Hey. I got an A in that class. I worked damn hard to impress her. The fact that it didn't work is not pertinent to my current situation." She could hear Michael snickering under his breath. "Bro, why am I even here?"

"Because my wife could deliver your niece at any moment, remember?"

"Goddaughter. Tell Josie. If I'm expected to spoil her daughter rotten with puppies, princess dresses, and poker lessons, I expect to have that moniker."

"Interesting choices," Michael said. "What if she's not a girly girl?"

"Two out of three works for both. I'll just switch out the princess dresses for some dapper shit like miniature bowties and tiny combat boots."

"Fine, but you can't teach her to play poker. Josie will have my head on a platter if you do."

"I'll do it in secret. The girl's gonna need a side hustle. You can't live in Miami and not have a side hustle." Kennedy couldn't wait to be an aunt. She planned to take the role very seriously by pouring lots of love and money all over the newest Fleming. It seemed even more important since the little one would have to grow up without a grandfather. Kennedy wasn't sure her dad even knew there was a baby on the way, even though her impending birth had become an important topic of discussion when she visited him in the nursing home. Sometimes he seemed to understand what she was saying, or at least he'd look her in the eye when she spoke. But more often than not, each visit made it clear that the dementia was taking their father away from them at a much faster pace than expected. And looking at the strange mountain home she was standing in, Kennedy wondered what other surprises would pop up upon his death. Did she even know her own father? Like, really know him?

"Can you just sit tight until Monday?" Michael asked. "I haven't firmed up a meeting time with the agent, but I'll let you know ASAP."

"We're going to sell this place, right? Because I sure as hell don't want it."

"Oh, come on, Ken. That's just the Realtor in you talking. I don't remember it being so bad."

"Then you don't remember much," Kennedy said. "It's dated. It's a terrible design. And it's way too far from civilization for me.

I need people and traffic and a coffee shop on every corner. Not to mention good restaurants. Wait. Is there no TV in this place? How am I supposed to binge *Schitt's Creek* while I'm here?"

"You haven't watched that yet? Seriously, you need to catch up with the rest of the world."

"Well, I've been a little busy trying to break up with Miss Pet Hair, which I'd managed to put out of my mind until now, so thanks for bringing her up." If there was a silver lining to this trip from hell, it was that Kennedy was so far from civilization, her clingy ex-girlfriend would never be able to find her there. Not that she was stalking her, but the random texts with links to TikTok videos really needed to stop because A: they weren't an item anymore. And B: when it was over, it was over. None of this friendship bullshit. Straight people don't do that, so why should lesbians be forced to keep their exes in their lives? Kennedy didn't get it. She liked clean breaks. Unfortunately, she also liked hooking up with hot women who had feelings.

"Honestly, I can't wait to meet the woman you don't consider too clingy," Michael said. "She'll probably have to be in the Navy, serving her country on a nuclear submarine for nine months a year."

"That sounds hot. I love a woman in uniform. Do you happen to know any lady officers? Maybe a colonel? Ooh, she could bark orders at me and call me a petty officer. You know how much I love it when a woman tries to boss me around."

Michael laughed. "So...not bossy or clingy unless she's in the military. You're insufferable, you know that?"

Kennedy smiled. "Actually, I do know that. But I'm also kinda loveable. And I'm here, doing you this big-ass favor, which means I'm also a sucker." She caught a flash of something shiny just outside the window. "Gotta go, bro. Just keep your ringer turned up in case I need something."

"Wait, Ken. Just a word of warning. Don't get too friendly with the people next door. Dad's had some run-ins with the owner over the years."

She knew he was referring to the building next to the helicopter pad, but surely, "the people next door" didn't include hot redheads on balconies. Okay, fine. She hadn't been able to actually make out her features from a distance, but Kennedy had a soft spot for redheads.

"Ken? Did you hear me?"

"What? Oh yeah. Of course. Not a problem," she said. "I won't be here long enough to get friendly with anyone." Nor would she have time to get laid, no matter how cute the redhead turned out to be. "Bye, bro."

She put her phone in her pocket and stepped up to the window. A couple of guys in matching winter coats were wrapping yellow caution tape around trees. On closer inspection, it looked as though they were cordoning off her dad's property as if it was a crime scene. She couldn't be sure exactly where the property line was, but it obviously ended where the ski slope started on the west side. Or maybe it was the east side. She had no idea which way the house faced, but up the mountain from her, toward the helipad, they were cordoning off that area too. If she wasn't already freezing to death, she'd open the door and ask them what they were doing, but her time would be better spent trying to find a thermostat so she could get the heat going.

Nothing. Absolutely nothing happened when Kennedy moved the dial on the thermostat. She thought about calling Michael back, but then he'd tease her for being a city girl who couldn't take care of herself. She could take care of herself just fine. She'd just never lived in a building that didn't have a manager who took care of issues when they came up. For that matter, neither had Michael, so it wasn't as if he could've helped her anyway.

She did make a call. More than one, actually. She called every furnace repair company within fifty miles. For the record, that amounted to four repair companies. They all gave different versions of, "Lol. You know there's a big storm coming, right? There's no way we can get up the mountain now." Okay. She actually hadn't known there was a big storm coming. On call number three, she pointed out that she did know about the storm now. It was, in fact, her exact problem.

"Storm plus no heat equals problem," she said regrettably.

"What do you want us to do? Take a helicopter?"

Touché, Furnace Frankie, Tou-fucking-ché. Bottom line: No one was coming to fix the heat that day, but she had four confirmations for the next one.

Luckily, the house had a wood-burning stove and a fireplace. Even though she'd never camped a day in her life, she, along with the rest of the world, was one YouTube video away from being able to do just about anything. That was how she'd learned to use every smartphone she'd ever had. How to apply makeup and braid her own hair. How to make the perfect cup of tea, negotiate a contract, build a retaining wall, and wrap the perfect gift. There was a how-to video for everything but brain surgery. Actually, maybe even brain surgery was on there. She couldn't be sure since she'd never searched for that particular video, and even though she was curious, it would have to wait for another time because what she needed more than a brain tumor dissection was a how-to on fire building.

She grabbed her phone and grumbled when she realized she wouldn't be watching anything without Wi-Fi. Her mood had lightened a bit during the phone call, but standing there, staring at her options, she had the urge to call Michael back and scream at him until he sent another helicopter to get her off the mountain. "You can do this," she said to herself, feeling unconvinced. "Wood-stove or fireplace? Talk to me, ladies. Which one of you will set my world on fire?"

She deduced that the fireplace had been a part of the original cabin design, and the stove was added later. So maybe stoves did a better job of heating up a room? It was all guesswork, but she opened the little door on the stove. "It's you and me, girl. Let's warm each other up."

Chapter Two

K ennedy stood in front of the Boden Berg Lodge. Through the windows, it looked warm and cozy inside. She needed warm and cozy more than she'd ever needed it in her entire life. She needed warm and cozy more than she needed respect and admiration. More than she needed a nice wardrobe and her convertible BMW. She'd even trade in her soon-to-be bestowed title of godmother. Little What's-her-name could fend for herself in this big, bad, frigid world. Kennedy needed some heat.

Okay, so maybe putting logs that barely fit into the stove wasn't the best way to build a fire. Or maybe that damned stove was an old piece of crap. She'd go with the latter for now.

Smoke billowed from the lodge's chimney, and the scent of grilled meat—steak? It seemed like steak—filled the crisp air. No, not crisp. It was more apocalyptic than that. When Kennedy took a breath, she was certain she felt her lungs frost over. She would have held her breath altogether, but steak.

It smelled delicious. Whatever it was, she'd have it for lunch with a glass of red if they had a decent wine list. Then again, the trek she'd just made down the steep, winding, snow-covered driveway that she cursed her father for building, would be that much harder on the way back. Freezing to death while tipsy didn't sound the least bit appealing. Maybe she'd opt for some sort of decadent dessert instead of wine. Preferably something warm and chocolate-covered. Her mouth watered at the thought. Oh, hell.

She'd have both. Wine and dessert. That was clearly the best course of action. As she got to the front steps, she wondered if eyelash extensions broke off when frozen. No reason.

She opened the door and stomped the snow off her boots. They weren't actually *her* snow boots. They were her dad's. And they were several sizes too big. In fact, they were big enough that she easily wore her black leather ankle boots inside them, which would come in handy in about one minute.

A nice young man in a black turtleneck and matching fleece vest with the lodge logo embroidered on the left breast walked up to her. "May I check your parka, ma'am?"

The parka wasn't hers either, but boy, was she grateful to find it in her dad's closet, even if it made her feel like a bundled-up toddler going out to play in the snow. She pushed the hood off her head and gave him a smile. "Would you mind taking my boots as well?"

"Of course, ma'am."

She took off the bulky, army-green coat, but it turned out that the boots she'd easily slid into with her shoes on weren't so easy to take off. She sat on a bench and stuck her leg out tentatively. "Do you mind?"

He gave it a good tug and then another, but it was a no go. "My feet aren't really this big," she explained. "I have ankle boots on inside these boots." She hadn't thought it through when she'd stuck her feet into boots that didn't lace up. "It's fine. I'll keep them on." She'd have to wrestle with them back at the house later, but at least she wouldn't have an audience.

She stood and straightened her sweater. She always liked the way that particular sweater fit. It hugged her curves nicely—or so she'd been told by Miss Pet Hair. She'd had *some* good traits, one of which was that she never let a compliment go unsaid. Complimentary but clingy. Maybe Kennedy should change her nickname to CBC. Nah, she liked Miss Pet Hair better.

So the sweater was working in her favor. Her pants, on the other hand, had sagged over the edge of the boots, making her look from the waist down like a kid who'd been playing soldiers in their dad's clothes. She knew it was ridiculous to fret over the way she looked when starvation was imminent, as were hypothermia and apparently, a headache. But looking good was kind of Kennedy's jam. And yes, she knew it was shallow but so was turning heads when she walked into a room.

She'd turn some heads in this room too, but for all the wrong reasons. She mustered up the best smile she could, given the circumstances, and said, "Could you direct me to wherever that delicious smell is coming from?"

"Oh, it's coming from the Summit Room." He pointed to the right of the floor to ceiling stone fireplace that sat in the middle of the lobby and was surrounded on both sides by rustic furniture and comfy leather sofas. Kennedy realized then that this wasn't just any old ski lodge. This place catered to someone like her. Someone who appreciated excellent service and tipped well when she got it.

The two servers standing on the periphery, each with a tray in hand, was her first clue. She'd had that job back in high school when she'd worked at a country club, and when a guest held up their hand or snapped their fingers, she and her fellow servers would rush over and address them by their last name before taking their order or helping in whatever way they could.

At the time, she couldn't wait to grow up and be addressed as Ms. Fleming. Until she realized how the country club crowd actually was. *Talk about emotionally immature assholes with too much time on their hands.* But at the same time, those assholes bought and sold a lot of real estate, so in a sense, her job as a Realtor wasn't much different from that of a server. She still catered to the ultra-wealthy. She just had a better wardrobe now.

She pulled out her phone and searched for the Summit Room on Yelp. It didn't always work this way, but sometimes, if she saw a waiting line at a place where she wanted to get dinner, she'd get on the app and reserve a table, wait a minute or two, and go to the head of the line to be seated. She tapped a few buttons and voila! She had a table for one.

The lodge had a warm, cozy atmosphere. The furniture was all high-end. Real leather. Solid oak. Reading lamps strategically placed. The coasters on every table appeared to be slices of a tree branch, with the letters BB branded on the wood. Even the wineglasses and brandy snifters that guests were sipping from had those letters etched on them.

She appreciated that there weren't any dead animals mounted on the walls. She'd seen that sort of thing in enough ski lodges to know it was expected. Instead of a moose head adorning the fireplace, there was a large framed photo of a skier with a gold medal draped around his neck. A gold plaque identified him as Boden Berg, the lodge's namesake.

A few people turned their heads as she walked by. No one seemed to notice her clunky boots, but every step made her feel like the T-Rex in *Jurassic Park* whose tread was heard and felt from miles around. Or like that Fee, Fie, Fo, Fum guy, except it wasn't the blood of an Englishman she could smell, thank God. It was the scent of warm bread that tickled her nose.

There were a few people waiting outside the restaurant, but the place looked packed. She stopped at the hostess stand and announced herself. "Kennedy Fleming. I have a table for one reserved."

The young woman hesitated. Her eyes darted between Kennedy and the reservation list. "Did you say…Fleming?"

"I did. Kennedy Fleming."

Even if their system hadn't updated or Yelp happened to give her a reservation that wasn't available at all, a folded twenty-dollar bill discreetly placed on the stand usually took away any hesitation on their part. Unfortunately, this hostess was too busy whipping her head from side to side to notice it. Kennedy tapped her finger on the money and said, "Please check your list again. I'm sure you'll find me on there."

She could see an open table near another large fireplace that would suit her just fine. She rubbed her cold hands together in anticipation of the hot flames warming her from head to toe. The hostess had a hand over her headset, whispering something unintelligible. She seemed to be looking for something but not in the right direction.

Kennedy glanced at her nametag and leaned in. "Mackenzie, I'm so hungry, I can feel my stomach eating itself. My heat's out. I'm cold and wet, and these boots are so ridiculous," she kicked her leg out past the hostess stand so Mackenzie could see the men's size eleven clodhoppers she'd managed to weld to her feet. "The only thing that will make me feel better is a stiff drink and a huge meal. Please help me."

A woman stepped up to the desk. She gave Kennedy a tight smile but didn't say hello. Kennedy was pretty sure it was the redhead from the balcony. No, she was positive it was her. And yes, she was indeed beautiful. And tall. And the subtle freckles that dotted her nose made Kennedy feel like she could die a happy woman for just having seen them up close.

She held a strong resemblance to Boden Berg, the man from the photos in the lobby. Her hair was a darker red than his strawberry blond, but the eyes were the same shade of deep blue. What was strikingly similar was the dimple in their chins. She'd put money on her being the younger Berg.

The two women stepped away from the desk and whispered long enough for Kennedy to get another good long look. This day was starting to look up. She'd always had a thing for tall women. And a redhead to top it off? Yes, please. Except, there was the issue of Kennedy's attire. How the hell was she supposed to attract a woman dressed like this? She wasn't. Because she wasn't there to make friends, as Michael had reminded her. So should she care if this woman thought she had humongous feet? And a penchant for ugly shoes. Maybe everyone on the mountain wore boots inside boots. Or not, given the side-eye glare coming from the two of them while they whispered about who knew what.

Just in case there was a dress code or some rule that your shoes had to be "luxury mountain resort appropriate," whatever that meant, Kennedy took a step to the right so her boots would be hidden by the desk.

Viking Goddess of the North with the cute freckles stepped forward again. "Mrs. Fleming, there seems to have been some kind of mistake. We're completely booked up tonight."

"*Ms.* Fleming. And I'll happily sit at the bar if that works."

"I'm afraid that won't be possible."

Kennedy leaned to her left so she could see the bar area. There were several open seats. And the enticing scent of grilled steak, warm bread, and possibly some kind of hearty stew had her licking her chops like Pavlov's dog. "I think you can fit me in if you try." It didn't seem the kind of place that required bribery, but okay. She slapped another twenty on the desk and folded her arms, letting them both know she had no intention of being denied.

Mackenzie's eyes doubled in size but not with a look of delight at the tip she was about to receive. It was more a look of, *oh, shit, this isn't going to end well.*

But it was going to end well. Kennedy just needed to spell out what was going to happen next, so she lowered her voice and said, "I haven't eaten all day, so can we just act like the last thirty seconds never happened and pretend that you magically found a seat at the bar for me? That way, I won't have to give you a horrible Yelp review." Yeah, she pulled out the bad review card, but she was desperate and running out of patience.

"Please follow me," the Viking Goddess said.

A take-charge kind of gal. Kennedy had never thought of the alpha temptress as her type, so to speak, but she was willing to keep an open mind. Truth be told, she liked the bossiness a little bit. She started to follow but slowed when she realized the woman was going the wrong way. With tentative steps, she continued. Maybe there was a private dining area for VIPs. Then she saw the guy who'd taken her coat rush away. And the woman behind the front desk stared at her like she was a dead man walking. That was when she stopped.

The Nordic Queen turned and glared, but Kennedy didn't move. She couldn't decide which nickname she liked better. Queen. Goddess. Temptress. Or should she be more specific?

Athena? Aphrodite? Wait. They were Greek goddesses. That wasn't right. In any event, she realized the decision could wait until later. What she knew for sure? She was not going back out into the cold without some food in her stomach. And why the hell was she being treated so poorly anyway?

It was the boots. It had to be. God, how embarrassing. They didn't want her walking into their fancy restaurant looking like a member of *Duck Dynasty*. Was there a dress code that high up on a mountain? She glanced around at people's feet, and most of them were wearing little fur-lined moccasin booties with the BB logo on the side.

It was actually a clever idea to give every guest something to slip into when they came in from the slopes. It would keep the floors clean and dry, and there would be less wear and tear on the carpeted areas. Why in the world hadn't the guy at the front door offered her a pair?

They got to the back of the lodge and the redhead, who seemed a lot less goddess-like now, gestured toward a set of large glass doors that exited straight to the mountainside. The realization dawned on Kennedy. She was being straight-up, objectively, ass to the grass, thrown out. The only thing she didn't know was why.

"Is this about my boots? Because they're kind of stuck—"

She-Wolf Queen of the Mountain didn't let her finish. "If you don't leave now, Ms. Fleming, I'll be forced to call the sheriff, who, thanks to your husband, the lodge has an intimate relationship with. So you can either walk out that door or wait right here with security until the authorities arrive. Those are your choices. And in case it's not clear enough, you will not ever, under any circumstances, eat in my restaurant."

"Did you just say you'd call the sheriff?" Okay, so clearly, it wasn't about her boots. She put her hands up to signal she wasn't a threat. "I honestly didn't know bribes, I mean, hostess tips, were frowned upon here." She offered her hand. "I think we may have gotten off on the wrong foot. I'm Kennedy."

"Fleming," the woman added. "And like I said, you're not welcome here. Now, can I escort you through the door?"

"Only if it includes a kiss good night. I mean, after you introduce yourself, of course."

The comment threw She-Wolf. After a few seconds of shock, she said, "I'm Bridget Berg. Now, if you don't mind?"

"Bridget. Okay, now we're getting somewhere. Like I said before, I'm literally dying of hunger, and the kiss comment was purely an effort on my part to diffuse the situation. I don't actually want to, you know, anyway, I'm staying at my dad's cabin for a few days. Jerry Fleming?"

The Norse Handmaiden...wait. Referring to her as a handmaiden felt a little too creepy. She'd have to nix that one. Bridget Berg stepped closer but not in a friendly way. Her lips were pursed, and she had to glance around before she leaned in even closer and said, "The fact that you're that lowbrow Jerry Fleming's blood relative only worsens your position here, so your best move would be to leave peacefully."

Lowbrow? Since when were the Flemings considered lowbrow? This entire situation was so utterly humiliating, confusing, insane. Take your pick. And Kennedy's patience was almost gone. "Excuse me? I don't know what your problem is, but I won't have you insult my father."

"I can't say I know any other way to think of him. Now, please leave before we have to involve security." A large man dressed in black cargo pants and a light blue shirt arrived on the scene the moment Bridget Berg nodded in his direction, which could only mean he'd been standing a short distance behind Kennedy the entire time.

Sobered by his presence, Kennedy knew she'd have to swallow her pride and leave. The problem was, she had no way to get down the mountain, and DoorDash surely wasn't a thing at the top. She noticed a shop opposite the restaurant that looked like it sold food and drinks. "May I at least buy a few snacks from your shop? I haven't eaten all day, and I seem to be stuck up here."

"I'll buy them for you," Bridget said. "If you agree to leave quietly and leave my guests alone."

Bridget ended the statement with a once-over of Kennedy from head to toe. Aha. So she was judging her boots. It might not have been the reason she was 86'd, but it certainly couldn't have helped. Unfortunately, it wasn't possible to sashay to the shop at the moment. So with Bridget right behind her, she clomped her way to Elk Mountain Sundries and grabbed two bags of trail mix, a bottle of water, a sleeve of doughnuts, a Snickers bar, and... "Do you sell any of those mini bottles of liquor?"

"No, ma'am," the clerk replied. "You'd have to go into town to the state liquor store for that."

"Right. Of course. Because this is my life now." She reached into her purse for her wallet only to be stopped by a hand on her arm.

"Put this on the house account, Brenda. Ms. Fleming's money isn't good here."

Kennedy shook her head and sighed. If only She-Wolf Alpha Norse Goddess had put a hand on her for a different reason, something more friendly, then she wouldn't have had to turn to her and say, "If you don't take your hand off me, I might have to call the sheriff."

She'd used a pleasant, slightly flirtatious tone. Brenda's eyes got almost as big as poor Mackenzie's back at the hostess desk, and much to Kennedy's delight, the offender had turned bright red. "I apologize," she said, and took a step back.

Kennedy didn't wait for Brenda to bag her snacks. She gathered them up with both hands, turned, and leaned close to Bridget, who had clearly become just as uncomfortable with the situation as Kennedy. "It's okay," she whispered. "I kinda liked having your hand on my body."

And with that, she straightened her shoulders and clomped out of the shop, making a point to smile at anyone who dared make eye contact. The same guy was at the door, waiting for her with her parka open and ready. She was mad at him for not offering her a pair of those fancy moccasin slipper things, so it was a silent effort to juggle her snacks and slide her arms into her coat. Once she had them all tucked away in the pockets, she glanced back. Every employee had their eyes on her, along with several of the guests. She wanted to yell several profanities at them, but that would only give them justification for the way she'd been treated.

The second she got outside and took a deep breath of the frigid air, her bravado disappeared, and she knew she'd probably cry the whole way home, like a kid who'd just been bullied on the playground. And all that awaited her was a cold house and the crappy kind of trail mix that had carob chips instead of M&Ms, which she'd wash down with Aquafina instead of scotch. Great. Just great.

❖

Had Bridget done the right thing? She had no idea. It was bad enough that her dad had to deal with Jerry Fleming's bullshit all those years. Now his daughter was stirring things up too? And the nerve of her to think she could flirt with Bridget and get any kind of reaction other than disdain.

Yes, she'd done the right thing. She'd set the tone and made it clear that no Fleming, no matter who they were or how cute they were, was ever welcome inside her lodge. Her dad might have put up with Jerry's heavy-handed tactics and ridiculous outbursts, but she wouldn't. Those days were over.

She put the word out to all her employees that they shouldn't engage with Ms. Fleming at all. If Kennedy approached them, they should get on their radio and ask for Bridget's assistance by using the code words, "Hungry Hippo." Everyone seemed excited to use it, especially Harriet, who had been there the longest and witnessed the worst of the Fleming nightmare.

The nickname didn't really suit the brunette with the captivating brown eyes. Well, except for the hungry part. Kennedy was definitely hungry, or it was all a ruse to get her foot in the door and spy on them for her father. Either way, who knew Jerry had such an attractive daughter? That part was a big surprise. And so was Bridget's urge, which she wished she'd controlled better, to touch Kennedy. Just on the arm, and oh so briefly, but it hadn't been necessary. Her words would've sufficed.

Well, she wouldn't make that mistake again because surely, she'd humiliated Kennedy enough to keep her away for good.

Bridget stood at the lobby fireplace. She stared at her father's portrait and wondered for approximately the six-hundred-and-seventy-eighth billionth time what had started the feud with Jerry in the first place.

Her dad had always been coy about it, waving it off as a bad neighbor thing. "He's just a bit mixed up in the head," he'd say.

Bridget wondered if there was more to it than that. Her dad wasn't one to back down from a fight or take abuse from a guest or anyone else, no matter how wealthy and influential they were. He publicly and quite famously separated from a ski company endorsement because they wouldn't take a stance on environmental preservation. These days, it was called climate change, but in the eighties, it was just a skier turning down money because he couldn't stand to see what was happening to the land he loved. That was Boden Berg. A national hero, friend to everyone, and accidental climate activist. The guy stood up for what he believed in.

Except when it came to Jerry Fleming. And no one seemed to know why.

With her dad not there to help, Bridget would have to go by her own instincts, and they were telling her to stop the nonsense before the stress of it all killed her too. She'd have zero tolerance from here on out. If any Fleming so much as whispered boo to one of her guests, she'd take them to court. Get a restraining order. Whatever it took to keep them out of her business.

All her guests were in for the night. After a hard day of skiing, they usually went up to their rooms early. The gondola shut down at four, just before sunset at that time of year. After that, the bar and restaurant stayed packed for about four hours before tipsy tourists started to realize just how tired and sore they were. Not to mention the realization of a start time at seven a.m. the next morning. Even at peak season, the whole operation was usually shut down by ten.

Bridget made a habit of doing a final walkthrough before she went to her room for the night. She'd dim the overhead lights and turn off the reading lamps in the lobby. Pick up any stray gloves or scarves that had been left behind and put them in the lost and found box. And she always took a moment to stand under her dad's photograph and say good night.

This was the time of day she missed him most. Once the guests were all tucked in, he had time to read her stories or help with homework or talk about her latest crush or racing injury or whatever was going on in her life. This had always been their special time together. Now she was alone, left with a massive weight on her shoulders and a hot neighbor. Not hot. Irrational. Petulant. Overbearing. That was what she'd meant to say. Or think. What she hadn't meant to say out loud was, "What the F, Dad?"

She glanced around to make sure no one had heard her, then whispered it again. "I mean, seriously. What the F am I supposed to do with her?"

He didn't answer. Most likely because he was a portrait, but knowing her dad as she did, Bridget was still a little surprised that had stopped him. She blew him a kiss. "Night, Dad."

On her way to the stairs, she glanced at the live weather forecast that ran continuously on a monitor mounted to the wall behind the front desk. For a ski resort, it was must-have information, the equivalent of running the day's sports scores or airing twenty-four-seven news headlines. She knew there were places where discussing the weather was considered small talk. Elk Mountain was not one of them. At least a foot of snow was expected to fall overnight, with more to come in the next few days. That meant an excellent start to the season and hopefully, a fully booked resort.

She gave her night clerk a wave before she climbed the stairs to the top floor to check on the renovations her handyman had started in her dad's suite. With the same key she'd had since childhood, she unlocked the door and went inside. His was the only suite in the lodge that hadn't been converted to keycard.

"This is our home," he had explained. "And homes shouldn't have keycards."

She'd never felt the need to tell him homes actually had keypads and smart locks now. Besides, she liked the tradition of it, and every year, even once she became an adult, her dad would put a new keychain in her Christmas stocking. She had them all stored away somewhere. Everything from Hello Kitty to her gold and maroon lanyard that said, *Go Elks!* And yes, they were the Elk Mountain High School Elks. Because what else would their mascot be?

Oh, and there was the year she'd been super into 4H, and therefore, cowboy boots, so her dad got one of his friends who did leather work to make a miniature version of those boots for her keychain. The following year, she was into Doc Martins and fully expected to get another mini version of her purple Docs, but her dad went in a completely different direction and gave her a car. More specifically, a tiny, baby blue Jeep. Little did she know there was a real one waiting for her in the parking lot. That was probably the best day of her life up to that point and was still in the top five. That Jeep took her everywhere. It had gone with her to college and every ski resort in the west. She'd camped on the beaches of California and Oregon with it. She'd even had her first sexual experience with a woman in the back seat, under the stars, with the Santa Ana winds blowing through their hair.

Needless to say, when Baby Blue, as she'd called it, decided not to run anymore, she couldn't bring herself to get rid of it, so her dad had put it in one of the lodge's storage sheds. She had no idea if it was still there, and with so much snow on the ground, she'd have to wait until spring to find out.

Much like her dad's favorite belt buckle only smaller, his key fob was also a round metal disc wrapped in beaded leather. Hers changed every year, but his never did. He'd once told her that it slid into his pocket nicely and felt good in his hand. It was still in the suite, hanging on the hook by the door.

The last keychain he'd given her was a sterling silver B. Engraved on the back were the words, *My Greatest Joy.* She would cherish it forever, as she had every one of those keychains he'd given her. She'd probably buy a special box to put them in. Something she could keep tucked in a drawer.

As she'd always done before, she went into the suite and put her key on the hook next to his. With all of the artwork and framed photos taken down for painting and the big Navajo rugs rolled up and stood on end in the corner, the place looked devoid of her dad's presence. Even the lingering scent of his cologne was gone. All she could smell was fresh paint mixed with whatever cleaning products they'd used on the wood floors.

Had she done the wrong thing? That suite had been her home. The entire hotel had been her playground, but the suite, along with her small bedroom at the end of the hall, was her safe place, and she didn't even have that anymore. It was her own doing. She couldn't blame anyone for taking it away from her, but was it too soon? Had she dealt with her grief enough to move on?

The kitchen held so many good memories of her dad cooking, washing dishes, flipping pancakes, and cheering when he didn't drop one on the floor. He usually wore one of two outfits: a wool sweater and ski pants or a denim button-up shirt with jeans, brown leather boots, and a leather belt. Those clothes still hung in the closet. If she wanted to make the suite available to guests anytime soon, she'd have to go in there and pack it all up. Not a task she looked forward to.

A spiral staircase led up to the loft where she used to do her homework by the arched window. From there, she could watch the skiers come and go. On sunny days, her dad was often out there on the big deck, mingling with the guests who were relaxing in Adirondack chairs. He'd usually look up and blow her a kiss. Sometimes, he'd wave her down, and they'd ski a few runs together.

She hadn't decided what to do with that space yet. The easiest thing would be to replace all of the big pillows she'd used as a kid with a couple of mattresses for the families who booked the suite. She didn't have to decide right then. It could wait a couple more days. Besides, she'd start crying again if she climbed those stairs and found yet another reminder of her dad.

She went to the door and reached for her key, but instead of grabbing her own, it was her dad's she held in her hand. She stared at it, shocked that she'd made that mistake since it hadn't ever happened before. She rubbed her thumb over the tiny beads and wondered if it was a sign from her dad that he was still out there somewhere.

She locked the suite back up and slid his key into her pocket. He was right. It slid in nicely and felt good in her hand.

❖

Even when Kennedy turned the thermostat up as high as it could go, the furnace couldn't seem to warm the place. The weirdly vaulted ceiling probably didn't help. She cupped her hands around her mouth and shouted, "What were you thinking, old man?" With her hands on her hips and her eyes glued to the ceiling, she paced the room. The vault was clearly an add-on that served no purpose. It didn't increase window height to give the room a better view because the windows weren't on the high side. It didn't look like her dad had started to build a second level but had to stop for some reason, either. It seemed intentional in design.

From the outside, it looked like a normal cabin with a single-roof pitch from front to back, but then on one side, it had this tall, jutting, steeply pitched thing that created the vault on the inside.

There was nothing warm about what her father had built. It felt cold. Hollow. Lifeless. Compared to the Boden Berg Lodge... well, there really was no comparison. If only she could've booked a room there, she'd be enveloped in expensive Egyptian cotton sheets and a down comforter. At least, that was how she pictured it. In her mind, there was a jetted tub as well, and for a second, it featured a certain redhead until Kennedy reminded herself that said redhead had issues. Big ones.

She had to admit that she loved the aesthetic of the lodge. While being kicked out of the place, she'd noticed a mission-style rocking loveseat in the lobby that was clearly from another era. She guessed it dated back to the early sixties, and given the chance, she would've tested it out while sipping on a hot buttered rum. And if that certain redhead happened by, she'd pat the spot next to her, and they'd have a nice chat because in this version of reality, Bridget was actually a nice person. In real life, not so much.

On her second desperate attempt to get some warmth in the house, she opted to use the fireplace instead of the woodstove. She found an old phonebook from 2002 in the small desk in the bedroom. She assumed her dad must've saved it for the cover that celebrated Utah hosting its first Winter Olympics because what other reason would someone have to keep a phonebook that old? Or at all? She tore the cover off and put it back in the drawer where she'd found it. The rest of it, she'd use for the fire.

Fortunately, there was a decent stack of wood piled next to the fireplace. She tossed the phonebook in and placed several logs on top of it in an aesthetically pleasing manner, as they did with the fake logs in a gas fireplace. In other words, she tossed those in too. Random tossing seemed better than laying them out like sausage links. She'd never seen that look in any of the houses she'd sold, so it seemed logical there had to be some sort of point to the randomness.

She grabbed the same book of matches she'd used to light the logs in the stove and on the third try, managed to get the edges of the phonebook burning. She stood back and watched with her fingers crossed. The phonebook really started to burn, but she couldn't jump for joy just yet. A log had to catch fire before any celebration took place.

It didn't take long before she couldn't even see the logs for all of the smoke in the air. "What the hell?" She waved her hand in front of her face and coughed. It was only getting worse, and she was about to get a glass of water to put it out when she remembered that chimneys have a thing you're supposed to open.

She'd have to go in hard and fast if she had any chance of survival. She covered her mouth and nose with the crook of her elbow and reached in. Her hand flailed until she found a lever and pulled with all of her might, which sent her backward, landing hard on the floor. She propped herself up on her elbows and waited. When the smoke started to billow up into the chimney, she lay back down and stared at the ceiling.

It wasn't a sense of accomplishment she felt for managing to make the stupid fireplace work. It was more a sense of betrayal. She'd been duped by her brother. The first-class airline ticket, followed by a helicopter ride, had lulled her into believing he actually cared what happened to her while she ran his little errand. The truth as she saw it brought tears to her eyes, which she promptly wiped away because she'd be damned if she'd let Michael, or anyone else, get the better of her.

Once the smoke cleared, she pushed her dad's well-used recliner as close to the fireplace as she dared. She put his parka back on and wrapped a couple of blankets around her legs. The fire seemed to be burning well, but she'd have to keep it...what was that damn word? Oh, yeah. She'd have to keep the fire stoked.

If only she were stoked to be on Elk Mountain.

Chapter Three

The following morning, Kennedy had a better lay of the land. Their cabin was flanked on one side by the road and on the other by the ski slope. The front door faced downhill and the back door uphill. The lodge was higher up on the mountain where the road ended, and it sat about a hundred feet away from the ski slope, while the cabin was only about ten feet away from it.

By her estimation, she'd gone the long way to and from the lodge the day before. Going out the front door and down the driveway took her farther down the mountain before getting to the road and turning right just to hike back up.

From where she stood on the back porch, it looked to her like the lodge guests were using a trail to get onto the slopes that was much closer. All she'd have to do was hike up the groomed ski slope to the trail, and she'd almost be there. There was just one problem. Yellow crime scene tape. Okay, so it was just caution tape, but it might as well have said, *A serial killer lives here. Enter at your own peril.* And it was wrapped around what she could only assume was the entire perimeter of her dad's property.

Something had obviously gone down on this mountain. History she wasn't privy to but was being punished for. And in her discombobulated state the night before, she hadn't thought to grab a bottle of coffee from the cooler. No, all she'd grabbed was a bottle of water, which she didn't actually need since what came out of the tap tasted better than any bottled water she'd ever had.

Kennedy wasn't good at estimating snowfall but guessed that one-point-five shit-tons had fallen overnight, which lowered her chances of getting grocery delivery by one hundred and ten percent. Those were rough numbers, of course. She couldn't even confirm her guesstimate because she had no internet, and as it turned out, she couldn't just call the local grocery store and say hey, I need a few things, and I need them delivered way up on top of that mountain behind you.

Somehow, she needed to get into that lodge unnoticed and head straight for one of those leather sofas, where she was sure to be offered a cup of hot black heaven. And possibly a pastry of some kind. And maybe she could even warm up by the fire for a few minutes. After that, if she got kicked out on her ass again, so be it. At least she'd be well caffeinated. It could work. It had to work because there was literally nowhere else she could get to on foot. It was decided then, caution tape be damned.

She went back inside to get bundled up, but the thought of dressing up like a *South Park* character as she'd done the day before made her feel slightly nauseated. Or maybe that was just her tummy begging for sustenance. Either way, everyone would recognize her in that big green parka. And the huge boots would be a sure giveaway. In fact, those clothes probably reminded them all of her dad, and that was the last thing she needed.

She decided to wear the wool coat she'd arrived in, and maybe if she stayed on the groomed trail, her ankle boots would get her there just fine. But between the porch and the groomed trail was the same deep snow she'd tried to ski on when she'd first arrived. Trudging through that would require a thick pair of socks, so she went into the bedroom and found several pairs in the top of the chest of drawers. Her boots would never fit the same after squeezing into them wearing those socks, but it was that or risk losing a toe to frostbite.

By the time she'd made it through the knee-deep snow and onto the slope, a lodge employee was standing at the end of the caution tape about fifty feet away. Unfortunately, there was no casual way to walk up the edge of the ski slope as if she belonged there. A skier went by and did a double take, then stopped and shouted, "Are you lost?"

She gave the man a friendly wave. "No, I'm fine, thanks." *And please, for the love of God, go away.*

"Did you lose your skis? I can help you find them," he shouted back.

When he started to side-step his way back up the hill to her, she shouted, "Really, sir. I'm fine, okay?" She didn't want to be rude, but she needed this guy to stop bringing attention to her. He finally got the message and skied away, so she trudged up the hill as fast as she could and was able to get within twenty feet of the employee before he went for his radio. "Hey," she shouted. "Don't do that. I just need to ask a quick question."

He put up a hand. "Ma'am, I need you to stay off lodge property." He pointed at the caution tape. "It starts here."

He couldn't have been more than eighteen, and although he'd tried really hard to sound like a tough guy, the slight shake in his voice betrayed his lack of confidence. Also, his reasoning didn't make sense. "If it starts there, then I think you put the caution tape up wrong," she told him.

"I'm not sure what you mean, ma'am."

"You taped off the wrong property. You made it so no one could go on my dad's land, not yours."

"Oh," he exclaimed. "No, it's right. We do that so our guests don't accidentally ski on Mr. Fleming's property."

Kennedy scanned the area. The land between her dad's cabin and where they were standing was just open space. It wasn't as if he'd planted evergreen saplings or something else just as fragile. And it made sense that the skiers would want to use that area to access the slopes instead of the narrow trail that the tape ran along. "What happens if they do?" she asked.

"I haven't seen it for myself, but I've heard it's not good."

Oh God, why had she asked? It pained her to see her dad through those people's eyes. He wasn't a bad guy, and she refused to believe any of it without some sort of corroboration. Maybe he had a very good reason to keep people off his land, so she said, "Well, then, please make sure they don't."

She marched up the trail toward the lodge and heard him shout into his radio, "Hungry Hippo on the move."

What the hell? Well, that pissed her off, so she picked up her pace. She needed to get inside, plop herself down on a sofa, and refuse to move until she'd been caffeinated.

A group of skiers appeared out of nowhere. She tried to jump out of the way, but they knocked her to the ground. "Don't mind me," she shouted at them. Yelling at strangers wasn't exactly her MO. Then again, neither was being knocked on her ass.

She wondered how much worse the day could get, but she didn't have to wonder long because standing at the top of the trail with her hands behind her back and a killer glare on her face was Bridget Berg. "Shit," Kennedy whispered.

Her chances of getting into the lodge had just gone from slim to none. She got back on her feet and brushed the snow off her butt. Knowing that the not-so-cute little nickname was meant for her, she still felt the need to say, "Well, good morning. Kind of you to answer when called. Mind if I call you Hungry Hippo too? It has such a nice ring to it."

"They weren't referring to me, but I think you already know that." Bridget's expression didn't change, nor did she move an inch. She stood at the top of the trail like the gatekeeper of Valhalla.

"Oh. So, were you a fan of that game too?" she asked in a gleeful tone. "I used to love watching those little hippos eat the marbles." She knew it had nothing to do with the game, but feigning ignorance might've helped keep the conversation going.

"Fine," Kennedy said. "The hungry part is accurate. I'm starving my cold ass off, but the hippo part..."

Bridget cut her off. "May I help you with something, Ms. Fleming?"

Kennedy started up the trail. "Yes, as a matter of fact, you can."

"Let me rephrase that," Bridget said.

"Oh hell, no. You offered to help, and I'm taking you up on that offer come hell or a herd of hungry hippos."

"I misspoke."

"Seems to me that you've been misspeaking since the moment we met, which is why I want to file a complaint with the owner. I'm sure he'll be shocked by how rudely his daughter treats his guests."

If it was possible to intensify her expression, Bridget's killer glare morphed into a psycho, I chop people up for fun, glare. Kennedy summoned every inner demon she had to match it. She wouldn't back down this time. She'd get that coffee even if it meant brawling in the snow for it. Her fists tightened. Her jaw flexed. She was ready. *Bring it.*

"He's dead. And as long as I'm in charge, no member of the Fleming family is going to step one foot on my land." Bridget turned on her heel and walked away.

It took a moment for Kennedy to process this new information. Long enough that she'd have to run after Bridget to catch up to her. And since she felt like a total jackass, she chose to go back down the trail and ask the scared kid. "Hey. Is it true that Boden Berg passed away?"

He shook his head so hard, his beanie almost came off. "I'm really not supposed to talk to you, ma'am."

"Fine. Blink once if it's true."

He blinked and whispered, "He died last year."

Kennedy would have to apologize at some point, but that could wait. She reached into her pocket and pulled out a hundred-dollar bill. "This is yours if you get me two things. The lodge's Wi-Fi password and the biggest cup of coffee you can find."

"Trying to bribe my employees to sneak you into my hotel?" Bridget skied down the narrow trail and stopped in front of them. "Seth, go take your break."

Kennedy grabbed his arm. "No! It's not what it looks like. I offered him a hundred bucks to get me a coffee and your Wi-Fi password. That's it."

"Absolutely not. Go, Seth."

Kennedy kept a hold on his arm. "Okay, look. I'm desperate. And possibly addicted to both coffee and Wi-Fi, so before I go into withdrawal, could you please help me out here?"

"Your addictions are not my problem. Or Seth's. Or anyone's on this mountain, for that matter."

"What if I added in an apology for bringing up a painful subject? I honestly didn't know that Boden Berg had passed."

Bridget sidestepped on her skis until she was right in Kennedy's face. "I can appreciate that maybe you're not fully up to speed on the history our fathers have, but I am. And I refuse to let his daughter, or any member of his family, come up here and act like none of it ever happened and that we should all be buddies now. I don't trust you, and I don't want you on my property. Period."

A man skied down behind them. "Watch out," he shouted. "Coming through." Once he was out on the open space of the slope, he stopped and turned. "Are you heading down, Bridget? I'd love to ski a run with you."

She gave him a nod and pulled her goggles over her eyes. "Be right there, Zach."

Kennedy still felt the harsh glare, even though she couldn't see through the reflective lens. It didn't take away from the fact that Bridget Berg was a sight to behold, on skis or off, but those tight Lycra ski pants definitely brought her strong athleticism to the fore. Kennedy decided then and there that one way or another, she'd have those strong legs wrapped around her. Maybe in a hot tub or a steam room. Or maybe she was just freaking cold standing there, and that was why sex in a sauna sounded so good. She held up a finger and said, "Can I just say that you are so beautiful, and all I want is a hot cup of coffee?"

Kennedy had no idea what Bridget's eyes were doing behind those goggles. Were they looking her up and down? Because there wasn't much to see except a wool coat and highly inappropriate shoes for the terrain. "Did you just hear a thing I said?"

"Heard it. Felt it. Would love to hear more, but it's kinda cold out here, you know?" She wrapped her arms around herself and lowered her gaze while she waited for what she hoped would be a sympathetic reply. It gave her a chance to check out those tight ski pants again, and wow, did she have great legs.

"I'm going to go ski you off," Bridget finally said. And then added, "Seth, I'm going to ski her off. Don't you dare let her on the property, and don't take less than two hundred."

Seth turned back around and gave her a salute. In a kneejerk reaction, Kennedy did the same and said, "Thank you, Captain Stubing. I mean—"

Before she could finish, Bridget skied off and, yes, Kennedy did enjoy the view until she disappeared behind the pine trees. And then she shouted, "Yes. I get my coffee and Wi-Fi. Yes, yes, yes."

Seth came back down the trail, also looking pleased as punch. "Did she say two hundred?"

The wind picked up, causing a deep shiver to course through Kennedy's body. "Honestly, I don't know how you handle this cold. I'll throw in even more if you don't make me stand out here for too long."

"Yes, ma'am." Seth went to leave but turned back around. "This means I can buy my girlfriend that snowboard she's been eyeing for Christmas. She's gonna be so happy."

"Aw, that's sweet, Seth. Can you grab a muffin or a doughnut too? Actually, anything edible will be fine." Her standards for the world's most expensive breakfast had become shockingly low. "Oh, and one more thing. What did she mean when she said she was going to ski me off?"

"Oh, um…" He cleared his throat. "You know, like, working off the stresses of the day?"

"But the day's barely started." And then its meaning dawned on Kennedy. "Oh, right. I get it now. Hurry back."

Seth gave her a thumbs-up and started up the trail. If only she could follow him to that warm, comfy, delicious-smelling lodge. Who knew a person could actually covet a hotel lobby so much?

Like a good girl, she stayed right where she was. Heaven forbid Miss Sexy on Skis run into her again and have to *ski it off.*

❖

Bridget came out of the back office and motioned for Lola to follow her to the restaurant bar. "Is it five o'clock somewhere? Because it's been a hell of a day."

Lola glanced at her watch. "Close enough."

"How are things down the mountain?"

"Oh, the usual. People driving too fast for the road conditions. Some petty theft. Nothing exciting enough to report."

"I guess that's a good thing." Bridget pulled out two stools and gave the bartender a wave.

He came over with his hands up and said, "It wasn't me, Sheriff."

Lola quirked her head. "What do you mean?"

"Whatever you're up here for. It wasn't me."

"Oh. Well, ignore the uniform," Lola said. "I'm just here to have a drink with my friend."

He laughed. "I'm just messing with ya. What'll you have?"

Lola took her jacket off and unzipped her sweater. "I'm still on duty for another twenty minutes."

Bridget said, "A vodka and soda for me, Kevin. And a coffee for the sheriff."

Kevin put a couple of cocktail napkins on the bar. "Hey, Sheriff. My little sis is still crushing on you hard. Any chance you'd date a snowboarder? I know you skiers can be hardcore about these things."

Lola sat on the stool next to Bridget. "I'm not opposed to dating snowboarders. I'm opposed to dating women half my age."

Bridget shrugged. "It's a respectable stance, Lola."

"Meh. With my blown-out knee, I couldn't keep up with a twenty-year-old."

Kevin remained undeterred. "She's twenty-two. And a huge fan. Even has your *Sports Illustrated* cover hanging in her bedroom. And did I mention that she's really cute?" Kevin grabbed his phone and brought up a photo. "See?"

Lola leaned forward. "You're right. She is cute. But someone who's past their prime is more my speed. Someone like Bridget here."

"Hey!" Bridget pointed at Kevin. "Don't laugh or you're fired."

He jogged off to the other side of the bar and shook with laughter while he poured the coffee. Lola leaned in and said, "Now that he's gone, a little bird told me there's a new Fleming in town."

Bridget scoffed. "A little bird?"

"What? People still say little bird. It's totally a thing. You obviously just don't get out enough."

Bridget sighed. "You speak the truth, Lo. But what I meant is, you don't have to say little bird. I know you're talking about Harriet."

Of course it was Harriet. She was the only employee at the lodge that had Lola's cell number on speed dial. Rarely did they need to use it, but every once in a while, they'd have expensive ski gear go missing or a drunk guest who got a little too rowdy. Lola had a way about her that calmed people down. She never escalated a situation the way some of the other sheriffs would. So before calling 9-1-1, they called her.

"You know I can't reveal my sources," Lola said. "Besides, I like that Harriet has your back. With Boden gone, you need her. Especially when it comes to Jerry Fleming."

Bridget huffed. "Apparently, it's not just Jerry anymore. Will it never end with these people?"

"I was hoping the feud would die with Boden," Lola said. "In fact, I kind of imagined that Fleming would just abandon his place now that his nemesis is gone."

"I seriously doubt that woman is here to announce that they're abandoning the place." Kevin set their drinks in front of them. Bridget took a long sip of hers, hoping it would calm her nerves. She'd almost said beautiful woman. Had she done so, Lola would've jumped on it and wanted to know every little detail about her. How tall was she? Maybe 5'7"-ish. Was she attractive? Stunning, Bridget would've answered. Absolutely stunning. And then, Lola would've gotten that annoying expression on her face that screamed, you like a girl! As if they were in grade school and it was some big revelation that Bridget did indeed like girls. Thank God she hadn't divulged how beautiful Kennedy Fleming—aka, the lodge's mortal enemy—was.

"Any idea why she's here?" Lola asked.

Bridget lowered her voice. "Between you and me, I'm scared to death she's about to serve me with some bullshit lawsuit I can't afford to fight."

"Crap. You might be right. If she's anything like her father..."

Bridget cringed at the thought. "Don't tell me that, Lo. Not when I have employees who have little mouths to feed and bodies to clothe. I have to somehow make this place thrive without my dad. It's all on me. And then Hungry Hippo waltzes into town on a goddamned helicopter, the same way Jerry always has, and honestly, my heart can't take it." Lola laughed under her breath. "I'm serious, Lo. You've been in the thick of it with my dad. You know what they're capable of."

"Fair enough. If you're that worried about lawsuits, just try not to antagonize her, okay?"

"Well shit. You could have given that advice before I 86'd her."

Lola's eyes widened. "You threw her out?"

"Twice. With fanfare."

"All right. Well, let's just tone down the fanfare going forward."

"Fine. But I can't lose this place just because I let my guard down. I'd never forgive myself."

"You won't," Lola said. "I can't promise you much, but I have no doubt you'll be here long enough for your face to get all wrinkly and to have some sweet little kid bouncing around the owner's suite calling you grandma."

Bridget almost choked on her drink. "Are you trying to cheer me up? Because telling me that I'll be old and wrinkly soon isn't helping."

Lola laughed. "I was joking. You're closer in age to Kevin's little sister than I am. Why isn't he bothering you about it?"

"Oh, I don't know. Maybe because I don't have three Olympic medals and a *Sports Illustrated* cover?"

"The ladies do love that." Lola smirked. "It even worked on you, as I recall."

"Yeah. For about five minutes, Rico Suave. And for the record, I didn't date you for shallow reasons. Unless you consider the fact that you reminded me of Michelle Rodriguez to be a shallow reason."

"Ha. The shallowest reason of all, but I'll take it. Hey, Kevin. Do you have any of that spicy bridge mix?" She leaned closer to Bridget and lowered her voice. "I love that stuff. In fact, just wrap up a big bag of it and give it to me for Christmas. Also, a word of advice, don't ever sleep with a groupie. They're terrible in bed because all they can think about is how they'll announce their conquest to their friends. The star fuck is something they never get over. Not even in the moment."

Bridget knew Lola had plenty of conquests under her belt. At the top of her career, it was rare that she didn't have another Olympian on her arm. "Christmas gift and sex advice in one go? Why stop there?"

"Fine. Your gorgeous red hair could use a trim."

Bridget burst out laughing. "Nice try, Lo, but I had it trimmed two weeks ago."

Lola shrugged. "I just threw something out to see if it would stick."

Kevin put a small bowl of snack mix in front of Lola and gave her a wink. "Don't say I never gave you anything, Sheriff."

Lola popped a few in her mouth. "Feel free to join my Christmas gift list, Kevin. He's a flirty one, isn't he?"

"The guests adore him," Bridget said. "Oh, and last I checked, I'm fresh out of groupies. I would have had to medal for that."

Lola wrapped an arm around Bridget's shoulder. "It would've been yours, Bridge. If it hadn't been for that stupid knee, you probably would have gotten silver."

Bridget nudged her. "Silver? Please. I would have smoked your ass."

"And I would have loved seeing you try. Seriously. You were the best competition I ever had. And I bet you have plenty of groupies who never forgot how great you were, and you shouldn't either."

Bridget tried to shrug it off. "It hasn't mattered to me since Dad died. I can't think about what might have happened when I have this place to run. Did you know my dad charged fifteen hundred dollars to let a guest ski with him for two hours? No one would pay that much to ski with me."

"Have you tried it?"

"I wouldn't want to suffer the humiliation of no one ever booking time with me." Bridget's eyes lit up. "But they'd totally book time with you, Lo. We could put it on the website, and you could ski on your off days. We could even get some merch to sell in the gift shop right alongside Dad's. Oh my God. Why didn't I think of this sooner?"

"Woah, there, little lady."

Bridget threw a hand over her eyes. "Oh God. Not the terrible gunslinger accent."

Lola got off her stool, spread her legs and tucked her thumbs in her belt. "I'm the sheriff in these here parts, and I will not be pimped out by the likes of you." She rocked on her heels and pretended to spit chew out of her mouth.

Bridget motioned up and down Lola's body. "Does this schtick actually work for you? Because all I wanna do right now is take you back to the office and…" Bridget paused when Lola's eyes got big. She let her stand there and wonder for a moment before she said, "Talk to Harriet about getting you on the schedule."

Lola threw her hands in the air. "You couldn't give it to me, Bridge? Come on. It's kinda cute, right?"

Bridget chuckled. "Sure. Maybe you should try it on Kevin's sister."

"I'm done with the young ones. I need to find someone who doesn't require guidance. Someone classy and elegant. Someone like…"

Bridget raised an eyebrow. "If you say someone like my mom—"

"She's a handsome woman."

Lola had been teasing Bridget about hooking up with her mom for years. After all of the upheaval in her life over the past year, it was kind of nice to see that some things would never change. But she still feigned annoyance by rolling her eyes and downing the rest of her drink in one go. "Come on, cougar lover. I have someone I'd like to introduce you to. She has a new hairstyle I think you might find attractive." She grabbed Lola's coat and sweater and headed for the door.

Lola caught up to her. "Wait. Are you being serious?"

"Oh, yeah. She won't require any guidance. In fact, she'll boss you all over the bedroom. Window to the wall."

Lola grabbed her arm and stopped her. "Okay. I know where you're going with this. And it's not even a little bit funny."

Bridget gestured with her thumb and index finger. "Maybe a little bit funny? You? Harriet? Sparks flying?"

Lola threw a hand over her eyes. "I can't deal right now. She's like, I don't know…an auntie figure?"

"Yeah. It's kinda creepy. But we're going to her office anyway. We need to discuss getting you on the schedule up here."

"I thought you were the boss. It's your name on the building."

Bridget gave one of her younger guests a little wave as she went by. "Technically, I am. But nothing happens without Harriet's approval. You know that." Another young guest approached them, so Bridget threw her hand in the air. The boy made a running jump and tried to high-five her. "Good one, Max. You're almost there."

"Why are the cops here?" he asked.

"One cop. And she's my friend."

Lola offered her fist. "Hey, Max. Nice to meet you. Word of advice, Bridge? Don't tell Harriet what you just told me. You need to run this place like it's yours. Which it is. So own it, okay?"

Bridget didn't need any reminders that she was in charge or that everything to do with the lodge fell on her shoulders. She'd been carrying that load around for going on a year now. She stopped at Harriet's door and turned to Lola. "Trust me. I'm owning it when it counts. That hot Fleming chick will not get under my skin or anywhere near my…" She cringed when she realized she'd said it out loud. Maybe Lola would let it go. And maybe pigs would fly.

Lola smirked. "Hot, huh? Oh, and please finish that sentence. She won't get anywhere near your what?"

Bridget rolled her eyes. "Fill in the blank."

❖

Kennedy opened a kitchen cupboard and slammed it shut. She did the same thing with three more while she waited for her phone call to go through. She knew food wouldn't magically appear in one of them, but giving them a good slam every few hours seemed to help with her newly acquired anger management issues. She gave the empty fridge a good slam too.

"Ken? What's that noise?" Michael asked.

"I'm starving, okay? There's no food in this house, and no one will deliver because I'm on top of a fucking mountain, and the driveway hasn't been plowed. The only reason I can talk to you right now without the call dropping is because I bribed an employee at the lodge to give me their Wi-Fi password. Did you get the picture I sent of the cabin? Our father obviously lost his mind long before we knew he was losing his mind." It was a harsh thing to say about a man suffering from dementia, and Michael's silence told her it wasn't appreciated. "Sorry," she said. "That was uncalled for."

"Is that crime scene tape?"

"Oh, you noticed that too, huh? Doesn't blend in with the evergreens and snow well enough, apparently."

"What happened?" Michael asked.

"I happened. And when the fine people at the Boden Berg Lodge realized I was here, they put that tape up all around Dad's property. A fine welcome to the neighborhood, don't you think?" She slammed the last empty cupboard door shut. "Now, get me the hell out of here before an actual crime gets committed."

"Okay, look. You can't leave yet. I'll find someone to plow the driveway for you."

It didn't make sense. Michael could've worked with a real estate agent remotely. Kennedy did that in Miami all the time with out-of-state clients. And it wasn't as if they could sink a few grand into the house and make that much more of a profit. The place was dated. The design was horrible. The furnace was useless. The house was a total tear-down. Why not just take what they could get and walk away?

She sank back down in the recliner under a blanket. "Michael, our father is hated here. And the longer I stay, the more worried I get that I'm going to lose respect for a man I've admired my entire life. They literally hate him. And me by proxy. Why is that? What are you not telling me about this place?"

"You can't look at it as just a dated house on top of a mountain. Dad built that place back when there were only one or two ski runs on Elk Mountain. The people who skied there back then were diehard badasses who didn't care if the runs were groomed. They were there to ski the back country where the powder was deep, and there wasn't another soul around."

"Great story, bro, but here's a news flash. There still isn't another soul around, and the few who *are* here on top of this, this goddamned mountain won't feed me. Oh, and my luggage still hasn't arrived, so I have nothing but Dad's clothes to wear. Just kill me now, Michael." She sounded pathetic and spoiled, even to herself. But she hadn't put herself in this situation, Michael had. In fact, she'd worked her ass off just so she'd never have to deal with shit like this. She could pay someone else to stoke the fire and bring her food and whatever the hell else she needed. This was just plain bullshit.

After a long pause, Michael said, "I thought lesbians liked flannel."

It wasn't like Michael to make jokes about her sexuality. Why he chose that particular moment to make one, when she was cold and hungry, was beyond her. "You know what, Michael? You're lucky your wife is about to deliver my goddaughter because it's the only reason I'll still be talking to you after this. Good-bye." She wanted to throw her phone across the room, but then she'd truly be all alone.

CHAPTER FOUR

B ridget walked Lola to the door. "Thanks for stopping by. And give it some thought, Lo. I think some of our guests would jump at the chance to ski with you."

"And I think you're selling yourself short," Lola said. "But I have to say, the way you told Harriet what was what instead of asking her permission was kinda hot. Keep that up, okay?"

Bridget blushed. Even though their dating relationship had been short-lived, Bridget was grateful it hadn't ruined their friendship. She didn't know what she'd do without Lola in her life. She was about to reply when a strange voice came through her radio.

Please be advised that Hungry Hippo just sat at the bar, and she's about to order a martini on an empty stomach.

Bridget gasped. "How did she get hold of someone's radio?"

"That's her?" Lola asked with a laugh. "Hey, at least she has a sense of humor."

Harriet rushed toward them. "Bridge, maybe you should let Sheriff Johns handle her this time?"

Lola grinned. "I'd rather watch Bridget kick some ass. But in a really nice way because she's working on not being antagonistic."

Bridget fumed on the inside. Kicking ass was exactly what she wanted to do, but she gave Harriet a reassuring smile. "Take Lola to the security office. She can watch from there."

Lola winked before she turned to walk away. There was a certain level of comfort in knowing she'd be there if Bridget needed backup. Hopefully, it wouldn't come to that since the lobby had started to fill up with tired skiers ready to warm up by the fire with a cocktail. She made sure she smiled at her guests as she went while calming herself with a few deep breaths. The last thing she needed was a nasty scene right before the dinner hour.

Kennedy was indeed sitting at the bar with her arms folded tight against her body and a scowl on her face. She lifted her chin when she saw Bridget and said, "It's about time. Kevin would only serve me water until you arrived."

Bridget held out her hand. "The radio, please."

With a look of defiant reluctance, Kennedy took a radio from its hiding place between her legs and set it in Bridget's hand. "I got desperate when I couldn't find Seth."

Kennedy didn't make eye contact the way she had before. She folded her arms again and stared straight ahead. Bridget took it as a silent threat that she'd make a scene if she was asked to leave again. As much as she wanted to grab her by the arm and drag her out of there, a part of her also wanted to impress Harriet and Lola by diffusing the situation without their help. Didn't mean she couldn't still make the threat.

She leaned on the bar with one elbow and faced Kennedy. "If you're here to make trouble, you should probably know that Sheriff Johns is currently sitting in my security office."

"I bet his jail is warmer than my house. Maybe I should steal some food instead of going broke for it." She put up a finger and made eye contact. "Or maybe you should go to jail for charging me two hundred dollars for coffee and a muffin. I think they call that price gouging?"

Bridget tried to suppress a grin. The fact that Kennedy actually paid Seth that much made her want to laugh out loud. "The sheriff is a *she*, actually. And I wouldn't know how warm her jail is, but if you leave quietly, neither of us will ever have to find out."

Kennedy's eyes lit up. "Oh, I love a woman in a uniform. Especially one who's packing heat. What color is her uniform? I'm going to guess it's khaki green. Seems logical for someone whose territory is in the woods, wouldn't you agree, Bridget?"

For a moment, Bridget wondered if their close proximity and the flirty tone in Kennedy's voice was some sort of power play. Now that she had their Wi-Fi password, had she done her research? Did she know Bridget was a lesbian? Did she just assume she was also a sucker for a pretty face? She didn't want to think of Jerry Fleming's blood relative in those terms, but it was hard not to when they were so close to one another. When Bridget realized she'd let her eyes follow Kennedy's hand as she smoothed her hair over her ear and down the back of her neck, then rested it under her chin, she turned away.

"Oh God," Kennedy said. "You're going to make me wonder what color it is, aren't you? Well, for the love of all that's sacred, can I please get some bread and butter before I keel over on your floor, and you're forced to give me mouth-to-mouth?"

Bridget could've kicked herself when her eyes went directly to said mouth. It was as if she couldn't help herself from falling into every flirty trap Kennedy set for her. With a quick flick of her wrist, she waved a server over. "A basket of bread, please, Wendy."

"And a cheese board, Wendy. And a medium rare steak, if it's not too much trouble. Oh, and I don't know if word has gotten around, but I tip really well, especially when I'm on death's door. Can you see how hollow my cheeks have gotten? And my color is sort of gray, isn't it? Like I belong in a hospital bed getting last rites from my priest."

"Okay, that's enough." Bridget shooed Wendy away and turned back to Kennedy. "I'd appreciate it if you'd direct your comments to me and leave my staff out of it."

Kennedy leaned back in her chair and put her hands up. "Fine. At least you haven't kicked me out into that arctic gale that's picked up in the last hour. I guess I should be grateful for that much."

"Guilt trips won't work," Bridget said. "You'll eat your bread, and then you'll leave quietly. Now, what kind of soda do you like? I can't have you choking on the bread."

Kennedy leaned forward and rested her chin in her hand. "The vodka kind."

Bridget caught Kevin's eye and waved him over. "I'm not going to serve you alcohol on an empty stomach so you can wander out into the cold and die on a snowbank. I hate when that happens."

"Yeah, choking and hypothermia don't sound like much fun, but what if you try to kill me with food? A big fat steak and a baked potato covered in butter and cheese and bacon bits. Oh, and sour cream, obviously. I'd die for that. Hell, I'd kill for that. And you can sit right here on the stool next to me to make sure I behave." Kennedy threw her hands to the sky. "My God, I'm brilliant."

"What can I get for you?" Kevin asked.

Bridget stopped Kennedy from replying by putting her hand across the bar in front of her. "She'll have a Diet Coke on the house. No refills." She snapped her head around when she heard a chuckle and said, "I'm this close to kicking you out, so I wouldn't laugh if I were you."

Kennedy pursed her lips together and gave her a nod. "Thank you for buying me a drink. Very chivalrous of you."

"Don't say it like I just bought you a *drink* drink." Bridget grimaced at her own words. She felt flustered and feared she was getting red in the face. She wasn't sure what to do next. Should she stand there and watch the Hungry Hippo snarf down a mini loaf of bread? Should she walk away and hope she didn't go from table to table begging for scraps? Should she give in and let the woman eat? She pulled at her collar and wished she hadn't put a company sweater on over her button-up shirt.

"Holy hot sheriff," Kennedy said. "And I nailed it with the khaki green."

Bridget turned toward the entrance. She wasn't sure why Lola had felt the need to join them. She had the situation under control.

It irritated her slightly, but she tried not to let it show and waited until she was seated on the other side of Kennedy before she said, "Sheriff Johns, this is Kennedy Fleming, aka, Jerry's daughter. She'll be gone once her bread arrives, won't you, Ms. Fleming?"

Kennedy gave her a sly grin. "Careful, Ms. Berg. You might get me all hot and bothered with your tough talk." She offered a hand to Lola and said, "It's a pleasure to meet you, Sheriff Johns." She leaned back in her chair so the three of them had a view of each other and glanced between them as if watching a silent tennis match.

Lola reached into her shirt pocket and pulled out a business card. "I just came by to introduce myself. This is my direct number. If you have any issues, concerns, complaints, feel free to call me anytime."

Kennedy took the card and tucked it in her pocket. "That list would take some time to write, so how about we focus on my current complaint, which is the lack of service in this bar. Do you happen to have any pull with the boss, Sheriff?"

Lola smiled. "I try to save it for the really important stuff. You ladies have a good evening."

Kennedy offered her hand again. "So good to meet you, Sheriff. Feel free to stop by my place anytime. It's BYOB. Oh, and potluck. But not salad. I don't have time for salads anymore."

Bridget had heard enough. "Hey, Sheriff? Chef is making a special Sunday brunch tomorrow. You should join us if you can."

Lola rubbed her hands together. "Ooh…will he be making those hazelnut crepes I love so much? If so, I'm in."

"Great. See you tomorrow." Bridget gave Lola a pat on the shoulder as she went by and turned back to find Kennedy scowling at her. "I'll have the shop send over some provisions to your house in the morning. Can't have the neighbors going hungry."

"So I'll be eating tiny powdered doughnuts from your gift shop while you all have, what? Caviar? Stuffed French toast? Fresh ground espresso? Maybe an English muffin with marmalade?"

"Homemade English muffins. They're delicious. And don't forget about the caramel pecan cinnamon rolls and warm beignets dusted in powdered sugar." It gave Bridget such pleasure to say those words; she realized she was smiling in a gleeful way. Was that horrible? Did it make her a bad person? Probably, but she didn't care.

Wendy walked up with a to-go container. The look of fear in her eyes told Bridget that she'd realized who Kennedy was: Jerry the Jerk's daughter.

"Oh, look. Wendy put the bread in a to-go container for you, which means there's no reason for you to sit here any longer."

Kennedy picked up her glass and downed her drink. She stood and faced Bridget. "I wouldn't take that bread from you now if it was the last thing I had to eat."

Bridget raised an eyebrow. "It is, isn't it?"

With a final glare that Bridget assumed was meant to cover up the hurt in her eyes, Kennedy walked out of the restaurant. "Well, shit," Bridget whispered. She grabbed the bread and went after her. "You really should take the bread. Can't have you dying of starvation on my mountain," she quipped.

Kennedy sauntered through the lobby, never looking back before she went out the door. She didn't even stop in the store for some snacks. Lola came back out of the security office and stood next to Bridget. "Well, she's trouble with a capital T. *Hot* trouble."

Bridget huffed. "You're just saying that because you like the feisty type. Remember that girl from Sweden?"

"All legs and bad attitude," Lola said. "God, how I loved her." She nudged Bridget with her elbow. "Want me to take this one off your hands?"

Bridget gasped. "She's a Fleming, Lo. Please tell me you would never, in a million years, go there, or I might have to ban you from the property too."

Lola laughed. "I'm just messing with you. And I'm one call away if you need me." She put her coat on and zipped it all the way up. "It's getting bad out there. Better get going."

Bridget held up the to-go box. "I remember how much you like good toast in the morning."

Lola took the box. "Ooh, I have the perfect topping for it too. Aunt May just made a batch of her apple jalapeno jelly."

"Tell her to call Chef. He'll want to stock up."

"Will do."

She watched Lola brave the wind and snow until she was safe in her SUV. Snowfall was welcomed by all but combined with wind, made for some rough skiing. Bridget hoped it would die down by morning.

❖

Kennedy wasn't spending another miserable night in that cabin. She didn't care what Michael had to say about it. She opened the garage door and inspected the four-wheel ATV. It had a small snowplow attached to the front. She just had to figure out how to make the damn thing work so she could plow the driveway and get herself out of this godforsaken place.

She'd found the keys to her dad's Jeep in the bedroom, but even if she gunned it, she'd never get through the deep snow on the driveway. *Is that what you're supposed to do? Gun it? Or do you try to ease through it?* These weren't problems they had in Miami. She swung her leg over the seat and grabbed both handlebars. She'd only been on one once before, but that was years ago on a beach. *Turns out, if you barely cut yourself on some ocean rock, a cute lifeguard named Sarah Jane may just roll up and offer you a ride to the first aid office. She may also tell you to put your arms around her waist and hang on tight.* Kennedy had obliged, of course.

So, yes, she'd been on an ATV before; she just hadn't ever driven one. She was more of a boat girl. The kind that came with a driver and bartender. But really, how hard could it be? She was capable. She knew how to visualize. "Just close your eyes and imagine yourself plowing the hell out of that driveway," she said.

After a moment, she opened her eyes, took a deep breath, and pressed the start button. Nothing. She pressed it again and again, then jumped off the stupid thing. Was it out of gas? Or oil? Did it need to be primed? Dead battery? She flipped the headlight switch, and it lit up. Okay. The battery was fine. Oh, maybe it had one of those pull-cords like a lawn mower. She circled the ATV. No pull-cord. She didn't see a kickstart pedal either. She kicked the tire in frustration. "Ow. Damnit," she shouted as she hopped on one foot. She limped over to the door, switched off the lights, and went back inside. There was no Sarah Jane to rescue her now.

She hobbled back into the house, thinking of all the ways this was Bridget Berg's fault. To start with, if Bridget wasn't such a profoundly irrational person, Kennedy would be enjoying a warm meal and a cold drink right about then. Instead, she was looking at an evening of nursing her big toe in a freezing cold house that had all the warmth of one of those minimum-security prisons they filmed reality TV shows in. Not that Kennedy ever watched that sort of thing. Not often anyway. Unless Sundays, and also sometimes Saturdays, were considered to be often. One thing was certain. Bridget Berg would pay for her complete lack of humanity. Once Kennedy had the upper hand, she'd give her a taste of her own medicine. "Damn right, I will," she said out loud. "You haven't met revenge until you've met me, Bridget Berg."

Who was she kidding? She'd never plotted revenge against anyone in her life. She tilted her head and wondered what the first step would be. A narrowing of the eyes seemed right. And a tapping of an index finger on the chin. She wiggled her toe again because surely revenge required ten good toes. And strength. She'd need the strength a good warm meal would give her. But that wasn't likely to happen anytime soon.

Her thoughts turned to her dad. Was this all his fault? Sure, the man could fly off the handle. He'd been known to say hurtful things once in a while, but his heart was in the right place. Wasn't it? Kennedy found herself questioning everything now. Did all of their neighbors in Miami hate her dad too, and she just didn't know it? Was she the only person in the entire world who thought well of him? It seemed impossible. No, whatever had happened on this mountain was an isolated incident. And her dad must've had good reason for his actions, whatever they were.

Thoughts of him had her wishing she could see him. Hold his hand. Tell him how much she loved him and hope he understood her words one last time. She sucked back her emotions. Now was not the time to cry. Now was the time to flip all of these people off on her way down the mountain.

But that meant getting the damn driveway plowed. Kennedy had made multiple calls to different plow people, but none were willing to get to her until after the storm. And apparently, no one could bribe a county plow contractor to clear a driveway no matter how long and steep it was. And no matter how easy it would be to do when they were already doing the main road. Something about liability and turning the truck around, blah, blah, blah. If she was going to eat, she'd need to figure something out.

She'd searched "food near here" on her phone earlier that day. Of course, the lodge's restaurant with its stupid five stars and four diamonds came up first. After that, the search results revealed an actual store in town, a small market that would at least have enough to see her through. Equally important, the town of Elk Mountain had a coffee shop. Yes, please. According to the reviews—and four hundred or so photos—it even had good pastries. Not Boden Berg Lodge great, but still good, the reviews said. Because of course, someone had to mention the lodge in their stupid review.

She eased onto the floor in front of the fireplace so she could get her boot off. A whimper escaped her lips with the first tug, and then a high-pitched yelp when the edge of the boot grazed her injured toe. "Don't be broken," she whispered. "Please, big toe. Don't be broken." It was red and already starting to swell. She took a deep breath and tried to wiggle it. When it moved, she could have cried due to the pain but also because that usually meant the bone wasn't broken. "Thank you, big toe. Oh my God, thank you for not breaking." It was obvious she'd jammed it or sprained it or something, but at least it moved.

Since the ATV appeared to be a literal nonstarter, Kennedy weighed her other options for getting off the mountain. She could flag down one of the employees on their way home from work and beg for a ride into town. That would require another hike down that steep, winding driveway in deep snow. If she hadn't broken a bone yet, she surely would then. It also presented the possibility of a long wait in the cold since she had no idea when their shifts ended. Even if she did make it, would someone really help her out? In all likelihood, they'd probably see who she was and drive like hell to get away.

She put both feet near the fire and wiped a few tears away with her sleeve. Allergies, obviously. It wasn't like she was crying because she was frustrated or mad at her father or hungry or unable to figure out why the hot hotel lady hated her with a passion. Hell, everyone on the mountain hated her with a passion. Except maybe Seth, but he only liked her for her cash, and without an ATM nearby, she'd soon run out of that too.

None of it made sense. Maybe there was some bad blood over the Jerry Fleming Correctional Facility being built in the shadow of the lodge. She could see people being angry about that, but did that really warrant the hungry hippo business and her being kicked out so unceremoniously? It was an ugly house, but watching someone trapped in it without food or heat? That seemed a bit much, even for Bridget Berg. What was her deal? Did she think being an adorable, athletic, redheaded sex kitten would excuse bad behavior? Kennedy meant all that in an objective way, of course. Obviously.

For some reason, she felt the need to lie on her side with her legs curled up. But not in a fetal position or anything. That would have been pathetic. Again, it had nothing to do with her miserable situation. She simply enjoyed lying on cold hard floors while staring into flames, just like every other revenge-plotting person in the world.

If only those lodge people understood that being the daughter of the man who made the mountain ugly didn't automatically make her his cunning, manipulative, devil-horned offspring. Or worse, that she had bad taste. She'd already invested considerable time sitting in this cold house trying to figure out why and how and who had helped her dad put that ridiculous, monstrous thing on the roof.

She straightened her leg so she could check in on her swollen toe and said, "This house is awful, Big Toe. You could do a better job of designing a house than Dad did. Hell, your baby friend on the end there could do a better job. And now, I'm talking to my fucking toe. This is turning into a *Cast Away* situation. You're the volleyball, and I'm the one who's hungry."

She rolled onto her back and clasped her fingers on her very empty tummy. "She's beautiful, BT. That's what we're calling you now, Big Toe. BT Fleming the second. Anyway, Bridget Berg is beautiful. Stubborn. Smart. Sexy. But Jerry's Fucking Daughter—that's what we're calling me now—anyway, she, or me, can't seem to flirt her way into that woman's heart. I mean, her restaurant." She lifted her leg and wiggled her toe again. "I know. It's starting to get weird for me too. Glad you're feeling better, though."

She sat up because she really needed to get off this mountain and find a hotel with a warm bed and room service before she started talking to other body parts. Maybe there was a how-to video on YouTube she could watch. She took her phone out of her pocket and typed in the search bar, *How to start an ATV*. She went still when she heard something outside. It sounded like one of those snowmobiles she'd seen go by on the slopes, but it was coming from the other side of the house. Was someone riding up the driveway? Was she being rescued? She got up and promptly forgot about her injured toe when she took a step. "Shit, shit, shit." She hopped around for a second and then gingerly limped her way to the door.

She peered through the peephole. To say she was surprised by the visitor would have been an understatement. She'd have been less taken aback by the Publisher's Clearinghouse Prize Patrol showing up with a giant check. Instead, she watched Bridget Berg climb the steps while taking her hat and goggles off. Her shoulders were covered in snow. The tips of her hair were wet. Her cheeks were rosy. Kennedy opened the door and tried to act casual, even though she wanted to grab Bridget and cry in her arms because she was that glad to see that someone cared if she was alive or dead. Even if that someone had some serious issues.

She put her weight on her good foot and leaned against the door with her arms folded. Yeah. That looked casual. "This is a surprise. Unfortunately, I don't have a thing to offer you in the way of food or drink, but you already know that."

"May I come in for a moment? It won't take long."

Her softer tone surprised Kennedy. "Um, yeah. Of course." Before closing the door, she noticed that the snow was coming down harder than before. "Is it going to do that all night?"

"All weekend, if we're lucky." Bridget stomped her feet on the door mat.

Lucky for you, maybe. Kennedy closed the door and turned to find Bridget staring at the place. "Have you never been inside before?"

Bridget shook her head. "I imagined something quite different."

"Not exactly up to my standards, either. Can I take your coat?"

"I'm not staying," Bridget snapped back.

Okay, so the kinder tone had lasted all of five seconds. "Of course not," Kennedy said. "How silly of me to think that this was a friendly visit."

Bridget turned back to the door as if she was about to leave but stopped and turned around. "I'm not a cruel person. In fact, I wouldn't let my worst enemy go hungry, and since you seem to be the closest thing I have to one of those, I brought you dinner." She took off her backpack and pulled out an insulated shopping bag.

Part of Kennedy wanted to decline the offer with, "I wouldn't take food from you if it was the last thing left to eat on Earth."

But that part of Kennedy was not her stomach. Instead, she was ready to shed tears of gratitude. She imagined herself falling into Bridget's arms and kissing her rosy cheek. She'd unzip her parka and slide her arms around her waist and bask in this little moment of kindness and connection. But that might scare her away, and more than anything, she wanted Bridget to stay a little longer. Okay, evidently, the hunger had taken hold of Kennedy's grasp on reality. She wasn't actually crushing on this horrible woman. She couldn't be.

She took the bag and said, "Thank you. That's very kind of you." She'd have to limp her way to the kitchen with one bare foot. It wouldn't be the least bit sexy, but she needed to get Bridget away from the door so she couldn't make a quick exit. She limped away, hoping she'd follow her. "Is there any alcohol in this bag? I'd love to pour us a drink."

"I didn't come here to drink with you." Bridget turned to open the door.

"Why did you come here, Bridget? You could've sent someone else on this little errand, couldn't you?"

"This property is off-limits to my employees. Your father has seen to that."

"Why would he do that?"

"If you really don't know, you'll need to ask your father, Kennedy."

"Okay, secret squirrel. Have it your way. But they're banned, and you're not?"

"Technically, I am too, but I figured you'd overlook it for food."

It hadn't taken much time on the internet for Kennedy to confirm that the good sheriff and Bridget were both gay. Both were USA Ski Team members who had dated at one time. And both were sexy, hot, athletic women. She wondered if there was any chance her attraction to Bridget could be mutual. The chances were slim, given all the animosity, but when Bridget's eyes landed on Kennedy's bare foot, she decided that maybe being flirty wasn't the way to go at all. The sympathy card was worth a shot, so she held up her foot and said, "I may have broken my big toe."

It was a pitiful attempt, followed by an even more pitiful pushup onto the counter with a shy shrug added for good measure. She swung her foot out and waited.

Bridget didn't move from the door, but her internal struggle was obvious. Every second that passed gave Kennedy hope that she'd break through that thick armor, if only out of pity. Hey, she'd take it, or any other reason that kept Bridget firmly planted on this side of the door.

"It looks fine from here," Bridget said.

Kennedy tilted her head and frowned at her foot. "Really? Because you wouldn't believe how badly it's throbbing right now." Okay, so maybe other body parts were throbbing harder than her toe. And maybe as Bridget slowly approached, she lost her breath for a second or twelve.

She wouldn't have the background chatter of a busy restaurant to muffle whatever physical reactions she might have in the next few seconds. She'd have to control her breathing if Bridget actually touched her, or she'd know this was all a ruse to keep her there. And not just because she was maybe crushing on her slightly. She wanted her to stay long enough to see that Kennedy wasn't a threat to her or any of her guests. She wanted to chat. Get to know her.

Bridget stood in front of her, her hands tucked deep inside her coat pockets. "Wiggle it."

Kennedy ignored the request. She so badly wanted to reach out and wipe a melting snowflake from Bridget's brow. Maybe tuck her damp hair behind her ears and caress her cheek. The thought sent her heart into overdrive, causing her to take an unexpectedly short breath. Not quite a gasp for air but close. She disguised it as a sign of pain and wiggled her toe as best she could.

"You should ice it." Bridget turned and headed for the door.

"Said the ice queen."

Kennedy said it under her breath, but it stopped Bridget in her tracks. She turned back around, and Kennedy pointed. "See? Icy glare from the ice queen. Are you ever going to tell me why you have such hatred for someone you don't even know? Google me, Bridget. You'll see that I'm just a normal girl from Miami who sells real estate, has a passion for good wine, fine chocolate, and yappy little dogs I can carry in my purse. Oh, and I appreciate good architecture. So yeah, I know how awful that ridiculous add-on is."

Bridget lifted her eyes toward the ceiling. "Seeing it from the inside just confirms that Jerry really did make this house taller just to block the lodge's view of the valley. My dad used to love to take guests onto the balcony at night so they could see the city lights below. Don't forget to ice that toe."

"I'm not my father," Kennedy shouted. But it was too late. Bridget was already out the door.

❖

Womp. Bridget whipped around to see who had just thrown a snowball at her back. Any other time, she might have returned fire, but she wasn't in the mood "Seriously, Harriet? What are you doing out here, anyway?"

"I was just saying hi."

"By throwing a snowball at me?"

"Well, you didn't answer when I called your name," Harriet teased. "Where were you?"

Bridget reached under her beanie and took the AirPods out of her ears. She'd parked the snowmobile and sat there for a moment, listening to music and contemplating if she'd done the right thing. She hadn't needed to take off her parka to know how cold it was in that house. She could've asked where the thermostat was so she could check to see if it was working. She could've stoked the sad little fire Kennedy had built and had it roaring within minutes. But she hadn't done either of those things. Nor had she gotten close enough to know if the claim of having broken her toe was real or not. For all she knew, Kennedy would claim it had happened on lodge property and sue them for bodily injury.

It was so easy to dislike the woman because of who her father was and all the history. Easier than engaging her in conversation. Easier than asking why she was there. Easier than asking why Jerry *wasn't* there. She wasn't ready to confront the situation head-on out of fear it would turn into something bigger than she could handle. After all they'd been through with Jerry over the years, she'd be a fool to ever trust his daughter. Luckily, she was able to ignore the way Kennedy tried to look so cute when she hopped up on the counter and stuck out her foot. Bridget might have formed an image in her head of being between those legs and having them wrap around her while she explored a soft neck with her lips and maybe some tongue. She also might have heard the breathy gasps for air and felt fingernails dig into her shoulders, but it was all very short-lived. A split second, really. A flash of passion she'd chastised herself for even thinking because, no. Just…God, no.

"I took some food to our neighbor," she said. "And don't tell me I'm a sucker for a pretty face. It's not about that."

"No," Harriet said. "It's because just like your father, you have a big heart. That's why everyone adored him. But I thought we'd decided not to feed the animal so she'd seek food down valley. What changed?"

"After she walked out of here with nothing to eat, I felt so guilty. And with all this snow coming down, I knew no one in their right mind would deliver food all the way up here, no matter how much she offered to tip them."

Harriet looked at the sky. "A few more inches and they'll close the road until morning anyway. Oh, that reminds me. I turned on the heat in the bunkhouse. I'm sure some of the staff will want to spend the night. Also, I may have had them move everything out of your dad's closet and into your room. I got the feeling you'd been putting it off."

Bridget gave her a smile. "I had. Thanks, Harriet. I'd be lost without you."

"Well, we both know that's true. Hey, do you mind if I stay in the penthouse tonight? I noticed that the bedrooms have been made up."

It was a weird request. Harriet would drive through a blizzard to get back to her cats. She always said she knew the road so well, she could drive it blindfolded. "Of course," Bridget said. "But what about Luke and Laura?"

"My neighbor will feed them." She pointed at Bridget. "But you, my dear, should stop feeding the animals. Got it?"

Bridget bent down and grabbed a handful of snow. "Get outta here before I return fire."

"Don't you dare." Harriet made a quick retreat back into the lodge.

On her way inside, Bridget stopped where she had a view of the Fleming cabin. She'd done the right thing, but Harriet was right. Eventually, a wild animal would bite the hand that fed them.

Chapter Five

Bridget bent and zipped up little Ruby Gallagher's coat. "Did you fill up on Chef Lawrence's French toast?"

Ruby gave her a big nod. "And my favorite bacon. I'm sorry your daddy had to die. I miss him."

Leave it to a six-year-old kid to express her love for bacon and at the same time, offer her condolences. The Gallagher family had been coming to the lodge for so long that Bridget had become friends with Ruby's dad when they were both about eight years old. She kissed Ruby's forehead and said, "I miss him too, sweetie, but I'll let you in on a secret, and only you and I will ever know, so you have to promise not to tell anyone, okay?"

Ruby grinned. "I keep the best secrets."

"Good. You know the really big deer out back with the huge horns? It's called an elk, and that was Uncle Boden's favorite animal in the whole world."

"I like that statue," Ruby said. "Every year, my daddy puts me on his back and takes a picture."

"Well, when I'm missing my dad, I go out there, and I rub Mr. Elk's nose. You could do that too, if you want."

Ruby grinned. "I will. Right now."

Bridget stood and gave Ruby's parents a wave as they left. She heard someone clear their throat behind her, so she turned. She was shocked and mildly annoyed to see that Kennedy Fleming had managed to get a seat at one of the small tables near the bar. "How much did that cost you?" she asked.

"The table? Or having Seth carry me most of the way on his back?"

Oh, what the hell, Bridget thought. Might as well sit down for this one. She pulled out a chair and sat sideways with her back against the wall so she wouldn't have to look Kennedy in the eye. "I thought I made it clear that we don't serve your kind here."

"What kind is that?"

"The kind that attack without warning, even when unprovoked. Also, it's a health and safety code violation to have animals near the buffet line. So how about you skedaddle on out of here?"

Kennedy leaned back in her chair and grinned. "You really do have one of the smartest mouths I've ever encountered. God, it's a turn-on."

Bridget rolled her eyes. "How did you get in here?"

"Oh, now, don't be mad at Seth. It's not his fault he can't resist my wily hippo charms."

"Don't you mean your money?" Bridget folded her arms. "How much did it take?"

"Two hundred. I would've paid five to see you again, but he didn't haggle." Bridget shot her a glare. Kennedy raised a hand. "Wait. Don't look at me until I explain a few things."

Bridget turned away again. "Oh, thank God. For a second there, I thought you were going to try to win me over with those wily hippo charms."

"I have a feeling you wouldn't fall so easily. Especially when I look like this, which is why I wanted to tell you that the airline lost my luggage, so all I arrived with was the clothes on my back and my skis."

"Excellent news. The roads are closed, but you can ski down the mountain and never have to see that house you hate so much again."

Kennedy lifted her leg and put her foot on Bridget's knee. "I'm wearing my dad's old Levi's. Luckily, he's always been a skinny man." She tugged at her collar. "And flannel doesn't really suit me, but it's all I could find in the closet."

Bridget eyed the big boot resting on her leg. For a split second, she wondered how the toe was doing, but then she pushed Kennedy's foot off with the back of her hand and said, "Oh, but it does suit you. To a tee." She loved flannel shirts, but she figured that someone as feminine as Kennedy would take her comment as an insult, which was perfect. And the brief flicker of insecurity in her eyes told her it was true.

Kennedy blinked a few times, but she seemed to remain undeterred. "Also, I can't do anything with my hair. Everything was—"

"In your luggage," Bridget said. "I'm picking up on the theme here, but you really should stick with the Joe Jonas look."

Bridget was about to get up when a server blocked her way with a carafe of coffee and a plate of beignets that she set on the table, and with fear in her eyes, said, "Seth told me to do it."

"I'm sure he did." Bridget gave her a tight smile. "It's fine." As soon as the server was out of earshot, she turned back to Kennedy. "Wow, you have some nerve."

"My nerve is right up there with your quick insults." Kennedy took a bite of a beignet and moaned so loudly, it made Bridget cringe.

"Okay, do you have to do that? This is a family friendly hotel."

Kennedy wiped her mouth with a napkin. "You should've heard me last night with that hamburger you delivered. Me and Ms. Burger got. It. On."

Bridget leaned on the table and shaded her eyes with her hand so she wouldn't have to watch Kevin snicker at them from behind the bar. "Like father, like daughter," she said. "Always trying to provoke, disrupt, and ruin everyone's day." She pulled her radio off her waistband and set it on the table.

Kennedy's eyes widened. "Are we going to scuffle?"

"What?"

"You know, in the movies, when guys get ready to fight, they usually take something off, like their jacket or their watch or if it's a western, their gun holster. You just took off your walkie-talkie, which makes me think we're about to get into it."

"It was poking into my side, but if we did *scuffle*, I would kick your ass all over this mountain."

Kennedy nodded. "I have no doubt about that, but isn't walkie-talkie a great name? I love saying it. Walkie-talkie."

"It's a radio. Walkie-talkies are for kids. But by all means, stop the talkie thing, so you can do the walkie thing right on out of here before I have to do the kicky thing, and you end up face-first in a snowbank." Bridget got up and pointed at Kevin on her way out the door. "Stop laughing, Kevin."

"Speaking of great asses," Kennedy said, loud enough for the guests seated around them to hear.

Bridget stopped. She took a deep breath and resisted the temptation to turn around and grab Kennedy by the arm and drag her out of there. But she did saunter back and stand over her with her arms crossed. It was time to know the truth. "Why are you here, Kennedy?"

"I'm here to meet with a real estate agent."

Bridget stopped breathing. Could it be that Jerry was ready to sell now that Bridget's dad was gone? Was the fight no longer fun for him? Would he take no pleasure in tormenting Boden's daughter? It seemed like too much to wish for. "You're...you're going to sell the place?"

"My brother could tell you more. He's the one who's been handling this, but he and his wife are busy having a baby right now. And after sending me on this nightmare of an errand, he'll make her my goddaughter if he knows what's good for him."

"I see."

"That makes one of us," Kennedy said. "Personally, I think he could've handled it from home, and this is his way of getting back at me for that time I stole his girlfriend. Please let me know when I've made enough references to being a lesbian."

"Didn't have to say a word. The flannel shirt and 501s gave you away."

For the first time, it seemed like they were having a moment of mutual amusement and extended eye contact that wasn't a prolonged glare to see who would break first. Kennedy had a gorgeous smile and a sparkle in her eye that Bridget hadn't noticed before. It felt like one of those fairytales where the Hungry Hippo turned into a beautiful, flannel-wearing lesbian right before the other lesbian's eyes. Lady-on-lady fairytales. That classic trope.

But it could be a trick. She was still a Fleming, after all, but she couldn't totally squelch her enthusiasm for the first measure of hope in twenty-five years. And Bridget couldn't wait to share the news with Harriet. So in a much kinder tone, she said, "Enjoy your breakfast," and walked away.

As soon as she hit the lobby, she speed walked to Harriet's office, threw her door open, and said, "You won't believe what just happened."

Harriet shot out of her chair, grabbed her chest, and sat back down. "You can't scare an old woman like that, Bridge."

"Sorry. It's just…big. Really big."

"Well, have a seat, then."

"I can't. I need to pace and jump up and down, and oh my God, Harriet, if this is the real thing, I'll be over the moon."

Harriet chuckled. "Let me guess. The love of your life just walked through the door, and you leaned in and whispered to whoever was standing next to you that one day, you'd marry that woman, and they laughed because said woman is a country music superstar?"

"Um, no. You watch too many Hallmark movies."

Harriet sighed. "I'm still thinking about the singer's tight Wrangler jeans, but do you like how I turned it into a lesbian romance for you?"

Bridget leaned on her desk with both hands. "I need you to focus, Harriet. This is about my nemesis, who snuck into the restaurant again."

Harriet leaned in. "Right. So we're going more Harlequin romance. I have some experience with those too, but let me fill you in on real life. When someone falls in love with their nemesis, one of them usually suffers an unexpected death."

Bridget straightened and threw her arms in the air. "What are you talking about? I'm not falling in love with her, and no one is dying. On the contrary. We can actually start living again. No more frivolous lawsuits. No more crazy neighbor shit. No more constant worry about what he's going to say or do to the guests. Harriet, Jerry is going to sell his cabin, and we have to find a way to buy it so we can tear the damn thing down."

Harriet sat there in silence as if taking it all in. "So we aren't going to have a new show called, The Flemings Versus the Bergs, the Next Generation? Because I've already pitched the idea to a producer in Hollywood. He really liked the lesbian aspect. Much more titillating than two old guys duking it out over property lines and all that who-loved-her-first tension."

Bridget raised her fists and groaned. Then it dawned on her what Harriet had just said. "Wait. What do you mean, who loved her first?"

Harriet waved it off. "Oh, Boden never would admit it, but I think this whole thing with Jerry started because they both loved the same woman. They used to be the best of friends, and quick caveat, this was all before my time, so I can't confirm any of it. In fact, forget I even brought it up."

Bridget needed to pace again. Best of friends? How was that even possible? Jerry and Boden were complete opposites. She'd need some sort of confirmation beyond Harriet's assumptions before she'd believe such a claim. It was probably just idle gossip from an employee. Harriet was an expert at that.

Bridget sat with the hope that Harriet would start taking her seriously. "So? What do you think? Can we find a way to buy Jerry's place?"

"Honey, I don't want you to get your hopes up. The house might be ugly, but that land is worth a small fortune. So maybe you should focus some positive energy on the universe giving us a nicer neighbor than Jerry."

It felt like a soul-crushing answer, but Bridget tried to hide her disappointment. She didn't need Harriet thinking she didn't have a clue about real estate and mortgages, even though she didn't have a clue about real estate and mortgages. "You're right. You're right. Either way, it's a win for us."

Harriet flashed her a grin. "Exactly. One less weight on all our shoulders. You know, your dad had a great time running this place, in spite of Jerry. I hope you will too, Bridge."

Bridget returned the smile. "Me too."

Harriet was right, of course. Still, Bridget felt like she had a new spring in her step as she walked back into the lobby and stood under her dad's larger-than-life photo. Maybe she'd find a photo of the two of them and hang it in the lobby as well. After all, she did own the place now.

❖

Getting off the mountain couldn't be that hard. Sure, it had snowed all night, but Kennedy was literally feet away from a ski run that would take her to the bottom of the mountain. She could catch an Uber into town where a nice warm hotel room would be waiting for her. Hopefully, she could use points for the room and maybe book a massage at the spa. And if she were really lucky, the airline would finally deliver her suitcase so she could get back to feeling like herself again.

She felt giddy just thinking about the dinner she'd order that night. Steak with thick-cut french fries and a bottle of her favorite red. She'd get so full, she'd have to spread out on the bed and channel surf for at least an hour. Maybe two.

But before any of that could happen, she had to get her sore toe into a ski boot. She'd decided she could endure the freezing temperatures in the wrong ski clothes long enough to get down the mountain. Couldn't be worse than the igloo she was currently calling home. She also had to strap her carry-on bag to her body because she sure as hell wasn't leaving the only bag she had behind.

She'd look like a fool trying to ski with a small suitcase on her back, but at this point, did she really care about things like pride and dignity? Hell no. Not when the satiated, full feeling she'd left the lodge with would soon turn into stomach growls so loud, they were sure to cause a small avalanche.

The brief moment of kindness on Bridget's part was not something Kennedy could count on happening again. And the attraction didn't seem to be mutual. No matter how many times Kennedy had alluded to her own sexuality or flirted or undressed Bridget with her eyes, the woman hadn't even flinched.

It wasn't as if the attraction was real anyway. Kennedy knew it was just her legendary inability to back down from a challenge that kept her interest. Well, maybe not legendary, but she was pretty sure it was a thing with her. She would never be legitimately attracted to someone with such an unpleasant demeanor, no matter how disarming the woman looked in a ski sweater. She was very capable of setting aside her affection for tall redheads in tight ski pants who seemed so sweet and charming to everyone else. Yep. It was strictly the challenge for Kennedy. Obviously.

Not one to get down on herself, Kennedy chalked up Bridget's total lack of interest in her to her lumberjack attire and unkempt hair. Not everyone was into the grunge look. Oh, and also, the irritable innkeeper hated her. It was neither here nor there, of course, because she needed to get off that mountain while she had the strength and energy to do so.

And so it was decided. She'd ski out of there a few hundred dollars poorer and definitely worse for wear, both of which Michael would hear about until his dying day.

With her carry-on packed, she used some rope she'd found in the garage to loop through the handle. That way seemed more secure than the way she'd held it the first time she'd tried this. She'd carry it like an extremely large cross-body purse and let it hang behind her as much as possible. It would work. It had to work.

The snow was coming down hard again. What few skiers she saw go by were bundled up with goggles and face masks. She had neither of those things, so she'd have to get by with her designer sunglasses and her dad's old beanie.

She'd looked at the trail map. If she stayed to the left, close to the tree line, and followed the signs, she'd avoid the black diamond runs and hopefully end up on a smooth trail called "The Easy Does It" that crisscrossed the mountain. It didn't seem like it would take that long. Maybe an hour if she went slowly. Of course, she'd have to trudge through even deeper snow than the day before to get to the groomed run. That would not be an easy task since she'd also have to carry her skis and poles.

She considered her second set of terrible options for the day. If the road hadn't been plowed, it would be easier to navigate than the mountain. She'd just follow the reflective snow-depth poles she'd seen along the side of the road. No chance of getting lost. No chance of ending up in a field of moguls taller than she was. And best of all, she wouldn't have to trudge through anything. She could just walk out the front door, put on her skis, and head down the driveway. She'd called the lodge—anonymously, of course, and possibly with an affected Southern accent—to confirm that the road hadn't been plowed.

"No, ma'am. I'm afraid not." The desk attendant had struck an apologetic tone. "We don't expect them to make it up here until this evening. I'm so sorry."

"Well, darlin', that makes one of us," Kennedy had drawled in what she thought was a pretty convincing accent. She gathered her things. If she was apprehensive, it was tempered by her enthusiasm for a little bit of hospitality and heat. Besides, she always loved to put a plan into action. Now she just had to get her foot into that ski boot. Once it was in, the hardness of the boot would protect her toe. Sure, it might throb a bit, but she wouldn't hit it on anything and cause further damage.

With a big intake of breath, she shoved her foot in and screamed bloody murder. She panted with her eyes squeezed shut until the pain lessened a bit. She wiped the sweat from her forehead with her sleeve, put on the other boot, then buckled the latches.

She should've put something between her teeth like they did in the movies when they had to stitch up their own wounds with dental floss and a fish hook. At that moment, she was pretty sure the grit it took to slide into that boot ranked up there with resetting a bone or pulling out your own tooth. "You are a badass, Kennedy Fleming. You can fucking do this," she shouted, hoping it would echo back at her due to that stupid vault in the ceiling.

She still couldn't believe her dad had added on to the cabin for the sole purpose of blocking the lodge's view. It was one more reason to get out of there before someone took out years of hatred and frustration on her. People sometimes snapped over the smallest things. Like a wife who'd taken years of physical abuse but ended up stabbing her husband with a carving knife on Thanksgiving Day because he told her the stuffing was dry.

Kennedy had been poking the bear for two days. In a sense, harassing both Bridget and her employees. It was time to move on before someone spiked her coffee with rat poison.

With her carry-on slung over her shoulder, she tucked her phone in her coat pocket and gingerly stepped out onto the front porch where her skis and poles awaited her. The remnants of Bridget's snowmobile tracks were still visible. If she stayed inside the tracks, she wouldn't veer off in the wrong direction. It was perfect. She'd be down the mountain in no time. She clicked into her skis and put on an old pair of leather gloves that she'd found in the garage. With a final glance in the direction of the lodge, Kennedy felt a slight pang of disappointment in herself. Even with her dad's bullshit hanging over her head, she should've been able to somehow win over the other lesbian on the mountain. If they had gotten together, it would've been hot. And so sexy. And also, hot.

She grabbed her poles and inhaled deeply a few times, just like the real skiers would do at the starting gate. "You got this," she whispered before pushing off.

It was slow at first, but once she got over the flat part of the driveway, she picked up speed, so she spread the back of her skis to slow herself down. The driveway had a hairpin turn near the bottom that she managed to navigate well. "You got this," she said, a little louder as her excitement grew. When she made it to the road, she threw her arms up and let out a big whoop. She'd done it. And the rest would be cake.

❖

Bridget smiled when she saw who was calling her. "Hope you're on your way up. Brunch is almost over, and I have the best news."

"I've run into a problem," Lola whispered. "I'm not really sure what to do with her since the hotels are all full."

"Since when do you have a problem with kicking someone out of your bed? Especially with Chef Lawrence's chicken and waffles on the line? Just do it and get up here."

"Wait. He does a gourmet chicken and waffle? That's my fave."

"It's a new item on the brunch menu, so kiss the girl good-bye and get your ass up here. The snowplow just went by about half an hour ago. It might have helped that I promised to send brunch back down with them if they prioritized us, but hey, you gotta do what you gotta do, right?"

"Yeah, Bridge. Here's the thing. I found someone who got buried by the snowplow. I saw an arm and a ski sticking out of the snowbank, and who knows how long she would've lasted if I hadn't come by? I can't really take her back up to her house because she says she doesn't have any heat."

Bridget headed for the front door. "Oh God. Are we talking about—"

"Yeah. Look, she was going to ski down the road with her suitcase roped to her body."

Bridget's eyes widened. "How far did she get?"

"I found her at the bottom of her driveway, but I had to cut the rope and leave the suitcase there. I couldn't save both of them."

"I get that, but why didn't you choose the suitcase?"

"Don't make me laugh," Lola whispered. "She's in my car, and she's super humiliated about the whole thing, which is understandable."

"Yeah, it's understandable. Who the hell skis down a road?" Bridget said with a giggle. She waited for Lola to respond, but all she got was silence on the other end. She whispered into the phone, "You're trying really hard not to laugh, aren't you?"

"You should've seen it. You'd be dying too. Stop. Wait. I have to get control of myself before I turn around...okay, I'm good now. Anyway, can I bring her in and let her warm up there?"

"Oh, dear God, yes. I wouldn't miss this for the world. We might even change our tagline. Come for the chicken and waffles, stay for the abject humiliation."

"It's probably for the best if I don't laugh at that one," Lola whispered. "So put a pin in, and we'll revisit, but in the meantime, I think you should tread carefully here."

"You're probably right. Bring her in, but only because I'm in a great mood, and I can't wait to share the news with you over a cup of coffee." Bridget went out the front door. "I had a feeling you were already parked out front."

Lola tucked her phone in her pocket. "I wanted to give you the chance to say no."

Bridget smirked. "And if I had?"

"Eh, I probably would've arrested her for impeding a snowplow and thrown her in jail for the night. Any chance you'd take care of her while I order breakfast?"

"What am I supposed to do with her? I don't have a jail cell here, you know. Although now that you mention it, it wouldn't be the worst idea."

"Sit her down by the fire and let her thaw out, Bridge. After that, maybe you could have one of your employees drive her back to the airport while you tell me this great news, which I assume is something about having met the love of your life, given I haven't heard that kind of excitement in your voice in quite some time."

Bridget glanced over at Lola's SUV. "Yeah? Well, this one better not ruin my day." She put up a hand. "Fine. I'll be gracious. Well, maybe not gracious, but I won't be unkind. She can warm up and get something to eat. However, I refuse to help her get to the airport. The road's plowed now. She can call a cab." She opened the door for Lola. "Go order your chicken and waffles before it's too late."

Lola leaned in and said, "You have no idea how hungry I am after digging her out."

Bridget went to the car and opened the passenger door. The muddy snow the plow had apparently buried Kennedy in had started to melt in the warm car. Dark droplets dripped from her hair to her cheeks and nose, leaving streaks on her face. It reminded Bridget of that press conference Rudy Giuliani gave when his hair dye seeped down his face. Her bare hands were shaking. She couldn't have looked more pitiful if she'd tried. And without turning to look Bridget in the eye, she said, "I know you don't want me here."

Bridget wanted to agree, but she bit her tongue.

"I...my wallet...my phone...they were here." Kennedy dug into her coat pocket and came up empty.

The image of Kennedy getting pummeled by a wall of dirty wet snow should have had Bridget holding in her laughter, and a plethora of snide comments, but what she found herself trying to hold back was sympathy. She actually felt sorry for her. That was when she learned how much she hated feeling sorry for her. "Seth will be disappointed," she quipped.

Kennedy still hadn't looked at Bridget. Apparently, she'd left that defiant, flirty, aggravating attitude in a pile of snow at the bottom of her driveway. Bridget could work with that. If nothing else, it would make what she was about to do a little less painful. She held out her hand and said, "Come with me."

Kennedy turned, her eyes full of surprise. "Where?"

"I haven't figured that out yet. You're too dirty to thaw out in the lobby. You look like Linus on an episode of *South Park*."

"Who?"

"You know, Linus. From the *South Park* cartoon."

"You mean *Peanuts*. And Linus was the thumb-sucking snoozy one. I'm pretty sure you're referring to Pigpen. Did you have a childhood at all?"

"I didn't watch a lot of cartoons. I was, you know, training and stuff."

"Oh right. The Olympics."

So Kennedy *had* looked her up. Huh. Not that it was a secret, but Bridget the would-be Olympian with the busted knee wasn't exactly a household name. "Fine. Pigpen. Are you really going to argue with me right now?" Bridget wiggled her outstretched fingers. "You can't stay in Lola's car forever."

Kennedy seemed to hesitate before reaching for Bridget's outstretched hand. "Lola's a pretty name for a sheriff. Makes me think of Barry Manilow. And my grandma. My grandma loved Barry Manilow."

Bridget laughed. "Don't tell Lola that. And whatever you do, don't start singing that song in her presence. She hates it with a passion."

"Noted."

Kennedy's hand was ice cold. She gripped Bridget tightly as she limped up to the lodge in her clunky ski boots. "Did you injure yourself again?"

"No. Same old toe thing."

"Can you manage the steps?"

"You might need to hold on to me a little tighter."

Bridget gave her a quick glance, sure that Kennedy was back to her flirtatious ways. But all she saw in those big brown eyes was pain. She let go of her hand and wrapped an arm around her shoulders. "Here, take my other hand."

Kennedy held on tightly until they made it to the door, then let go and lifted her chin. "Thank you. I can do the rest on my own."

Bridget knew that look. How many times had she been on those same steps after a hard fall, determined to prove to her dad that she could be a champion downhiller just like he was? Of course, this incident had nothing to do with actual skiing so she still had to suppress a grin while images of Snowplow versus Fleming—the GIF—flashed through her brain. She held the door open and said, "After you, then."

Kennedy went straight for the nearest bench and buried her face in her hands. Sure that she'd begun to cry, Bridget whispered, "Shit," and waved one of her employees over to help. "Eric, please help her get her boots off. And be gentle. She has an injured toe."

"Yes, ma'am."

It wasn't the first time they'd had a half-frozen guest unable to control their emotions once they felt like they were back in a warm safe place. For the weekend warriors who only ventured out onto the slopes once or twice a year, the mountain could feel overwhelming at times. Especially when visibility was low, and they'd lost their way. And also when they'd stubbed their toe and had the crap beat out of them by the offshoot of a snowplow.

Bridget sat next to her and tried to think of something comforting to say. She shooed Harriet and a few other concerned employees away. No need to add to Kennedy's embarrassment by having an audience. She leaned in and said, "What do you need first? Food? Water? To sit by the fireplace?"

Kennedy turned, and with tear-filled eyes, she whispered, "I need you to not kick me out again. Or poison me."

A wave of guilt engulfed Bridget. She shook her head and said, "No. That won't happen. Did you say poison? Never mind. I'll...we'll...someone...will take care of you."

In reality, only Bridget could decide how to take care of her. The lodge was completely booked. Not a single room would be available until Tuesday. There was the bunkhouse, but four of her employees had spent the night there and most likely would again if it kept snowing as hard as it had been. They were young, so to them, it seemed fun to shack up together and ski the powder for free when they weren't working. Plus, Bridget couldn't quite imagine housing such a spectacularly enchanting woman in the bunkhouse. Spectacularly enchanting? She wondered where that came from. That would be an obnoxious thing to say even if Kennedy was tolerable. She didn't mean enchanting. She meant arrogant. Or presumptuous. Or just a total pain in the ass.

To Kennedy, the bunkhouse might actually be a slight step up from that cold house she'd been in but not much of one. And besides, Bridget thought it best to keep her as far away from her employees as possible. She stood and offered her hand again. "We're booked solid, but you can shower in my room. I'll even lend you a bathrobe until we can get your clothes washed."

Kennedy looked like she was ready to break when she whispered, "Thank you," and took Bridget's hand again.

They stood face-to-face for a moment, their hands joined. Just long enough for Bridget to question whether or not it was a tear running down Kennedy's cheek or just more snow melting from her hair. The urge to wipe it away was almost as strong as the urge to keep hold of her hand, both of which made absolutely zero sense. She could be a kindhearted person without making the situation personal. Couldn't she? She cleared her throat and said, "No problem. Follow me to the elevator."

She turned on her heel and hoped her thoughts had not been plastered on her forehead because the last thing she wanted was for Kennedy Fleming to think that any of her flirtatiousness had had an effect, which it hadn't. Obviously. Kennedy wasn't her type. Not even close. She preferred women whose last names weren't Fleming. Literally anyone but a Fleming could be her type. *Calling all non-Fleming women, Bridget Berg is open for business.* Smiths, Jacksons, Joneses, and Garcias were all welcome to apply. Last name Lively? Um, you bet. In the past, there'd been a Bradley, a Patel, and an extremely brief Baldwin. Fine, maybe there was one Johns too, of the county sheriff variety. Repeats of the names, if not the people, were fine. Because all of them had one thing in common. They were not named Fleming.

She got to the elevator and realized Kennedy was slowly limping her way behind her. By the looks of it, the toe had definitely gotten worse. She rushed back and offered her a hand. Kennedy gave her a tired smile and leaned heavily on her arm.

Once inside the main elevator, Bridget waited until Kennedy seemed stable against the wall before she pushed the button. "Is the toe getting worse?" she asked.

Kennedy gave her a nod, followed by a grimace. "Probably wasn't the best idea to shove it into a ski boot."

"Or ski down a mountain road."

Kennedy cringed. "Right."

"I'll call for some ice while you shower. In fact, it might be best if you soak it in a bucket of ice water."

Kennedy grimaced again. "Great. More ice."

"I know it sounds awful, but the pain will only get worse as your foot warms up. It'd probably be good to take some ibuprofen too. You're going to feel this tomorrow. Trust me, I know what I'm talking about."

She helped Kennedy down the hall to her room and put her keycard in the slot. It was only when she opened the door that she remembered her room was cluttered with cardboard boxes full of her father's belongings stacked three and four high on what little floor space her room had. "Crap," she whispered.

"It's okay," Kennedy said. "As long as this storage room has a shower, I'll be fine."

"It's not a…this is my room. I forgot about all this stuff."

"Oh." Kennedy turned to her. "You live here?"

"Don't forget, I've seen your cabin. I'm not sure you're in a position to judge."

"You're right. Of course." She looked around the room, and her eyes seemed to settle on the bed. "Listen, I don't mean to ask for more. Except I do." She hesitated.

"Yes?" Bridget assumed the woman would ask for a steak or a scotch like she always did.

"I'm just wondering if I could lie on your bed for a little while after I shower."

Bridget shut the door and said, "This won't work. I'm just not comfortable with that."

"But I thought you said you're all booked. Please, I won't be in there long, and I promise not to touch anything."

Promises or not, there was no way Bridget would let Kennedy be in a room alone with all her dad's belongings. There was only one other option, and the thought of it caused Bridget to sigh deeply. "Trust me," she said. "You'll like this so much better."

She closed the door and started down the long hallway to the penthouse suite. It became obvious fairly quickly that if she didn't do something to expedite the process, they'd arrive around dinner time. She got in front of Kennedy and crouched so she could give her a piggyback ride to the other end of the lodge. When nothing happened, she turned her head and found Kennedy staring right at her ass. "Are you going to get on or what? It's a long walk down the hall."

"Oh. I wasn't sure what you were doing there. I thought maybe you were getting into your skier's crouch, but you want me to hop on your back? I mean, it's no hot shower, but yeah, I think I might like it just as much."

Bridget groaned internally. "Just get on my back, would you?"

"Fine, but you keep telling me to trust you, and it's kinda scaring me. I mean, you could be taking me anywhere right now. You could be leading me to the dungeon where there's no food or drink. This is a pattern with you, isn't it? You like to starve and torture vulnerable, classy, hot women."

Bridget straightened and turned. Kennedy had moved in enough that they were almost nose to chin. "All I see right now is a dirty woman who's limping on a bad foot. Vulnerable, yes. But classy? I'd say that's pushing it."

"Huh. You didn't weigh in on hot. So hot vulnerable women who are short on class." Kennedy batted those big brown eyes and in a coy tone asked, "Just your type?"

Bridget smirked. "Far from it, but at least you've got your sense of humor back. Now, get on."

Kennedy wasn't a heavy load at all. In fact, Bridget could've easily jogged down the hall, but she decided to grunt a few times for effect. Strong fingers squeezed her shoulders even tighter. "You don't have to grip so tightly. I'm not going to drop you."

"Is this better?"

Kennedy had leaned in closer and wrapped her arms around Bridget. She could feel her warm breath graze her cheek, but that was the only warm thing about her. The rest of her felt damp and cold against Bridget's back. Having grown up on the slopes, she knew that feeling well. Sometimes, no matter how warmly you dressed, heavy wet snow could seep through your clothes and weigh you down, zapping your energy. Kennedy needed to take a warm shower, hydrate, and eat something. And the sooner, the better.

Bridget stopped at her dad's penthouse door and waited for her passenger to slide off, but she stayed where she was with her arms wrapped around Bridget's shoulders and her legs gripping her hips. Bridget turned slightly and said, "You can dismount now."

"I'm afraid to. What's behind that unmarked door? There's no number on it, which means my death could be imminent."

"Are you for real? I'm trying to help you, not kill you."

"Then maybe I'd prefer to be carried over the threshold."

"You have exactly one second before I drop you on that ass of yours."

"Fine." Kennedy slid off her back. "Thanks for the ride. You make a fine steed."

Bridget gave her a side-eye and pulled her dad's key fob out of her pocket. Kennedy took a step back. "Whoa," she said. "I'm not going in there when that door doesn't even have a keycard. Where does it lead to? What's behind it?"

The fear in Kennedy's eyes seemed genuine. Was she really afraid something bad was about to happen? Bridget softened her tone. "It doesn't have a keycard because it's my dad's suite. It's where I grew up." She unlocked the door and held it open. "See?"

Bridget hadn't seen the suite since it had been put back together. With all the upgrades, it looked amazing. It still had her dad's warm, rustic aesthetic. His Navajo rug had been hung back up, along with framed photos and a few original paintings of western scenes he'd collected. The bookshelves still held all his favorites. And the view out the large vaulted window was still spectacular. All it lacked now was the scent of his cologne that seemed to have permeated everything over the years. It was something Bridget hoped she'd still experience when she opened those boxes. She wondered if she could find a way to bottle it. Then she laughed at the drama of her own grief. *It's cologne, genius. It literally comes in a bottle.*

She could've given in to the temptation to wax nostalgic and tell Kennedy that she'd had it renovated but that she hadn't had the heart to rent it out yet, but that felt too personal. So, in as casual a tone as she could muster, she lied. "The guests who booked this suite have been delayed due to the snow, so you've got a couple of hours to rest and clean up."

Kennedy's expression was one of awe. "This is amazing. Are there more rooms like this?" She limped toward the window.

"No. This one is special." God, Bridget wanted to tell her more. So much more. It would've been so easy to follow Kennedy to the window and tell her about the time they were snowed in for a week when she was ten. She'd spent most of the time right under that window, reading books and listening to music, a bag of peanut M&Ms by her side.

It was that same winter when she'd had her first crush on a woman. Just as it always had, the memory caused Bridget to cringe a little. She'd shamelessly followed the single older woman around like a lovesick puppy during her stay at the lodge, a fact her dad had never let her forget. She was so beautiful, though. So sophisticated. She'd even smelled sophisticated, if sophistication had a scent to it. And Bridget was totally taken by her. Cassie. Cassie Colcraft. That was her name. Bridget now realized the woman probably hadn't been older than twenty-five. At the time, that had placed her squarely in the category of experienced seductress. And to ten-year-old Bridget, seducing meant showing off her ski moves and possibly playing video games.

Cassie was the reason Bridget had grown up assuming she'd end up spending her life with someone older than she was. But she'd soon realized that lesbians weren't like straight men, in that they weren't usually willing to suffer the inexperience of someone much younger just because her breasts were perky. Sure, plenty of couples found love in the age gap, but rarely was it about perky breasts. Most lesbians were smarter than that. Okay, maybe not most. But some.

A perfect example was Lola. She could've had anyone she wanted during the height of her Olympic fame. She still could. The way she carried herself in that sheriff's uniform with such confidence and swagger seemed to make all the young lesbians' hearts beat faster. But Lola wanted substance. Commitment. Permanence. She'd welcome all forms of genius too. She'd bought a season subscription during her time with the Salt Lake Symphony's concertmaster. And the PhD in molecular biophysics she'd dated? Lola hung on her every word, even if she hadn't understood them all.

Bridget realized she was similar. Not that her "type" was focused on women at the top of their fields. It was more like she knew she wanted someone as passionate about their interests as they were about her. She wanted someone on equal footing, someone she could grow with. The kind of person who'd challenge her to be better but only if she could do the same for them. Casual dating and one-night stands no longer held any appeal. Ironically, after a lifetime of fierce competition, all Bridget wanted in a relationship was a level playing field.

At the moment, however, all Bridget wanted was a reason to stay in the penthouse suite because God, how she loved that view. Seeing it again filled her with a sense of gratitude that she'd always have it. If she could carry on like her father, she'd always have the lodge and all of its memories. It was up to her to make it work.

And if that meant sharing the best view in the whole building with others, she'd do it. For her dad and for herself, she'd do it.

Kennedy turned around. "As much as I'd like to stand here all day and take in this view, I should probably—"

"Shower," Bridget said. So lost in her own thoughts, Bridget wasn't sure how long they'd stood there in silence. She hoped Kennedy didn't think that they shared the hobby of ass staring. "Take the smaller room at the end of the hall," she said. "I'll be back with some ice for that toe."

Kennedy gave her a nod and whispered, "Thank you. Really, thank you, Bridget. I won't ever forget this kindness."

It seemed like a sincere reply, but the truth was, Bridget wished that was exactly what Kennedy, and any other Fleming, would do. She wished they'd all forget about Elk Mountain and sell that hideous house so she could tear it down and reclaim the view they'd had of the valley. She knew it was asking for too much. Too much to even hope for. She knew what her dad would say: *Now is not the time to trust a Fleming.*

❖

Just as Bridget closed the penthouse door behind her, Lola rounded the corner with a take-out container in hand. "Bridge? Why are you bright red?"

"Jesus, Lo, I don't know." Bridget sighed. "Could be anything. The heavy load I just carried, stress over the fact that I can't bring myself to rent out the penthouse even though it would bring in great money. Or the goddamn snowplow-ee you left on my doorstep. Can't you stay for brunch?"

"Wait, what did you call her? The snowplow-ee? What the hell is that?"

"One who has been snowplowed. Obviously."

Lola gave her a sly grin. "Not just plowed?"

"No! Get your mind out of the gutter, Sheriff. Are you staying for brunch or what?"

"Wish I could, but duty calls," Lola said. "Honestly, I can't remember the last time my meal wasn't interrupted by some emergency. This time, it's a loose horse out by Highway Nine. So how is the snowplow-ee?"

"Feeling very victimized, I imagine. I'm letting her shower and rest in Dad's suite because my room is full of boxes."

"Huh," Lola said with a raised eyebrow. "That's very generous."

"Hey, you're the one who brought her here."

"You mentioned that. But I thought you'd have her thaw out by the fireplace downstairs while I enjoyed my chicken and waffles. And then, I'd take her back down the mountain with me."

"Take her where? Your place? The whole town is booked up."

"Oh God, no. Not my place. Now that I have Eddie, it's completely off-limits to lesbians. He can smell them a mile away and won't let them near me. For that, I'm grateful."

Bridget snorted. "Your rescue dachshund doesn't like lesbians?" She put up a hand. "Wait. How do you know Kennedy's a lesbian?"

"As you may recall, I spent a significant amount of time fine-tuning my lesbian detection skills at the police academy."

"I'm pretty sure sleeping with your instructor at the academy doesn't qualify as intensive lesbian-detection training, but tell me how you knew."

Lola shrugged. "I may have noticed the way she looks at you."

With a firm shake of her head, Bridget said, "No. Absolutely not. Are you kidding me right now?" She glanced back at the door and whispered, "She's a Fleming. The only way she looks at me is the same way I look at her. With utter contempt."

That wasn't completely true, and Bridget knew it. Kennedy had been flirting up a storm the entire time. Lola took her by the arm and led her away from the door. "Maybe it's not such a bad idea to let her stay up here. That way, she can get someone to plow that driveway and get an HVAC guy up here to fix her furnace. A little goodwill can go a long way."

Bridget considered it for a moment. "Yeah, I guess, if they really are selling."

Lola gasped. "What?"

Bridget led her toward the elevators. "That was my news. She said she's here to sell her dad's property."

Lola opened her arms. "Well, get in here, girl."

Bridget felt so giddy, she wrapped her arms around Lola's waist and picked her up. "Ow. Bad idea." She set her down and rubbed the spot on her tummy where Lola's duty belt had poked her.

"And you almost spilled my chicken and waffles."

"Sorry. I'm just so psyched about it, you know?"

Lola pushed the button on the elevator. "I'd love to stay and celebrate, but I really do need to go, Bridge."

Bridget glanced down the hallway. "I'll try to stay civil, but keep your phone close. You'll be my first call if I accidentally kill someone."

Lola sighed. "How many times have we covered this? When you announce that you might accidentally kill someone, especially to the sheriff, it's called premeditation. Say it with me. Pre-med-i-tay-tion."

Bridget shooed her away. "Yeah, yeah. Get going, champ. Before you get snowed in, and we're *all* trapped up here. You've got a horse to save."

Lola raised her hand and made the call-me sign as she backed away. "Good luck."

"Thanks. God knows I'll need it."

Chapter Six

K ennedy leaned over the tub and twisted the hot water handle until it was fully open. She should've been giddy that she was finally going to be warm and comfortable, but Bridget's reaction annoyed her. *Tell a neighbor you're selling your house, and they suddenly become helpful and friendly? What kind of condescending bullshit is that?* Kennedy and Bridget hadn't actually been neighbors, but still, it was yet another insult added to her many injuries, both physical and emotional.

She imagined everyone in the lodge knew by now that she'd been assaulted and buried by a snowplow going full speed up the mountain. Freezing dirty snow had come at her like a tsunami before she could do anything about it. Had she skied down the driveway five seconds slower, she would've been fine. Well, a slightly out of control version of fine, but she would've maneuvered the sharp left onto the road just fine and already been at a hotel enjoying that steak she'd imagined. Instead, she'd been pummeled with a mixture of snow and rock salt that felt like tiny knives digging into her face. No doubt the Boden Berg Lodge's staff would talk about her for years to come. Snowplow Fleming, they'd probably call her. At least it would be an upgrade from Hungry Hippo.

If she'd stayed on the slopes, she'd have probably been home by now too. Well, not home, but home free. Free to hail a cab and get the hell outta Dodge. She sunk a little lower in the tub and wrapped her arms around herself, wishing she could hide here until she found a way down the mountain. One that didn't involve complete humiliation, the likes of which she couldn't recall ever experiencing before. But the lucky guests who'd booked the penthouse suite would be there in a few hours, and she'd once again have nowhere to go.

Her dad never would've let her suffer like this. He would've made sure she was safe and warm and not hungry, just as he'd done her entire childhood. But she was stuck in this alternate reality where her beloved father was the much-maligned Jerry Fleming, and everyone said his name as if they needed to wash their mouth out afterward.

It didn't make sense. And even worse, she couldn't call him and have him explain the situation. The thought brought tears to her eyes because her dad, who she loved so dearly, would never be able to comfort her again. He'd never console her with his kind husky voice or offer a strong shoulder to lean on while she worked through something difficult. Why would he when most of the time, he didn't even know who she was? He knew his nurse better than he knew Kennedy, and even that wasn't saying much. Olive was a kind soul, but her dad routinely confused her with his own mother. The fact was, her dad was failing, and his mind was quite a bit further along than his body.

A good cry in the tub wouldn't bring him back to her, but maybe letting go of some pent-up emotions would help her get through whatever came next. She hated feeling so out of control of her own life. Trusting in the kindness of strangers wasn't her strong suit, and these weren't exactly kind strangers anyway. Most days, they were happy for her to starve and freeze to death rather than set foot in their precious lodge. Thank God today wasn't one of those days.

She stood and grabbed a towel to wipe the tears away and dry her body. Rather than cry in the tub, she'd get some sleep in that bed that looked so soft and comfy. Sure, they'd have to change the sheets before the other guests arrived, but oh well. She would enjoy it while she could. She'd pay for the sheets if she had to. Hopefully, they took Zelle.

The sheets were so soft, she felt the need to make a few snow angels before she settled on her back, took in a deep breath, and slowly exhaled.

❖

The semi-loud hellos hadn't garnered a response from the snowplow-ee. The sandwich Bridget had ordered for her remained untouched on the table. She walked down the hallway with a light step and saw that the bedroom door was ajar. She opened it and found Kennedy fast asleep on the bed.

Her inclination to shut the door and walk away was overpowered by a desire to stay right where she was for a moment, if only to enjoy the silence she'd yet to associate with Kennedy Fleming. The woman could be so annoying that it was hard to see past that and take in the rest of her. She snored, but it was more of a purr. She had the sheets and blankets pulled to her chest, one hand clutching them and the other resting on the pillow above her head. Bridget wondered if her position was a visual interpretation of her current state of mind, as if she half expected someone to barge in, rip the covers off her, and kick her out again.

Since Kennedy hadn't stirred in the slightest, Bridget leaned against the door frame and folded her arms. It was probably the first good sleep she'd gotten since she'd arrived on the mountain. The soft fluffy bedding was no doubt a huge step-up from the scratchy wool blankets and flat pillows she imagined were on Jerry's bed.

Stripped of the baggy clothes and arrogant, entitled attitude, Kennedy looked quite stunning lying there, her hair damp and a serene expression on her face. It could've been a scene from a movie, given the spectacular view from the large windows that flanked both sides of the bed. It hadn't stopped snowing and probably wouldn't for another day or so, according to the weather reports. Not that Bridget was looking out the windows.

Maybe she could get some solid deep sleep later too. Watching Kennedy, she found herself wishing she had someone to crawl into a warm bed with. Someone to hold while she fell asleep. It had been a while since she'd experienced the kind of comfort that only came from knowing someone would be there for her at the end of a long day. And the beginning of the next one.

Since taking over the lodge, Bridget could no longer come and go as she pleased. No more last-minute trips with friends. No more meeting up in the city for dinner and drinks. She'd become a fixture for the entire season, so her dating options had narrowed quite a bit. Besides, the list of women who wanted to live at the top of a mountain with a girlfriend who worked all hours of the day and night had to be a pretty short one.

She flinched when she took herself out of her thoughts and found Kennedy staring at her. "Sorry," she said, sure her face was about to turn bright red. Again. Ugh. "I didn't mean to wake you." She pointed behind her with her thumb. "I'll just..." She lost her words when Kennedy sat up. She kept the sheet tucked under her arms, but there was enough skin showing to render Bridget somewhat speechless. A tan line was barely visible across her chest, along with a subtle amount of cleavage. How was it possible, Bridget thought, that this scene wasn't in a movie? They really didn't make enough queer content. The proof? This scene with Kennedy and the skin and the stretching and the perfectly placed sheets that left just enough to Bridget's imagination and left her absolutely thirsting for more. And that was when she realized super-sexy bed lady was glaring at her.

"Is it that time already?" Kennedy asked in a clipped tone.

"Time?"

"You came here to kick me out, right?"

"No, I just came to check on you," she said.

They stared at each other for a few seconds before Kennedy made a move to get up but stopped short. "Do you mind? I don't have anything on under here."

Bridget felt a blush crawl up her neck. "Of course. Sorry." She shut the door and rushed down the hallway to the living room, where she paced from the window to the sofa while chiding herself for getting caught in the act. Was Kennedy aware of how long she'd been standing there? God, she hoped not. But her sarcastic tone indicated that, yes, she'd been awake longer than Bridget had realized.

Maybe listening to Lola was a bad idea. Keep things civil? How could she possibly do that when Kennedy couldn't show the least bit of gratitude? No, she'd shown enough kindness. And she sure as hell should've insisted Lola take her down the mountain.

Bridget had her hand on the door and was about to leave when she heard the bedroom door open. She turned, and there stood Kennedy, wrapped in a towel. There was even more skin showing. Sexy, tanned legs. And a very purple big toe that she protected by flexing her foot as she limped down the hall.

She stopped a few feet away and said, "First of all, thank you for helping me. I'm sure you know I was fresh out of options, so this has been a welcome ceasefire."

"It was my pleasure," Bridget stammered. "I mean, our pleasure."

"I'm sure you're exaggerating the pleasure part, but it's kind of you to say that." Kennedy gave her a smile that was equal parts sheepish and slight. "I'm a very proud person, so it kills me to say this, but I really thought I was going to die out there, and I realize that someone who flies down mountains at eighty-three miles per hour couldn't possibly relate to the fear I felt."

"You're wrong about that," Bridget said. "Fear keeps you alive. It's the thrill seekers who *aren't* afraid that end up dying before their time." She narrowed her eyes. "But I find it interesting that you were able to quote my fastest speed in the downhill."

"Hmm. Lucky guess, I suppose. Is that fast?"

Bridget made a concerted effort to not let her eyes wander over Kennedy's body when she said, "I think you know how fast it is."

She should've let her eyes wander. It would've been better than seeing the flirtatious glint in Kennedy's eyes when she said, "You're right, I do."

Bridget tucked her hair behind her ears and folded her arms. "Look, I get it. After my worst crash on the mountain, I wanted to burn everything I'd been wearing. So maybe we should throw away those clothes. Jerry won't miss them, will he?"

Kennedy dropped her gaze. After a pause, she said, "You know what? I'm sure he's forgotten he even had them."

Was it just the trauma of the day that had Kennedy bouncing from hostility to flirtation to her voice cracking with emotion? And the speed with which she hobbled back down the hall made Bridget think she'd have sprinted away if she could. Was she about to cry but didn't want to be seen doing it because of that pride she'd mentioned? Should Bridget follow her and find out?

With every step, she told herself she'd done enough for this frustrating, confounding woman. She'd put herself at risk by even letting her walk through the door of the penthouse suite. Or limp, as it were.

Even though the place had been renovated, it was still her home. Her dad's home. Where she'd grown up. Their inner sanctum. And she'd let the enemy waltz right in as if it was nothing. She stopped and listened at the open door. She heard Kennedy sniffling. With reluctance, she walked in, and in a bolder voice than intended, she said, "If I get you some clean clothes, will you cheer up?"

Kennedy was perched on the edge of the bathtub. She looked both pitiful and beautiful, her face blotchy and tear-stained. But her eyes still held a glint of humor when she said, "Those are words I never thought I'd hear past the age of five."

Bridget sat next to her on the tub. "Those are words I never thought I'd hear myself say until I had children. God. Did I just sound like a total mom?"

"A mean mom. Unsympathetic. I mean, where's my kiss on the forehead? Or are you the type of mom who'd put her hands on her hips and say, you shouldn't have been trying to ski down the road, young lady? It's your own fault you got in the way of that snowplow. Oh, and you're grounded for two weeks."

Bridget smiled. "While it's true that you shouldn't have been trying to ski down the road, I hear you weren't actually on the road when that snowplow went by. It's no different than if you were walking down the sidewalk, and some jerk sped through a puddle of water and soaked you. So the answer is no, I wouldn't be that type of mom. But I would be the kind of mom who points out that the snowplow already grounded your ass."

Kennedy returned the smile. "Okay, so you're in charge of dad jokes. What about my forehead kiss?"

Bridget shook her head at the ceiling. Why did Jerry Fleming's daughter have to be so damned cute? She took one more look at the post-plowed beauty, then stood and left the bathroom. "Flirt with me again and you're grounded for two weeks," she shouted over her shoulder.

"I'm already grounded," Kennedy shouted back. "Or stranded. Naked and afraid, like the TV show. Hey, are you going to bring some clothes back for me?"

Bridget stopped and tried to suppress a grin before she turned. "I'll be back shortly. Don't break anything while I'm gone."

"If I break another toe, can I have another piggyback ride?"

She should've kept going. Bridget knew that. Her better angels or demons or whatever were yelling, "Keep going." But Bridget turned back and marched right up to Kennedy, who was now leaning against the door frame. To do what, she wasn't sure. Was she about to lay into Kennedy? Or was she about to lay *onto* Kennedy? Or just lay Kennedy? There were so many options, and Bridget had no idea which one was the frontrunner. Her confusion became irrelevant once she let her eyes drop to that bare chest. Kennedy saw it, and maybe even felt it, if her quick intake of breath was any indication.

After a few seconds of holding her own breath, Bridget took a few steps back. What did they call that thing she just felt? Oh yeah. Chemistry. And wow, was it strong. It would have been so easy to lean in and kiss those soft lips without a care in the world. If she ever lacked confidence romantically, this was not that time. Looking at Kennedy's expression, she had no doubt her interests would have been reciprocated. She knew she could retrace her steps into that whirlwind of sexual desire and mixed-up emotions and take her right up against the door. But Bridget also knew that would inevitably turn out to be the worst decision she'd ever make in her life.

She turned to leave, but Kennedy stopped her. "You had me at a disadvantage."

Bridget glanced at the long slender fingers gripping her forearm. "How so?"

"If we'd kissed just now, this towel might've fallen off when I reached up and ran my fingers through your hair, and we can't have that now, can we?"

It didn't actually need to happen for Bridget to imagine that she'd see a similar tan line below like she'd seen up top. "No. That would be awkward for everyone."

Kennedy let go of her arm and turned to go into the bedroom. "Has anyone ever told you you're cute when you blush?" she asked over her shoulder.

"No. Because I'm not blushing. I'm a redhead, so I'm naturally pink. Obvi."

As the bathroom door shut, Bridget heard a muffled chuckle and Kennedy shout, "Obvi."

Bridget rushed into the guest bathroom and looked at herself in the mirror. Of course, she was bright red. Anyone would think that after living her entire life with fair skin, she'd stop trying to deny it. And why did the need to pee have to hit her just because she'd walked into a bathroom?

There were really only two downsides to being a redhead: sunburns and everyone knowing exactly what got her worked up. Unfortunately, a beautiful woman flirting would do it every time. But Jackass Jerry's daughter? How did it get to the point where she was seriously considering telling Kennedy that the only thing she had to lend her was a skintight pair of ski pants and an even tighter T-shirt? This needed to stop. Kennedy had somewhere to be. An Econo Lodge or something. And Bridget needed to attend to her guests. Or something. Whatever excuse it took to get her out of that suite and back on solid ground.

When she came out of the bathroom, Kennedy wasn't there, so she went straight to the door and snuck out of her own suite. *Real brave, Bridge. Real brave.*

❖

Kennedy finally felt clean, warm, and more like herself. Minus her makeup, perfume, phone, wallet, handbag, and most importantly, her own clothing. She wasn't surprised when an employee delivered the clothes instead of Bridget. Still, they smelled like her. Something subtle, with light floral tones. She'd have to remind herself not to sniff the collar of the red quarter-zip ski sweater in public. The dark jeans were a little bit long but fit perfectly otherwise.

And best of all, she'd finally been deemed worthy of having the complimentary Boden Berg Lodge moccasins with the fleece lining. She sucked in a breath while she slipped one over her injured toe, expecting it to hurt like hell. When it didn't hurt at all, she exhaled and said, "Thank you for thinking I have big feet, Bridget Berg."

Anywhere else, it would've bothered her to walk around sans makeup and hair products, but on this mountain, she couldn't imagine any of the other guests fussing over their appearance after a long day of skiing. Judging from the few times she'd been able to stay in the restaurant longer than two minutes, she already knew she'd fit right in. When she'd lumbered around in her father's clothes, she'd no doubt given off a vibe of total shitshow. Now that she had more appropriate attire, she hoped she could even go unnoticed. If she was lucky. Just another tired, hungry guest in need of food and drink who sniffed her sweater from time to time. And maybe that was the point of the clothes Bridget had chosen. Not the sniffing part. That would be weird. But the inconspicuous part. Maybe she wanted Kennedy to feel like she belonged so she wouldn't cause any trouble.

"Ha! If she only knew how much trouble I want to get into with her." She took a few timid steps to the bathroom and decided the two-sizes-too-big slipper-shoes would be fine as long as she walked on the back of her heel. She looked in the mirror and pushed her somewhat unruly hair this way and that. With longer hair, she'd just tuck it behind her ears. This shorter cut she hadn't quite gotten used to yet. She ran her fingers through it and smoothed down the sides, which seemed to do the trick.

Kennedy had always worn red well. Losing the military-issue parka that a small family could fit in comfortably gave her a burst of confidence. Which wasn't to say she was ever lacking in it, more that the events of the week had taken their toll. That, along with the fact that the sweater was just tight enough to show off her assets, was a plus, since Bridget seemed to be a breast girl. It was total speculation on Kennedy's part, but in her experience, a woman's eyes—and where they lingered—didn't usually lie.

Even if Bridget wanted to deny it to her dying day, there was something smoldering between them. Kennedy was certain of it. Her anger regarding a certain snowplow had morphed into a feeling of gratitude that she'd had a reason to be in Bridget's presence wearing nothing but a towel. When Kennedy had been stripped of her dad's old clothes, it seemed like Bridget saw not just more of her body, but maybe more of who she really was. Not a threat. Not a horrible person. Someone worth knowing. Maybe?

If nothing else, Kennedy was someone who did not leave a mess for someone else to clean up. So she tidied up the bathroom as best she could, wiping down the countertops and rinsing out the tub. She knew housekeeping would come in before the next guests arrived, but she still wanted to leave things as put together as possible. She found a trash bag under the kitchen sink to put her dirty clothes in and took a final look around. If she'd had her phone, she would've booked the suite for the following season just so she'd have a reason to come back when she could fully enjoy it. Then again, the Boden Berg Lodge probably had a block on anyone with the last name of Fleming. She might have to change her name.

Despite every effort to shed the vagabond image she'd so thoroughly cultivated up to that point, Kennedy left the suite with the trash bag slung over her shoulder. A few doors down, a housekeeping cart sat unattended, so she tossed the bag into the trash bin and grabbed a few chocolates off the cart. With haste, she unwrapped one and shoved it into her mouth, but before she could even bite down, she froze at the sound of giggling coming from behind her. She turned around to find two housekeepers snickering, which could only mean one thing. *Everyone* knew about her incident with the snowplow. And they just saw her offload trash and steal candy. Fantastic. The fact that she could continue to walk through the lodge with her head held high was really just a sign of her denial at that point.

She limped to the elevator while shoving the remaining chocolates in her mouth. She hoped the housekeepers would at least be pleasantly surprised when they saw she hadn't left a big mess. She imagined they'd expect a lot less of her, given her undeserved reputation.

She breathed a sigh of relief when the doors opened to an empty elevator. If she could make it to the restaurant without incident, it'd be a miracle, but she was determined to keep her head down and do just that. No eye contact, no conversing, just getting to the bar and ordering some food from Kevin and asking if he knew anyone she could bum a ride off of to get down the mountain. But then she noticed a framed ad with the day's events hanging on the wall of the elevator. It advertised private skiing sessions with Sheriff Lola. And that got Kennedy thinking. Could there be private sessions with Bridget too?

She'd stay on the mountain for that, even if it meant going back to her dad's cold, lonely cabin. Maybe she could take Bridget with her, and they could have their private session there. They'd keep each other warm by the fire. Get to know each other better. Cuddle and drink wine. Kennedy might even get bold and lean in for a kiss. And they'd keep kissing until their tongues touched. That was when Kennedy would probably pull away and say, "God, how I want you, Bridget Berg."

She didn't realize she'd closed her eyes until she heard someone clear their throat. She also didn't realize she'd crossed her legs to relieve the pressure on her throbbing clit. She really needed to stop having fantasies about a woman who was only being nice out of pity. Kennedy Fleming, pitiful Floridian who would be talked about for years on Elk Mountain. The only woman who'd ever been buried alive by a snowplow. "Sorry," she said, limping off the elevator while the guy who'd cleared his throat gave her a smarmy grin.

The lobby was abuzz with activity. All of the comfy leather chairs were taken by skiers trying to warm up by the fire. Without her phone, she had no idea what time it was, but she guessed it was nearing five o'clock. A feeling of panic had her reach for the wall and lean against it. She had literally nothing that belonged to her, down to the sports bra and panties Bridget had sent up from the skiwear shop. She felt isolated, naked without her phone and at least one credit card. But didn't everyone these days? A phone and a credit card were really all a person needed to survive in the modern world.

To prove her point to herself, she scanned the lobby and estimated that at least eighty percent of the people had a phone in their hands or sitting on the table in front of them. She also estimated that most, if not all, would also experience fear, rage, and a profound sense of loss if that phone disappeared. None of this mattered. It wasn't as if there was a snowmobile version of the rentable scooters and bicycles found in most cities these days. But there was Seth. And as he approached with a big smile on his face, Kennedy's mind raced with the possibilities.

"Ms. Fleming. Can I offer you some assistance?"

The sweet kid offered his arm, but Kennedy didn't take it. "Look, I know I've set a precedent with big tips for small mercies, but I don't have any money on me right now." She leaned in and lowered her voice. "Also, could you not shout that name across the lobby? Just call me Kennedy, okay? Or even Hungry Hippo. Just not...Fleming. For some reason, it doesn't seem to be a popular name around here."

He gave her a fervent nod. "Right. Okay. You just looked like you could use some help."

She took his arm and said, "Yeah, that's kind of been my M.O. since I got here, and I gotta tell ya, Seth, I'm hating every second of it because where I live, I'm actually a very capable... who's that guy?"

In their path, about twenty feet away, Bridget Berg in all her sexy, redheaded glory, stood face-to-face with a tall, overly groomed guy. His wavy hair was slicked back the way a hedge fund manager who spent his free time killing innocent animals with Don Junior and Eric would style it. He had a lowball glass in one hand, and with the other, he seemed to be telling a very animated story.

Kennedy hated him and his stupid story that, in her opinion, required way too much hand movement. If he wasn't careful, that drink would end up on Bridget, and then all hell would break loose because if there was one thing Kennedy hated more than a sloppy drunk guy, it was a sloppy drunk guy trying to pick up a gay woman, something she'd experienced far too many times in her life.

Just as her hackles started to rise, Bridget turned, and their eyes met. They held each other's gaze for a few seconds before the guy also turned, and it became a three-way staring contest. The guy leaned in and said something to Bridget, to which she replied with a nod. The guy raised his glass to Kennedy and chuckled, then walked away.

"Crap," she whispered. "Well, I guess that solidifies it."

"Solidifies what?" Seth asked.

Kennedy huffed. "What's my nickname this time? Oh, come on, Seth. Just tell me now so I don't have to hear it over someone's radio."

"Um..." He stifled whatever he was going to say when Bridget moved toward them.

Kennedy couldn't read her expression. Was she glad to see her, or was she simply amused by it all?

She stopped in front of them and gave Kennedy a once-over. Again, her expression, though pleasant, told her nothing. "I'll take it from here, Seth."

The tone in her voice was much more telling. It wasn't like before, when she'd been called in to rescue her employee from an unruly guest. This time, the easy smile and friendly tone matched up perfectly. And Kennedy's first thought was, don't blow this by saying something stupid.

She let go of Seth's arm and watched him walk away. She needed a few seconds to catch her breath because every thought in her head, if said out loud, could ruin everything. Things like, hey, I'm totally jealous of that guy, which means I've probably got a major crush on you, and I'll be devastated if you don't like me too. Yeah, because the truth worked so well in junior high, why not try it again?

She needed a reason to avert her gaze for a little longer, so she said, "Seth is a great employee. You should keep him. Looks like the lobby is full of happy guests. Lots of conversation and drinking and posting selfies to Instagram. Do you offer private skiing sessions too, or is it just the sheriff?"

And then, silence. No reply at all. She had no choice but to turn and meet Bridget's gaze. Her arms were folded, but she was still smiling. "Where are you headed?" she asked.

"Anywhere you'd like to take me." It wasn't a flirty reply so much as just the simple truth, but she still felt the need to apologize. "Sorry. I'm going to sound like a broken record, but I really need to eat something."

Bridget offered her right arm. Kennedy wrapped her hand around a toned bicep and felt instantly at home. God. She really had fallen hard, which made her wonder how hard it would be to get back up.

Unrequited love was a given for most gay kids, or probably most kids in general, but in Kennedy's adult life, it had only happened once. And boy had it hurt when Bella Corso-Sanchez had told her it was never, ever going to happen. And yes, she'd actually used the words, never, ever. Granted, Kennedy was only twenty-one at the time. Surely, she'd handle it better in her thirties. Or maybe falling hard for someone only to get her heart broken would never get easier. And maybe most people were smart enough to know that someone who loathed their father, and by proxy, them, was a recipe for love disaster.

Attraction was one thing. And Kennedy had every reason to be attracted to Bridget. But what was going on inside her was more than attraction. Feelings were swirling. The images in her head had gone from just soft-core sex scenes between the two of them to much more intimate moments. The clasping of hands while kissing. Whispering something in her ear. Even walking arm in arm, similar to the way they were now, only closer.

Would it be wrong to move her hand from Bridget's arm to her waist? Or rest it on the small of her back? Or even just slide it from her bicep to her forearm? She didn't do any of those things because the only reason they were touching in the first place was because of her damned toe. Any other touching would be unwarranted and most likely unwanted. But the desire to let everyone in the room know, especially the handsome guy, that they were not enemies, and that this was much more than an effort to avoid a slip and fall lawsuit, was strong. So strong that Kennedy did the only thing she dared, which was to glance at Bridget and hope the big smile on her face was returned. Then they'd all know, but more importantly, she'd know that, if nothing else, at least they were no longer bitter enemies.

"What?" Bridget asked, returning the smile.

To recap, she returned the smile. As in, Kennedy smiled at Bridget, and Bridget. Smiled. Back. And it wasn't just any old smile either. It was the kind of smile that consumed electricity and real estate. A megawatt, how in the hell was this woman not famous, soul-nourishing grin. How weird that no one else seemed to notice it.

Kennedy shook her head. "Nothing. It's just...I can smell the freshly baked bread from here." Given her circumstances, it seemed like a good cover for the grin, and one that Bridget seemed to accept. The fact that Bridget's instinct was to return the smile was what would likely consume Kennedy's thoughts for at least a week.

"I reserved a spot for you at the bar," she said. "Order anything you want. Oh, and I'm working on a place for you to sleep tonight."

Before she could stop herself, Kennedy pulled Bridget into a hug and said, "I'm so grateful, and I know we don't exactly have a hugging history yet, but I just need to hold on to you for a few seconds, and then I promise to let go, okay?"

The truth was, that hug had nothing to do with who happened to be looking their way. Kennedy just couldn't go another second without knowing what it felt like to hold Bridget Berg in her arms. And it would've felt perfect if the hug had been returned. Just one arm would've been enough. Even just a light pat on her back would've soothed the ache in her heart. But there was no reaction at all. Before she let go and walked away, she whispered, "Thank you, Bridget. And please remember, I'm not my father."

❖

Bridget caught a quick glimpse of herself in the bathroom mirror as she hurried into a stall. Of course, she was bright red, but at least she was having a good hair day.

Seeing Harriet, who wasn't even supposed to be there, stop and stare from across the lobby while Kennedy clung to her, had paralyzed her so much that she hadn't returned the hug. How could she not return the hug, even slightly? And why the hell was Harriet there on her day off? And what did Kennedy mean when she said they didn't have a hugging history yet. Yet? That implied future hugs. She knew Kennedy was flirtatious, but she assumed that was part of her magnetic personality. No, not magnetic. Annoying. That was the word she'd meant to think. Wasn't it?

And the most important question of all: why hadn't Bridget let Seth walk Kennedy to the restaurant? Clearly, he didn't know that his sugar mama's wallet was still buried in a snowbank. But that wasn't why she'd freed him from the task. She'd done it without thinking, as if it was the most natural thing in the world to offer Kennedy her arm. And it felt really good until the surprise hug happened. The one that would be the first of…an unknown number of additional hugs, apparently. She had so many questions. How many additional hugs? Where? When did Kennedy expect these to begin? Would they always be wearing clothes? Was she overthinking the word yet?

As for their first hug, Bridget was caught way off guard by it. Not just a little bit off guard, but way the fuck off guard. It followed a surprising moment when Kennedy had grinned at her like they'd mattered to each other forever, and Bridget's body—and mouth— reacted instinctively. She felt like she had returned the gesture times a thousand without a thought, care, or reservation. But the hug was different. They were touching, and Bridget panicked. The fact that Harriet and every other employee witnessed it left her not knowing what to do except stand there like a statue and then make a run for the bathroom.

She needed a moment to get her thoughts together and let the blush on her face calm down. Was she shaking? She spread her fingers to confirm it and groaned. Kennedy Fleming was getting under her skin. This time, in the best way, which was also possibly the worst way. Surely, a few moments spent hiding in a bathroom stall would help.

"Bridge? You okay?"

Great. Harriet had just walked into the bathroom. Bridget cleared her throat. "Um, yeah. I'm fine. I thought you were taking the weekend off."

Harriet's boots became visible under the door. "I heard about the snowplow and decided to hell with it, I'm going up there and taking that crazy woman off this mountain. She's too much of a liability."

Bridget rolled her eyes. The lodge had obviously become a big gossip mill over the last few days, and on top of that, Harriet didn't trust her to handle it. "How did you get up here? Aren't the roads terrible right now?"

"Terrible. But I know the twists and turns like the back of my hand."

"Harriet, you shouldn't have come back. What were you thinking?"

"After what I just witnessed, I'm glad I did."

She hadn't witnessed anything. It was just a hug. A long, lingering hug, followed by a whisper in her ear that might have seemed intimate and certainly made Bridget's ear tingle, but it wasn't anything intimate. As hugs went, it was entirely appropriate. Bridget opened the stall door. "Let's be clear about this, Harriet. Kennedy was just thanking me for the help we've given her."

Harriet had disbelief written all over her face. "I'll just say one more thing, and then I'll leave you to do your business," she said. "Number one, don't let her walk all over you. And number two, it's time we stopped living in fear of what the Flemings will do next. She may or may not be just like her father, but you need to let her know that you're not just like Boden. I'm not going to say your father acted like a doormat at times, but there certainly were instances where he behaved like a mat. That happened to be in front of a door. All the nonsense stops with you. Period."

"You realize there's no special parking spot for the Bossiest Employee of the Month, right?"

"Very funny. You know I'm telling you this because I love you like you're my own. And this place means the world to me. I'll give you your privacy now."

Once she was sure Harriet was gone, Bridget checked herself in the mirror. The flush in her cheeks had faded some, so she straightened her shoulders and gave herself a nod. "Harriet's right. The nonsense stops now. No matter how attracted you are to her, you need to hold the line. For everyone's sake."

With those words ringing in her head, Bridget headed back into the restaurant. She'd inform Kennedy that the plan had changed, and she'd be going down the mountain with Harriet later that night. She stopped short at the doorway and froze when she saw the scene in front of her.

Kennedy had an audience. Guests and employees had gathered around as she reenacted what could only have been her incident with the snowplow. When they all erupted in laughter, Bridget found herself giggling too, even though she couldn't hear what Kennedy had said. She didn't need to. The words didn't matter. It was the expression of joy, the light in her eyes—those were the things that solidified in Bridget's mind that this beautiful woman was indeed not her father. Not even close. And on top of that, Harriet had overstepped her bounds. Maybe this would be a good time to let her know who actually owned the lodge and therefore, made the final decisions.

Chapter Seven

Stop giving me that mother look. I didn't ask you to come up here." Bridget closed Harriet's office door behind her. "You're not driving back down the mountain when at least two more inches has fallen in just the last hour."

Harriet huffed. "I know you gave the penthouse to that woman, and I'm not sleeping in the bunkroom with those kids. I made that mistake once. Didn't get a wink of sleep."

"I wouldn't ask you to do that. You can take my room."

Harriet raised an eyebrow. "And just where will you sleep?"

They were interrupted by a knock on the door. Bridget shouted, "Enter."

Harriet raised both eyebrows, which caused Bridget to turn to find Kennedy standing there. She stood and said, "Hi," in a soft tone she usually reserved for puppies and kittens. She tried to cover it up with a more forceful tone when she added, "I mean, hi. What's up? What can we do for you?"

"Sorry if I'm interrupting, but Seth said he'd found a ride down the mountain for me and that I should knock on the manager's door." She looked at the door again and tapped the sign with her finger. "Yep, I'm in the right place. Hi, I'm Kennedy Fleming. I don't think we've been introduced."

She stepped forward and offered her hand. Much to Bridget's surprise, Harriet actually stood and shook it. "I'm Harriet, and

Seth, bless his little heart, didn't do anything, so don't you dare tip him."

Kennedy put up her hands. "I couldn't even if I wanted to, but am I to understand that he was wrong?"

"I'll leave that up to the boss." Harriet got up and headed for the door. "But Seth is all mine."

"Don't be too hard on him," Bridget said. "He just wants to impress his girlfriend with a nice Christmas gift."

Harriet popped her head back in and said, "You can't buy love," before she ducked out again.

Kennedy quirked her head. "That's funny. My whole life, I assumed that you *could* buy love."

"God knows there are plenty of people out there who seem to think everything has a price, even love. Heck, they're half our target market."

Kennedy leaned against the wall, right by the door, probably to take the weight off her bad toe. Bridget turned a chair toward her, but Kennedy waved it off. "And what do you think, Bridget?"

"I think you can't buy your way into love any more than you can buy your way out of heartbreak," Bridget said. "But, yeah, pretty much everything else has a price."

"If that's true, why can't I buy my way off this mountain? I've made every effort I can think of—at great humiliation, I might add—to get myself off this mountain, and yet, neither of us can figure out how to get me back down to civilization."

"If you're trying to insinuate that I'm somehow keeping you here…"

"I'm not insinuating anything. Truly, I'm not."

Bridget wasn't so sure, but she wasn't in the mood to argue. "I can get you back down the mountain," she said. "I'll take you myself if necessary. Just not tonight."

"Hey, I'm good with that, but now that I've had a taste of the good life, I don't think I can go back to that freezing cold cabin. I'll sleep in the lobby if I have to. Just give me a bear rug to wrap up in, and I'll be happy as a clam right in front of the fire."

Bridget considered it for a moment, but out in the open like that, who knew what Kennedy would get up to? "Turns out, I'm not in possession of a bear rug, so I guess you'll have to stay in the penthouse with me, and Harriet will sleep in my room."

Kennedy raised her eyebrows. "I thought you had guests arriving tonight."

Bridget lowered her gaze. "I may have lied about that."

"Bridget Berg. I'm shocked, just shocked. And here I thought we had a relationship built on the principles of honesty, trust, and food withholding."

Bridget pointed at the chair again. "Will you please sit down? You look miserable standing on one foot."

Kennedy limped over to the chair. "Do you think Harriet would mind if I put my foot up on her desk? It's throbbing like a motherfu...dger."

Bridget sat in the other chair. "You just noticed the big, "absolutely no foul language" sign, didn't you?"

Kennedy nodded. "How could I have missed it?"

"It's mostly for the younger employees. She says that if their own parents can't teach them manners, then it's her job to try. But that was a nice save with the motherfudger thing. I'll have to remember that one."

"It saved my butt on more than one occasion, but I'd still get a stink eye from my dad. Sorry, I didn't mean to mention him."

"No, it's a great segue into why I lied to you. The suite I let you use today, it's my dad's place. It's where I grew up. My home. I just had it renovated thinking I'd rent it out, but I haven't been able to bring myself to do it, even though it would be quite lucrative."

Kennedy turned in her chair so they were face-to-face. "Money isn't always the most important thing."

"Says the woman who throws it around like beads at a Mardi Gras parade."

"Hey, now. I require exactly zero flashing of breasts before throwing my money around, thank you very much."

Kennedy leaned on the arm of her chair, rested her fist under her chin, and unabashedly flirted with those big brown eyes by letting them flit from Bridget's eyes to her lips, her chest, and back again. If Harriet walked in, she'd probably run into a wall of lesbian chemistry so thick, she'd start speaking in Indigo Girls lyrics.

Bridget looked away first and said in a casual tone not befitting her heart rate, "In any event, money is what we desperately need to keep this place running, so one of these days, I'm going to have to suck it up and rent out the penthouse."

"Did I sleep in your room?" Kennedy asked.

Bridget gave her a nod. "Yeah."

Kennedy patted her hand. "You'll get there. Don't be so hard on yourself." Her eyes stayed firmly focused on their hands until she pulled hers away and cheerfully announced, "And in the meantime, slumber party!"

Bridget breathed a sigh of relief. She'd needed the energy in the room to lighten up. "Please don't expect any pillow fights or scary movies," she said. "How 'bout we just aim to be civil?"

"You've got a deal." Kennedy stuck out her hand to formalize their extremely important agreement.

Bridget feigned annoyance and rolled her eyes before she shook it. "I suppose you'll need pajamas? I usually sleep in thermal underwear in the winter."

"I'll take whatever you're offering, but in those soft sheets, I'm also just fine with sleeping in my birthday suit. Your choice."

"Thank you for appreciating them. Linens are one of our biggest expenses." Bridget reached into her pocket. "Here's the key. Make yourself at home, and I'll send up some snacks later."

"Will you be joining me? Maybe we could watch a straight rom-com while munching on peanut M&Ms and caramel popcorn, which I happen to know you sell in your little store downstairs."

"Why a straight rom-com?"

Kennedy threw her palms up. "Because, hello, that's all there is out there."

"There's *Imagine Me & You.*"

"Okay, there's one. And I'm over it. I can't take that scene where she's giving her husband's speech at their wedding anymore. I mean, it's so obvious that she's not in love with him, and yet, she marries him anyway."

Bridget shook her head. "Yeah. That's straight people for you."

"Also, who kisses a girl *right* after telling her it absolutely cannot happen?"

"Isn't that basically when most kisses happen?" Bridget asked.

"In movies, sure. Maybe in romance novels. But in real life? Not so much."

"Fine," Bridget said. "But who would seriously say, 'I dare you to love me' to a straight married person?"

"Um. In my experience, most lesbians have tried that at one time or another."

"Maybe not in so many words, but I get your point. Also, is that really what a lily symbolizes?"

"Obviously," Kennedy exclaimed. "Only a wanker wouldn't know that. Actually, I don't have a clue, but God, I love that movie so much."

Bridget sighed. "Yeah, me too."

After a brief pause, Kennedy threw a finger in the air and said, "Wait, I've got it. We could watch *All the Jingle Ladies.* You know, it's that Hallmark-y lesbian Christmas movie that came out last year. Oh my God, I must've watched it ten times in a row. Lacey Matthews is just so…"

Bridget knew who Lacey Matthews was. Every lesbian on the planet knew who she was. But she hadn't seen the movie Kennedy was referring to. "Did you say, *All the Jingle Ladies?*"

Kennedy put her hand up. "I know, it's a cheesy title for the best made-for-TV lesbian movie ever, but I'm telling you, it's so adorable and romantic. Oh, and did I mention Lacey Matthews is one of the leads?"

Bridget grinned. "A couple of times now." She stood and said, "As intriguing as you make it sound, I probably won't be able to watch it with you tonight. I don't know if you've noticed, but the fun never stops when you're running a ski lodge. Sadly, there won't be any *Dance Dance Revolution* or Lacey Matthews for us tonight." It didn't sound intriguing; watching a romantic movie with Kennedy sounded downright dangerous. Bridget couldn't go there. Ever.

"Fine." Kennedy got up and limped to the door. "At the very least, I should warn you that this thing between us absolutely cannot happen. And now I'm going to leave and slam the door, so brace yourself for what comes next."

"Wait, what?" Not sure if Kennedy was joking or if she actually planned to come barreling back into the office only to have them land on a nonexistent bed of roses and rip each other's clothes off, Bridget leaned on the edge of the desk, crossed her legs, and folded her arms. She laughed under her breath at the silliness, but at the same time, she found herself hoping that Kennedy really would burst through that door just so she could say, "Did you really think I'd be bracing myself for a passionate kiss?" And then Kennedy would say something like, "Hey, it was worth a try."

Her heart leapt when the door flew open. The euphoria lasted for all of one second when she realized it was Harriet. "Why are you grinning like the Cheshire Cat?"

Bridget might have been smiling, due to her current state of amusement, but she was *not* grinning like some cartoon. She leaned to the side to see if Kennedy was standing behind Mrs. Harriet Buzzkill or if she'd scared her off. Irritated that no one was there, Bridget pushed herself off the desk and mumbled, "I don't know what you're talking about," as she left the office.

❖

Kennedy stood at Bridget's bedroom door inside the penthouse. She couldn't think of a time she'd ever stood outside a door for this long. Should she knock, or would it be better to leave Bridget alone after such a long day? She glanced at her watch again, even though she knew it would still be ten past eleven. Which was exactly zero minutes past the last time she had looked.

She'd waited until she heard the shower turn off, then waited a few more minutes to give Bridget time to get into bed. All movement had stopped at nine past eleven, which meant she needed to knock or bail. Otherwise, she risked waking Bridget up.

She lifted her hand and knocked. "Bridget? Are you still up?"

"Come in."

She opened the door to find Bridget sitting up in bed. "Am I disturbing you?"

"Not at all. I thought you were asleep."

Kennedy shut the door behind her. "Can't sleep." She pointed at the bed. "Mind if I sit for a minute?"

Bridget patted the edge of the bed. "Is everything okay?"

"Yeah. Everything's fine." She put one leg up so she could face Bridget. The only light in the room came from the bathroom, but as Kennedy's eyes adjusted to the dark, she could tell by her relaxed expression that Bridget wasn't annoyed. That was a relief since she didn't have a good reason for the disturbance, other than a strong need to be near her again. After their conversation about movies they'd probably never watch together, Kennedy had felt like she was limping on clouds. Sure, she was disappointed that they couldn't spend the evening together. Nonetheless, they'd had a great conversation, and if she wasn't mistaken, the huge wall Bridget had put up between them was starting to show cracks. And she sure as hell wouldn't be able to get a wink of sleep until she could determine if she was right. "Long day for you, huh?"

Bridget sighed and leaned back against her pillow. "I think Harriet was determined to keep me downstairs for as long as possible."

Having just been given the perfect segue only five seconds into their conversation, Kennedy put up a finger. "Speaking of Harriet. I don't want you to think I'd left you hanging earlier."

"That's assuming, of course, that I had indeed braced myself for what was about to happen."

Kennedy hesitated. Bridget had been so quick to respond, it made her think that she wasn't the only who wondered what would've happened if she'd gone back in that office. She tilted her head and said, "Did you?"

"Did I what?"

"Brace yourself. I mean, a slightly wider stance would've been enough, so if there was any foot movement whatsoever, I'm gonna call it a win."

Bridget gave her a sly grin. "Oh, I was ready for you. Just not in the way you're imagining."

Kennedy slumped her shoulders. "Damn. I thought it was a genius move, but it turns out, I could've crashed and burned so hard, there would've been no coming back." She clasped her hands together and looked upward. "Whoever's up there, thank you for intervening on my behalf when I so clearly needed it."

Bridget giggled. "Amen."

It was the cutest giggle Kennedy had ever heard, and she wanted to hear it again, but she could tell that Bridget needed a good night's rest. So she stood and said, "Sleep well, Bridget Berg."

"You too, Kennedy Fleming."

Kennedy put a hand on her hip. "Wow, am I off my game. I thought for sure you'd sit up, reach for my hand, and tell me not to leave." She threw her hands in the air and turned. "It must be the altitude. I'm like a cake mix that you have to add more flour or oil or something to this high up."

"Kennedy?"

She stopped at the door and turned back. Bridget was sitting up again, but she didn't have her hand outstretched. Kennedy stayed where she was and said, "See, the way this works is, you have to reach for me, or I might misinterpret why you just said my name." She lifted her arm to demonstrate. "See, like this, as if you're desperate to touch me."

Bridget shook her head and laughed under her breath. "I was just going to say that I'll have someone dig your stuff out of the snowbank tomorrow."

"Oh. Or we could leave it for future generations to find. I think they'd be enthralled by my choice of facial cleanser and eyeliner, don't you?"

"Except that it does eventually get warm here, and by late spring, it'll just be a dirty suitcase lying on the side of the road."

"Right. Right! This isn't Siberia, and we're not Neanderthal women." Kennedy pointed at the door. "I think I'm just gonna go and brush up on my geology, maybe look at a few weather patterns. So I guess, um, nighty, night." She closed the door behind her and limped as fast as she could back to her room where she threw the covers over her head and groaned. "I really need to stop making a fool of myself." And she wasn't even referring to the "nighty night" thing, although, once she'd thought of it, what in the actual hell was that?

She shot back up and turned her ear to the door. Yep, Bridget was calling her. She went back to Bridget's door and in a casual tone, asked, "Did you say something?"

"Sorry for yelling for you. I was too lazy to get out of bed."

Kennedy closed the door again and went to the bed. Bridget had a bottle of lotion in one hand. "Is this where you ask me to apply suntan lotion to your entire body, and then I get turned on, and then you get turned on, and then we cut to tomorrow morning, and you have this glow about you that Kevin the bartender notices?"

Bridget grimaced. "Um, just kill me now if any of my employees know when I've had sex."

"Did I say sex? With me?" Kennedy pointed at herself. "Well, if we must, but remember that it was your idea." She started to loosen the tie on her robe, but Bridget fell over on her side in a fit of laughter. She tightened her robe and sat on the bed. "Seriously, though. What did you need?"

Bridget rolled over. Her face was bright red, and she had tears in her eyes. "Apparently, I needed a good laugh." She held on to her tummy while she caught her breath. "God, you're hilarious, Kennedy."

"Thanks, but I'm not quite sure how to feel about the fact that you find the idea of it so funny."

Bridget leaned up on her hands. "No, it was the way you flipped it around on me and started that little striptease." She sat up and crossed her legs under her. "You have this way of being both funny and sexy at the same time."

Kennedy couldn't suppress the huge, cheesy grin that no doubt took over her face. Clearly, her flirtatious jackhammer had indeed put some rather large cracks in that big wall. Or maybe it was simpler than that. Maybe Bridget was finally seeing Kennedy for who she really was. She turned away long enough to regain a bit of composure and then met her gaze again and said, "Right back atcha."

"But I can't," Bridget said. "Even if…"

She covered her eyes, so Kennedy finished the sentence for her. "Even if you wanted to?"

Bridget uncovered her eyes. "It's bigger than this right here."

Kennedy turned away again. She didn't want Bridget to see her frustration. "I don't know. This feels pretty big." Bridget didn't reply, so Kennedy stood and stuffed her hands into her robe pockets. "But I'll take what I can get." She offered her hand. "Friends?"

"I'd like that." Bridget took her hand and didn't let go for a moment. "I'll even throw in the robe and slippers."

Kennedy smiled. "I was going to steal them anyway." Bridget still had hold of her hand. It felt warm and comfortable and right. One tug of that soft hand was all it would take for her to crawl onto the bed and straddle Bridget. She said it in her head a few times. *Tug on my hand, Bridget. Come on, one tug, and I'm yours for the night.* Or longer. No, definitely longer. One night with Bridget Berg would never be enough. She'd need at least five nights to memorize every part of her body. Every little freckle. Every scar. There were bound to be a few scars from all her years of competitive skiing, and Kennedy wanted to kiss each and every one. Five nights would be enough time to get to know her body, but she'd need more than that if she wanted to know her heart. Her mind. She couldn't put a number on that one. Thirty nights? Three hundred? A lifetime?

Kennedy was getting ahead of herself. The tug she longed for wasn't going to happen, so with their hands still joined she said, "What's that saying? Love me or let me go? I'd prefer the former, but—" Bridget let go. "Okay, then. Good night." Kennedy backed away. "It's bittersweet, me leaving. You know that, right?"

Bridget pointed at her. "See? Sexy and funny."

"Oh, please keep saying that word. Only slower this time. And with more..." Her back hit the door. "Okay. I'm really leaving now. Good-bye, Bridget. May we meet again in the afterlife. Or tomorrow morning. Whichever comes first. I mean, I'll probably come first when I get back to my room, but...don't forget me, okay?"

Bridget grinned. "I won't remember anything else."

Kennedy clapped her hands like one of those movie slates. "And scene. God, we've both watched that movie too many times."

"Maybe some time, we can watch it together."

Kennedy opened the door. "I'm holding you to that one, Bridget Berg. Nighty night." There it was again, the stupid nighty night thing.

Just as Kennedy was about to kick herself all the way down the hall for saying it again, Bridget replied, "Nighty night."

For some reason, the reply made Kennedy cover her heart with her hand as she closed the door. She stood there for a moment, hoping it wouldn't be the first and last time she heard Bridget say those words.

Chapter Eight

Bridget rounded a corner on her way to the office and stopped short when she almost collided with Harriet. "Good morning."

Harriet eyed her for a few seconds and exclaimed, "Oh, thank God."

"What?"

"You don't have that post-sex thing going on, which means you didn't lose your mind last night, which also means I can call off the intervention."

Intervention? While it was true that Bridget neither wanted nor needed the drama and gossip that would surely make its way through the entire lodge at lightning speed, Harriet had crossed a line. Bridget lowered her voice and said, "That is wholly unnecessary, unwelcome, and last but most certainly not least, none of your damn business." They eyed each other for a few seconds, and then Harriet took her phone out of her pocket. "Please don't tell me you're now texting someone about this so-called intervention."

"Lola. Who else would I call in?"

"I shudder to think." Bridget headed to the office in the hope of losing Harriet along the way. At some point, they'd need to have a Come to Jesus conversation about all this. Thinking of Jesus reminded her of Kennedy's prayer last night, and that made her smile. She was so adorable when she tried to flirt and failed.

Failed was a strong word, considering that it had almost worked. Bridget had to resist hard to not put her hand out. She wanted to. Not because she thought they'd make out because that was certainly not going to happen. It was more that she wanted someone to fall asleep with.

Not someone. She wanted to fall asleep with Kennedy. But how did she ask someone who was obviously attracted to her, and her to them, to just cuddle? *Oh, and please don't get turned on. Just...hold me. You know, because it's cold and stuff. And also because you seem like you'd fit nicely.* Yeah. That wouldn't be awkward at all.

The truth was, Bridget didn't trust herself to not get turned on either, and she was pretty sure that under Kennedy's hotel bathrobe, there was nothing but soft sexy curves. She loved the curves on a woman. And she loved to run her fingers over those curves.

She'd done the right thing. But not for Harriet's sake. And was Harriet still on her tail, furiously texting with Lola? She glanced over her shoulder and said, "You really just need one word written three times. A-B-O-R-T. Lola's a smart girl. She'll understand."

"I'm just letting her know that your dignity is still intact."

Shocked, Bridget stopped and turned. "My dignity?" She pointed down the hall. "Your office. Now."

Apparently, that Jesus convo couldn't wait. Bridget shut the door behind them and folded her arms. "You've crossed a line, Harriet. When it comes to my personal life, you need to be a bit more thoughtful before you act."

Harriet glared at her for a few seconds before she went and stood behind her desk. "You haven't always been around, Bridge. You don't know everything your dad put up with."

"I know enough."

Harriet raised her hands. "Okay. I'll stay out of it from now on, but I may have already asked a friend to come up and fix the Fleming's furnace. Oh, and he's buying some groceries for her too." She held up a hand again. "I know what you're going to say, but he has a big truck with studded snow tires. He'll be just fine."

Bridget did her best to hold back her anger. "Can I assume the lodge will be paying for this?"

"It's in the lodge's best interests to get Kennedy Fleming back on her own turf. Oh, and Mack is down there right now, plowing their driveway."

Harriet's self-satisfied expression indicated she was waiting for a thank you of some sort, but Bridget didn't feel grateful. Her dad had always handled the Fleming situation and so would she, if Harriet would just stay out of it and stop treating her like a starry-eyed, clueless teenager. "Well, Harriet, I guess you have it all figured out, then. Any chance you told Mack that there's a suitcase in that snowbank?"

Harriet's eyes widened. "No. I forgot about that."

Bridget grabbed a radio from the charging station. "Let's hope it's not too late." She rushed out of the lodge and was halfway down the steps when she heard her name. She turned around, and like a starry-eyed, clueless teenager, she kind of, sort of, swooned at the sight in front of her. Because there stood Kennedy, looking as gorgeous as ever, even with her damp hair all slicked back. She had on the clothes Bridget had left out for her, dark jeans that she'd rolled at the cuff, a long flannel button-up, and a black puffer vest with the lodge's logo on the chest. She almost looked like she worked there or at the very least, was the smokin' hot girlfriend of the owner.

No, no, no. Bridget couldn't think those kinds of thoughts. She needed to wipe the grin from her face and use her pleasant lodge-owner voice when she climbed back up a few steps and said, "Good morning. Did you get some breakfast? How did you sleep?"

Kennedy used Bridget's shoulder to steady herself as she took a step down, putting them face-to-face. "I'm not sure why, but the toe is a little worse this morning."

Bridget took her elbow. "Maybe you shouldn't walk on it. Let's get you back inside."

"Wait," Kennedy said. "I was thinking maybe you could grab one of those snowmobiles and take me down to the scene of my embarrassing accident? I really need to find my phone."

Bridget furrowed her brow. "About that." She paused and looked to see if a snowmobile was available. "You know what? I'll tell you on the way. Put your arm over my shoulder." She took a step down and wrapped her arm around Kennedy's waist. "I've got you. Just do one step at a time."

When they got to the bottom step, Kennedy hopped on one leg. She almost lost her balance, but Bridget grabbed her so she wouldn't fall. That put them face-to-face again with her hands on Kennedy's waist, and when their eyes met, Bridget whipped her head to the left. And then to the right. She needed something else to look at. Something not desirable or sexy or warm and inviting. She needed different images in her mind. Harriet! That was who she'd think about. Except that was kind of mean. And weird. She could think about payroll taxes. That would do the trick.

"Uh, Bridget?"

"What? I mean, huh?"

"If we keep standing like this with my leg up, people are going to start to wonder if you'll ever be brave enough to actually kiss me."

Bridget took a quick look at her leg, and sure enough, she was in the kissing pose that one saw in old movies. And Kennedy obviously found the situation comical. "Very funny. Now, just stay right here. Can you do that? Can you put your leg down and stay upright for a minute?"

Kennedy demurred as she lowered her leg. "I suppose I can manage."

Bridget narrowed her eyes. "Is your foot really worse off today or—"

"Or what?"

"Or are you just looking for a reason to—"

"To what?"

Bridget wasn't buying Kennedy's innocent tone, but she didn't want to accuse her outright of using her injury to bring them physically closer. "Never mind," she said. "Just don't tip over while I'm gone."

She hurried to the parking lot and brushed the snow off a two-seater. She needed to get down there before Mack pushed that suitcase even deeper into the snowbank. Or worse, ripped it wide open with the plow blade and ruined its contents.

When she pulled up to the lodge, Kennedy put a hand up. "Don't get off. I can do it on my own."

Bridget offered her hand for support. "Easy does it."

With surprising agility, Kennedy mounted the machine with her good leg and eased in behind Bridget. "Where do I hang on?"

"You don't," Bridget said. "Hands straight up in the air like you're riding a roller coaster but don't you dare fall off."

"Ha. For a second there, I thought you were serious, but I realized that was just code for, slide closer and hold on to me as tight as you can." She wrapped her arms around Bridget's waist and tucked her hands into her coat pockets. "Okay, I'm ready to stay like this for an hour, so take the long way."

Bridget turned slightly and said, "If I go the long way, your suitcase might be toast."

"Well, I may have realized that I'm already toast, so my suitcase is the least of my worries."

Bridget turned around even more. "What do you mean?"

"I mean…" Kennedy stopped. She shook her head and rested her forehead on Bridget's shoulder. "Just go the short way."

Bridget turned back around and put her hands on the grips. She waited for Kennedy to put her hands back in her pockets, but she didn't make any contact at all. "You good?" she asked without turning her head.

"All good."

Was she hanging on to the back of the snowmobile? Bridget revved the engine, causing them to jerk forward just enough for those arms to grab her around the waist again. She smiled to herself and shouted, "Sorry about that."

It was a very short ride down to the Flemings' driveway. Mack was out of his truck, picking up pieces of clothing. Bridget stopped and said, "Damnit. It looks like we're too late."

Kennedy shouted, "Hey. Don't worry about that stuff. You shouldn't have to clean up this mess."

"No worries, ma'am. I already found your purse. Set it on the porch up there." He gestured toward the cabin. "Unfortunately, your suitcase seems to have exploded on impact, so I'm just gathering up your, um…" He held up a pair of panties "Unmentionables."

Bridget got off the snowmobile and stood in front of Kennedy to block her view. "I'll handle this. Just stay right here, okay?"

She grabbed Bridget's coat sleeve. "I'd really rather do it myself."

"It's fine."

"No, it's not," Kennedy snapped back.

Bridget raised an eyebrow. "You're acting like one of those people who gets stopped by customs in *To Catch a Drug Mule*."

"It's called *To Catch a Smuggler*, and I am not."

"You're not acting like that, or you're not a drug mule?"

"Bridget, stop him. Please."

"So you are a drug mule."

"Oh. My. God. I just don't want a stranger going through my things, okay?"

Seth's head popped up from behind a snowbank. "I found the phone," he shouted. "And this." He proudly held up a bright pink vibrator.

Bridget covered her mouth, but it didn't really muffle her laughter. Kennedy shot up off the seat. "Hey, leave that…woah." She wasn't able to get the words out before her arms started to flail in an effort to regain her balance. Bridget lunged for her, but Kennedy tipped forward and grabbed the handlebars, managing to squeeze the thumb throttle in the process. The snowmobile shot forward.

Bridget grabbed on to the back and screamed, "Take your hands off." She lost her footing but managed to hang on long enough to shout a more specific instruction. "Take your hand off the throttle!"

The snowmobile came to a stop a few feet away from Mack's truck. Bridget let go of the bar and rolled onto her back so she could catch her breath. Kennedy got off and dropped to her knees, a look of sheer panic on her face. "Are you okay?"

She was fine. They were both fine. But it needed to be said. "My God, you're a hot mess, Kennedy Fleming."

They shared a laugh that turned into a few seconds of silence before Kennedy said, "If I kissed you right now…"

Bridget hesitated for not more than a couple of seconds, but it was long enough for Kennedy to regret the question and try to pull away, but Bridget stopped her. Aside from the world ending, did the consequences of one kiss really matter? It seemed like the regret she'd most likely have for the rest of her life if she let the moment slip by would be a much higher price to pay. She wanted that kiss, so she whispered, "Just do it."

Their lips had barely touched when Seth dropped to his knees next to them.

"Woah, that was scary," he said. "I thought for sure you were going to smack right into that truck."

Kennedy made a noise that sounded a lot like, "Motherfudger," said through gritted teeth before she let Seth help her to her feet. She stomped a few feet away and with her back to them, threw her hands to the sky.

Bridget shared her frustration. Just the brushing of their lips together had her feeling all sorts of things. Mainly, a strong motivation to make sure it happened again, maybe somewhere a little bit more private. She pushed herself to a sitting position and brushed the snow from her body. Seth moved to help her, but she put up a hand. "No. Just hang on to Hot Mess so she doesn't cause any more trouble."

Seth stifled a laugh. "Can we use that one on the radio?"

Bridget got up and faced him. "You can call her anything you want as long as you don't say a word about what you just saw."

"Hey, I didn't see a thing." He cleared his throat and added, "Except for this personal massager."

Kennedy marched back over and grabbed it from his hand. "You didn't see this either. Got it?"

Kennedy had turned bright red. Possibly from the cold air. Or maybe it was from the almost kiss. Bridget wanted to think it was the latter, but it was most likely from embarrassment. She didn't want to add to it so she stifled a giggle and said, "Is it safe to assume it's okay for Seth to take the rest of your belongings to the cabin?"

Kennedy gave them a nod. "Thank you, Seth."

"Yes, ma'am. I'll check on the furnace guy while I'm there. He showed up right as Mack made his first pass up the driveway." Before leaving, he took Kennedy by the arm and led her the few steps to Bridget. "Can you hang on to Hot Mess while I'm gone, boss?"

Kennedy gasped. "Is that what you're calling me now?"

Seth took off giggling and Kennedy shrugged. "I guess it's better than the previous nickname. She turned to Bridget. "Especially if you gave it to me."

Bridget suppressed a grin. "Nah, it was Harriet. I think she might have a crush on you." She steadied Kennedy while she got back on the snowmobile.

"Yeah. I totally get that vibe from her. It must be the way she glares at me from across the lobby like I'm a possible suspect in a shoplifting gang that's been terrorizing the mountain."

Bridget laughed because she knew the look, and Kennedy's description was pretty accurate. Also, she looked so damned cute sitting there on the snowmobile. Her hair had dried into sort of a messy look. Kennedy would probably try to smooth it out if she looked in a mirror, but Bridget found it adorable and sexy. "Still want that long ride?" she asked.

Kennedy spread her legs wider, making room for Bridget to sit in front of her. "Hop on, cowgirl."

The consequences of the kiss became evident about a minute after they took off for higher ground. Kennedy pushed her entire body up against Bridget, her hands tucked into her pockets again.

And for Bridget's part, certain body parts had been awakened and were begging for attention. If a simple brush of lips had done that to her, what would a real kiss do?

Was it because it had been a minute since she'd been with anyone that she got so turned on? Or was it that her attraction to Kennedy was just that strong?

They went over a bump, which caused Kennedy's hands to bounce up in Bridget's pockets and graze her breasts. It only made the situation worse because then she imagined unzipping her jacket enough for Kennedy to reach in and touch her deliberately. To massage her breast and play with her nipple.

Her hand could go lower too. It could slide into her pants and then her underwear. A finger could glide into her wetness and find her aching clit, and—

"Where are we going?" Kennedy shouted.

Bridget stopped in the middle of the narrow trail and cut the engine. She didn't have a destination in mind. She just wanted to have those arms wrapped around her for a little while longer.

Kennedy put her chin on Bridget's shoulder. "Not that it matters," she said. "You can take me wherever you want."

Bridget got up, turned around, and straddled the seat so they were face-to-face. "Anywhere?"

Kennedy's lips parted as if she was about to answer, but she glanced from side to side. "Actually, I kinda like it right here."

Bridget also took a look around. As long as she lived, she'd never get over the natural beauty that surrounded her every day. "My dad once told me that most people think the best view of the mountains is from the bottom, but he saw it differently. He said that to really appreciate the majesty and grandeur of a mountain, you need to be on top of it, feeling scared to death that you're going to fall."

Kennedy rested her hands on Bridget's knees. "I'm not afraid to fall."

"That doesn't surprise me."

"Wait. You're the one who races down mountains. Are you telling me you're scared to death every time you do it?"

"I didn't realize we were talking about skiing." Bridget turned away. She shouldn't have said that. And she probably shouldn't have followed up with, "Earlier, you were going to ask me a question. You said, 'If I kissed you right now...'"

Kennedy raised a hand to Bridget's cheek and held it. "I wanted to know if you'd kiss me back."

Bridget didn't purposely delay her answer. She just needed a moment to take it all in. It was all so perfect. So sexy. And so different. It was just the two of them in the middle of nowhere with nothing to stop them from experiencing the pleasure of a shared kiss.

Kennedy started to remove her hand, but Bridget caught it and kept it on her cheek while she held her gaze. The tension between them heightened to the point where she felt like she'd lose her breath, so she raised her other hand and cupped Kennedy's cheek. "Are you still not afraid to fall?" she asked.

Kennedy's breathing quickened. "I'm scared shitless, but if somebody doesn't kiss somebody soon—"

Their lips touched again, but this time with a gentle force that sent shockwaves through Bridget's body. She held back a moan, but Kennedy didn't. She let hers reverberate on their lips before she pulled away just long enough to say, "Thank God this finally happened."

Bridget found herself in agreement and also very lost in Kennedy's scent. The kiss was everything she'd hoped it would be. It went from frantic to gentle and then back again. Her heart pounded, and other parts of her ached for attention. She wanted Kennedy in a way she had never experienced. She wanted all of her. She wanted her naked and open and wet and warm. She wanted to be inside her so much, she was tempted to stop what they were doing and race back to her cabin. But if felt too good to stop.

The combination of Kennedy's fingers running through her hair and her tongue exploring her mouth made her feel lightheaded.

She wondered if Kennedy was just as lost in the feeling of Bridget massaging her ass while she took her bottom lip into her mouth and sucked on it. The deep, throaty moan she elicited told her she was.

The kiss was everything Bridget had imagined and more. It was hot and passionate, and had they not been sitting on a snowmobile, it was the kind of kiss that could've led to so much more. And Bridget absolutely wanted more.

Kennedy kissed her way to Bridget's ear and buried her face in her shoulder. "You've got me so turned on right now, I don't know which way is up."

Bridget smiled. "I know the feeling. It's almost like I'm tipsy."

Kennedy lifted her head. "I'm drunk on you too. Also, parts of me are on fire, and other parts of me might never thaw out."

It hadn't occurred to Bridget that Kennedy wasn't exactly dressed for a long ride in the dead of winter. She glanced at her feet and gasped. "Oh my God. You're still wearing my slippers." She grabbed her cheeks and looked her in the eye. "We have to go back. Right now."

"One more kiss for the road?"

Bridget gave her a quick peck and got herself turned around. She started the engine and barked, "Hang on, and don't let go."

"Wow," Kennedy exclaimed. "That was a really short honeymoon period. Like, infinitesimal."

"You could have frostbite. Also, I'll make it up to you later, okay?"

Kennedy slid forward and wrapped her arms around Bridget. "I'm holding you to that. Also, my naked body. I'm going to hold you—whaaaa."

Bridget grabbed Kennedy's flailing leg as she gunned it and made a U-turn. "I meant it when I told you to hang on."

Frostbite was no joke. It also occurred to Bridget that the reason Kennedy hadn't complained about her toe since they'd left the lodge could be that it had gone numb from the cold. She needed to get her back home fast.

❖

Since it seemed like everyone at the lodge had orders to bend over backward for her now, being back in her dad's house again was not Kennedy's idea of a good time. She had a plowed driveway, heat blasting from the furnace, and although she hadn't looked yet, she'd been told that the fridge had been stocked with a few days' worth of groceries. If only they'd all been this kind when she'd first arrived. Now it felt like just when things were getting good, she was being told to take her toys and go home. But her toys were all broken, including her phone. And if her suspicions were correct, so was her toe.

So she sat there with her feet soaking in a pan of warm water while Bridget took a call outside. She rested her head on the back of the chair and turned toward the window so she could watch the skiers go by. The sun had finally come out. In fact, there wasn't a cloud in the sky. She wondered how long it would take for the giant icicles that hung from the roofline to start melting. She also wondered if Bridget's heart had begun the melting process or if that kiss was just raw attraction.

From the moment they'd met, Kennedy had felt the attraction, but it was so much more than that now. She couldn't even call it a crush anymore. It was whatever came between a crush and being madly in love. Like a lush. No. That wasn't right. Besides, she felt the scales were tipping slightly toward the latter due to that crazy hot kiss they'd shared. Kennedy's insides were still buzzing from it.

They hadn't had a chance to talk about it or even look each other in the eye, really. When they got back to the cabin, it was all rush, rush to get her feet warmed up and talk to the furnace guy, and take what was now Bridget's third phone call.

All Kennedy wanted was for Bridget to come back inside and stand in front of her so she could read her expression and get some idea of what she was—or wasn't—feeling. As if wishes came true, the door opened, and Kennedy's heart leapt. But it wasn't Bridget.

"Hello, Sheriff. What brings you up here?"

The sheriff stomped on the doormat and hung her coat on the rack. "You can call me Lola."

Kennedy shook her head. "Oh no. When you're looking so official in that fancy uniform, I will definitely use your title."

"Well, it's good to see you're back to your smartass old self again." She knelt on one knee and looked at Kennedy's foot. "Bridget said it's gotten worse."

Kennedy leaned forward. "I'm worried it's broken. What do you think, doc?"

"I think only a real doc could tell you that."

"Right. So why are you here? Sorry, that sounded rude."

The sheriff stood back up. "I have a friend who owns a B and B. She had a cancelation, so I thought I'd see if you wanted to get off this mountain."

She wanted to get off something, that was for sure. "Oh. Well, Bridget—"

As she said her name, Bridget walked in and stood next to the sheriff with her arms folded. "What do you think, Lo? Is it broken?"

"Only one way to find out."

Kennedy feared the worst. She didn't want to go down the mountain now. She wanted to stay close to Bridget, but only if Bridget wanted that too. And she really didn't know. No doubt it was a kiss for the ages, but it was impossible to gauge where Bridget's head was at, given that she'd spent most of their post-kiss time on the phone. She wanted to talk about it with Bridget and maybe, you know, also *not* talk about it with Bridget. She knew the chatter in her head was reaching peak lesbian. "You know what, I think it's feeling a little better now that it's warmed up." It was a lie, but she'd suffer through the pain if it meant she could stay right where she was. "Besides, you've done so much to make this place livable that I might as well stay. Right?" They both stared at her but gave no reaction. "Okay, fine. It hurts like hell, but there's all that food in the fridge, and, and…"

Bridget turned to the sheriff. "She needs an X-ray. Do you have time to drop her off at urgent care?"

Her tone was so businesslike, Kennedy wanted to wave her hand and say, Hey, it's me. The girl you passionately kissed about an hour ago. Remember that? But the two of them went over to the door and lowered their voices enough that she couldn't hear what was being said. And then Bridget was gone. The sheriff grabbed her coat along with Kennedy's and offered her hand. With a big dose of reluctance, Kennedy took it.

❖

Bridget stood outside the bed and breakfast known as the Corner Cottage. It was a ridiculously on-the-nose name since it was situated on a corner lot. She didn't know much about the place. Only that Lola had dated the owner a few times.

It was one of those tall, narrow, Victorian homes with three levels, which didn't bode well for someone with a foot injury. Or someone like Bridget, who had a weekender bag in one hand and a large pizza in the other.

She carefully navigated the steps, avoiding any spots that looked icy and breathed a sigh of relief when she made it to the front door with the pizza still in hand. A sign on the door said to "Come On In," so she set the bag down and opened the door. She spotted Kennedy sitting at a card table in the living room with three older women, shuffling the deck.

Bridget stepped inside and closed the door behind her. When they all turned, she said, "Don't trust her, ladies. She'll take everything you have and smile while doing it."

Kennedy's eyes lit up, but as quickly as they'd done so, her expression changed to something far more neutral.

One of the women stood and said, "Buy-in is twenty bucks. And you must be Lola's friend. I'm Iris. Come on in."

Iris had short graying hair and a nice smile. She was also at least twenty years older than Lola. A point she'd have to tease her about the next time they talked. She set the pizza on the desk and made the rounds, shaking everyone's hand until she came to Kennedy, who still didn't seem pleased to see her. "I hear you got some sort of boot for your foot."

Kennedy stuck her leg out. "The doc said it's probably overkill, but it'll keep my toe from bending when I walk."

"So it's not broken?"

"Hairline fracture." She gave Bridget a tight smile. "What are you doing here?"

"Well, I brought dinner and some clothes for you. Also, pajamas."

"Oh. That was nice of you."

All eyes were on them, so Bridget motioned with her thumb. "Can I maybe see where you're staying?"

"I gave her the back room so she wouldn't have to navigate the stairs," Iris said. "It's really only big enough for one person."

She said it in such a way that made Bridget feel unwelcome. And then Kennedy drove the point home when she stood and said, "Don't worry, she's not staying."

The boot, although clunky, allowed Kennedy to walk a little easier. Bridget followed her through the living room and the kitchen to a door that seemed way too short to be the entrance to a room one would rent out. Kennedy opened the door and said, "Watch your head."

Bridget didn't move. "You're kidding me, right?"

"Nope. After you."

It was a pantry. Lola had moved Kennedy into a pantry that had a twin bed and a tiny sink in the corner. And the light was a bare bulb in the ceiling with a long string hanging off it. She tossed the bag on the bed and turned back around. "I had no idea."

"Hey, at least I won't go hungry." Kennedy took a Mason jar off the shelf. "We've got peaches from last year's harvest, or if you're hankering for something savory, there's pot roast bottled in gravy over there on the other wall."

Bridget grimaced. "I've never heard of bottled meat."

"They call it canning, but it's really glass jars, which I feel is much more apropos because I find the whole thing jarring. Anyway, I'm happy to say I now know quite a bit about the process. The canasta club out there can explain it to you if it's something you'd like to take up during the off-season."

Bridget snorted. "I think I'm good. Is the bed comfortable?"

Kennedy tucked her hands in her back pockets, and for the first time since Bridget had arrived, she smiled. "Wanna find out?"

"I kinda got the feeling you weren't happy to see me. And now that I see your lodging situation, I can understand why. Although, I would like to remind you that this is Lola's fault."

"Oh, no. It's fine. They actually offered me a non-pantry room, the Martin van Buren Suite, to be exact, which is named after one of their late husbands. Whoever would have guessed Carol was a former First Lady? Anyway, the stairs just felt like way too much."

Bridget laughed. "Okay, but why the cold shoulder?"

"I just figured you wanted to keep whatever this is on the downlow. This morning with Lola, you seemed hell-bent on acting like you didn't know me. And then you sent me away to the Elk Mountain Senior Lesbians' Riding Club. And PS, all of these golden girls have slept with each other at some point in their lives."

Bridget threw a hand over her mouth to stifle a giggle. With the other, she waved Kennedy over and pulled her into her arms. Once she got her giggles under control, she nuzzled her ear and said, "I missed you today."

Kennedy squeezed her tighter and whispered. "Say that again. I didn't quite catch it the first time."

Bridget summoned what she hoped was her sexiest possible voice and whispered, "Martin van Buren was a widower."

Kennedy gave her a playful shove. "That's what you're going to whisper in my ear? And also, how do you possibly know that?"

"In sixth grade, we had to do a book report on a president. Mine was van Buren. His wife died before he took office, and the main reason I remember that is because her name was Hannah Hoes."

Kennedy scoffed. "You are making that up."

"I'm not. Look it up." Bridget crossed her arms and made a show of tapping her toe. "I'll wait."

"How 'bout I just choose to believe you?" Kennedy stepped back into Bridget's personal space, uncrossed her arms, and pulled her back into an embrace.

There was so much Bridget wanted to say. So much she wanted to apologize for. Including the way she'd handled things earlier. After that kiss, her emotions were running so high, she might've overcompensated in front of Lola by being downright rude when all she really wanted to do was take care of Kennedy for, like, ever. But she wasn't ready for that feeling to hit her so hard all at once. And she certainly didn't want Lola to see it in her eyes or feel it in the air. Kennedy was a Fleming after all.

She felt relieved that Kennedy hadn't held it against her. She must've understood on some level how complicated Bridget's feelings were, which in her mind was a sign of emotional maturity. And that could only mean that Jerry Fleming must not have been as horrible a father as he was a neighbor. And maybe one day, she'd tell him that.

Her interactions with Jerry had been limited. Bridget's dad had tried to keep him away from everyone, and most of the time, he succeeded in taking all the verbal abuse himself. But there were times when she'd witnessed his antagonism, especially in the last few years.

Holding Jackass Jerry's beautiful, kind, warm, smart daughter in her arms almost made it hard to believe that it had ever happened. What she could believe were her own words when she brushed her lips against Kennedy's cheek and said it again. "I missed you today."

Kennedy pulled back and looked her in the eye. "Not as much as I missed you."

Bridget wanted this kiss to be gentle, deliberate. She wanted it to say all the things she couldn't. Things like, I see you. I know how special you are. My eyes are wide open to the possibilities.

She also wanted it to say, I fucking love your tongue and your mouth, and I'll take good care of your clit if given the opportunity. Who was she kidding? She knew she'd be given the opportunity.

She moved in slow, with a kiss on the corner of her mouth, then a soft brush of their lips, followed by a light peck...and a loud knock on the door that sent them both through the roof like a cat that just spotted a cucumber. It scared Bridget so much, she was sure she'd blurted out at least three swear words in a random order that made no sense at all. Something about God's ass. And Kennedy was doubled over like someone about to vomit in the street.

"Hey, do you mind if we have a slice of pizza?" someone asked from the other side of the door.

Bridget realized Kennedy wasn't about to vomit; she was laughing hysterically. "Go ahead," Bridget shouted.

Once she could speak, Kennedy said, "God, fuck my ass." And then she dropped to her knees and continued with the hysteria. "I mean, if that's what you're into."

Okay, so maybe Bridget's profanity unintentionally made sense in a humiliating sort of way. "Uh, no. That was an exclamation related to your roommate's horrible timing."

"So not a request then?"

"No." Bridget laughed and sat on the edge of the bed, which caused the box springs to squeak. She bounced a few times just to make sure that the bed was indeed Pre-World War II before announcing, "We are not having sex for the first time on this bed."

Kennedy rolled onto her back and brought her knees to her chest. Her face was bright red, and she looked adorable lying there on the floor. "But eventually?" she asked. "Somewhere, when the world isn't so hell-bent on it not happening, it will...right?"

Bridget bent over and rested her elbows on her knees. "When we're not surrounded by hungry lesbians, I'd say it's a good possibility."

Kennedy rolled onto her tummy and gave Bridget a sexy grin. "I look forward to what will surely be a momentous occasion."

"I could take you back up the mountain tonight, but I have an early morning tomorrow. Most of the guests are checking out, and we have to get ready for the next round."

Kennedy waved it off. "Yeah, there's no way you'd be on top of your game right after a night of…everything I want to do to you for hours on end."

Bridget cleared her throat. "No. I would definitely not be on top of my game. I'd still be on top of *you* until you couldn't take anymore."

Kennedy bit her lip. "Be still my throbbing…heart."

Bridget stood. "Would you mind staying down there on the floor until I leave? I'm afraid if you get up, we might break that bed and send a spring flying into one of these bottles and knock the entire shelf down."

"You have quite the imagination."

"You have no idea."

Kennedy rolled onto her back and threw her arms above her head. "I'm just going to leave you with this image. Do with it what you will."

She looked lovely lying like that. Sexy. Beautiful. Ready. Bridget took a deep breath to try to calm her desire. She wanted Kennedy, but she didn't want their first time to be a quickie in the pantry of the Corner Cottage with four nosy lesbians on the other side of the door. She also didn't want it to be in the Fleming cabin. She wanted it to be perfect. Which was why she might have already told Harriet that she couldn't book the penthouse suite until after Christmas.

She reached out with one finger. Kennedy did the same, and for a few seconds, they locked those fingers together. "I have a meeting down here tomorrow afternoon. Can I take you to dinner afterward?"

"You know the answer to that," Kennedy said.

"Good. I'll be here around five thirty." Bridget's lawyer had called earlier that day saying they needed to address some things related to her dad's estate. Her desire to attend yet another probate paperwork meeting was nonexistent, but the promise of dinner with Kennedy afterward made the whole thing seem downright appealing.

"Are you sure I can't have one more kiss?"

"I couldn't stop at one. Could you?"

Kennedy dropped her hand. "Get out of here, Bridget Berg. And don't come back until you're ready to see what's under these clothes."

Bridget watched intently as Kennedy ran her hands down her sides and back up again. She slapped a hand over her eyes when it looked like Kennedy was about to pull her shirt up. "You're evil, Kennedy Fleming." She went to the door and didn't look back before she shut it.

CHAPTER NINE

With several bags of newly purchased shoes and clothes in hand, Kennedy went back into the T-Mobile store to pick up her new phone. It was her last stop before heading back to the B and B to get ready for dinner. The salesman's eyes widened when he saw her. "Wow. You got a lot of shopping done in two hours."

She dropped the bags by her feet. "Which begs the question, why does it take so long to get a new phone?"

"I had it ready an hour ago, and it's been dinging ever since." He handed it to her and not two seconds later, Michael's face popped up on the screen. "Hey, bro. Are you a daddy yet?"

"Where have you been? I've called a million times. I even called the hospital."

"There was an incident with a snowplow. My phone didn't survive."

"You should've called."

"I'm fine, thanks. And I just picked up my new phone. But you're right. I could've used someone else's, but I've been a bit preoccupied with having no food and no heat in the cabin and a huge snowstorm blocking the roads." So what if she failed to mention a certain redheaded preoccupation. Was there a law against omission? No. No there wasn't. Besides, it was none of his damn business.

"I know. And I'm sorry it's been so rough. I promise I'll make it up to you. But I'm glad I finally caught you. I need to give you some info about the meeting. You know it's in forty minutes, right?"

"Right. The real estate agent. Of course I know." The truth was, she'd completely forgotten about the real reason she was there. She'd been so wrapped up in one Bridget Berg, the rest of the world had stopped mattering.

"Ken, you're not meeting with a real estate agent."

❖

The bathrooms were on the left, the lawyer's office on the right. Should Kennedy go in there and vomit first, or just get the meeting over with? Would it be better to have her heart broken with a tummy full of strawberry crepes or devoid of everything? Did it even matter? Because either way, the outcome would be the same. Heart. Broken. Bridget. Gone.

She sucked in a breath and opened the office door. "Kennedy Fleming," she announced at the front desk. "Would you mind watching these bags for me?"

The receptionist took the bags and set them behind her desk. "Second door on the right. They're waiting for you."

Bad things happened in lawyers' conference rooms. Marriages ended. Contracts were broken. People who shouldn't be having sex on a conference table after working hours had sex on a conference table after working hours. Of course, Kennedy would think of that since all day long, she'd been thinking about having sex with Bridget. She'd even bought a sexy new bra and matching panties.

What she was walking into was all her dad's fault, and she found herself wanting to hate him for everything he'd done on Elk Mountain. Unfortunately, Michael didn't agree that it was time to let it all go, which made him just as bad as her father. Kennedy was about to lose him too. Because if he did what he planned to do, she'd never speak to him again. Or his child. He'd be dead to her. The only person she'd have left was her mother, but she wouldn't really have her since she'd abandoned the family when Kennedy was in grade school. It had been ten years since she'd even seen her, and now she had to consider what her dad's role had been in that.

All Kennedy wanted was the chance at a future with Bridget. Sure, they'd only kissed twice, but sometimes, that was all a person needed. How many of history's greatest love stories started before the first kiss? Maybe with just a look or a touch? Kennedy didn't know, but she was sure there had to be some. Unfortunately, with all the Fleming-Berg baggage, she already knew this was one case where love would not conquer all.

The poor kid at the T-Mobile store got to witness a total meltdown when Michael had told her what she was about to walk into. Leases and property line disputes and slope access. Just great. Michael claimed he'd never misled her about meeting with a real estate agent. Sure. He just said he'd set up a meeting about the "disposition of dad's property." Gee, why wouldn't she think that meant she was about to get thrown into some shootout between the Hatfields and McCoys? She wished they were more like the Montagues and Capulets, but she was pretty sure that in about two minutes, Bridget wasn't going to see Kennedy as her Romeo.

Apparently, under Utah law, when acting on behalf of a family member using a Power of Attorney, some member of the family must be physically present, even if it wasn't the person who had actual authority. In this case, that person was Michael. Kennedy was there simply to be the family representative. She was only following through on her agreement to go to this meeting in the hope that she could persuade Michael to let it go.

She opened the door and had three sets of eyes on her, but she could only focus on Bridget. And she looked confused. Kennedy imagined Bridget wanted to know why and how and when. All she could do was whisper, "I didn't know."

She felt like all of the blood had left her body, so she gripped the back of a chair. A woman stood and said, "You must be Kennedy. I'm Catherine Holmes, representing your father's interests."

The lawyer whose office it was also stood. "Ms. Fleming, I'm Peter Strand. I represent Ms. Berg. Now, enough with the suspense. Why are we here?"

Catherine interceded. "Kennedy, please have a seat, and we'll get your brother on speakerphone."

She pulled out the chair next to her, which put Kennedy sitting across the table from Bridget, who had a look of concern on her face. That seemed better than expected.

Bridget took a water glass from a tray and poured it half-full, then offered it to Kennedy. "You don't look so good. Drink this." Clearly, she didn't know how bad it was, or she'd have thrown the water in her face.

Michael's voice came through the speakerphone in the middle of the table. "Is everyone there?" he asked. "Ken?"

The words got stuck in her throat. "I'm…I'm here."

Bridget furrowed her brow again, but Kennedy couldn't hold her gaze. How could she when her family was about to tear Bridget's world apart?

"Go ahead, Catherine," Michael said.

"Okay, then. The contract between Jerry Fleming and Boden Berg, signed on December 1st, 1981, expired on December 1st, 2021. Therefore, any current use of said property is illegal and shall be terminated immediately."

Bridget leaned forward. "I'm sorry. What property are we talking about?"

Kennedy's lawyer pushed a piece of paper across the table with what looked like a surveyor's drawing on it. "It's the strip of land you and your guests use to access the ski trails."

Peter Strand piped up. "I had no idea this contract even existed, or I would've done something about it sooner."

"Nor did I," Kennedy said. "Bridget, look at me." But she wouldn't. She kept her eyes on the map. "May I see this contract?"

Catherine took two copies out of a manila folder. One for Bridget and one for her lawyer. Kennedy gestured for a copy of her own. It was a simple contract. One that allowed Boden Berg access to that tiny strip of land for forty years, and it appeared that Boden had paid Bridget's dad a lump sum of one hundred thousand dollars.

Underneath his signature, her dad had written, *We'll be old and gray when this expires, but I hope to God we'll still be best friends.*

Kennedy raised her head to find Bridget staring at her. "They were friends?" Bridget asked.

Kennedy shook her head; she was just as confused about the whole thing, and then Michael's voice came booming through the speaker. "Now that everyone's up to speed, here's our offer. Ms. Berg, can you hear me?"

Bridget turned toward the speaker. "Yes."

"Good. We'll sell the only access that the Boden Berg Lodge has to the ski resort for one million dollars, payable by January 1st, 2022, and we'll need a signed agreement to that affect, or we'll terminate your access starting tomorrow." He sounded so stern and businesslike, Kennedy hardly recognized him as her brother.

Bridget turned to her, then back to the speaker. "Are you serious? You want me to come up with a million dollars for a tiny strip of land in two weeks, or you'll cut me off tomorrow?"

"It may be a tiny strip of land, but I think you can see how valuable it is. If your guests can't access the slopes—"

"Michael, shut up," Kennedy said. "Bridget is well aware of how important that strip of land is to her business. Don't be so condescending."

Silence filled the room for a moment before Bridget said, "Where is Jerry, and why am I not dealing with him? If he and my dad were friends at one time, then I'm sure he'd be willing to work with me on this." She turned to Kennedy. "Where's your dad?"

"I...we...haven't had the chance to really—"

"Our father is in a home," Michael said. "I have full authority to represent his interests in this matter."

Bridget hadn't taken her eyes off Kennedy. "And who do you represent in this matter?"

Kennedy wanted to scream that she represented no one but herself and that she had nothing to do with this last-minute bombshell. "I honestly thought—"

"Ken, let Catherine handle this," Michael said.

"You have our terms," Catherine said. "Speak with your lawyer and get back to us."

Bridget turned to Peter. "Can they really do this?"

"Unfortunately, they can," he said.

"And we will," Catherine added. "You've been trespassing since December first."

"I didn't know that," Bridget said. "We're always careful about not trespassing on Jerry's property, but I thought that the trail to the slopes was ours."

"That's on you, not us," Catherine said. "And we have the right to secure that property immediately."

"Christmas is coming up. I'm fully booked. And I don't even know if that contract is real."

Peter opened a folder. "I've compared Boden's signatures. They match, Bridget. And the contract was notarized."

Bridget clasped her hands and lowered her gaze. Kennedy could only imagine the panic she was feeling. The fear that she was about to lose everything her dad had built. She needed to talk some sense into her brother. "Michael, this is ridiculous. I'm calling you, and you better pick up." She pushed back from the table and rushed out of the room. Luckily, she knew right where the bathroom was.

She locked herself in a stall and called him. "What the fuck, Michael?"

"Ken, calm down."

"Michael, I'm begging you, please don't do this. We can work this out with her. They were friends once, Dad and Boden.

Why can't we honor that friendship and let Bridget pay monthly or something?"

"From what I've found in Dad's paperwork, Boden has tried for years to get Dad to sell it to him, but he never would. That's the decision we should honor. And besides, you stand to gain as much from this as I do. We both inherit equally under Dad's will."

Kennedy closed her eyes. "You don't understand, Michael. I...love her."

Michael laughed. "Yeah. You always fall for the unavailable girls, which is why you're still single."

"Bridget is available. Very available. And I think she feels the same way. But if you do this to her, you'll break both our hearts."

"Listen to me, Ken. She's not available to you, okay? I know what Dad's plan was, and I'm following through on it."

"Why? It's not as if he's going to pat you on the back for ruining Bridget's life. He can't even..." She choked back her emotions. "Michael, he doesn't even know who we are anymore. We've lost him."

"That's not true. When I told Dad that I'd found the old contract, you know what he did? He smiled at me. He actually smiled. And then he said, 'bury that bastard.' So don't tell me he doesn't know what he wants."

"Oh, great. So you're telling me that the only thing Dad remembers about his life is his hatred for Boden Berg? Well, guess what, Michael, Boden is dead, and his daughter is an amazing person, and I will not let you hurt her because of some feud between two old men."

"You need to see the bigger picture, Ken. And it's a huge picture. Imagine how cheap that lodge will be when it has zero access to the slopes. Then imagine combining Dad's property with it, including all the land around the cabin. They'd have not a tiny strip of land with access but over a hundred feet of slope-side land. A developer would pay millions for that property. They could put a big hotel on it or condos or whatever."

His voice was filled with so much excitement, it sickened Kennedy. How could he find so much joy in ruining a person's life? Taking away their inheritance? Their home? Was this really who her family was, and somehow, she hadn't gotten the memo?

"I'm going to say it again, Michael. I love her. Does that mean nothing to you?"

"You've been there since Friday. It's Tuesday, Ken. Don't be such a teenager."

Her phone went dead. She dropped it into her purse and slumped against the wall. She gave herself a few minutes to pull herself together enough to go back out there, and just as she opened the door, she saw Bridget. And Bridget saw her, but she kept walking toward the exit. Kennedy caught up with her outside. "Bridget! Give me two minutes to explain. Please?"

Bridget turned around. "Are you serious? What could you possibly say that would make this okay? And why the hell didn't you tell me Jerry was in a home?"

"Because I tend to get a little upset when I have to tell people that my own father doesn't even recognize me anymore." Kennedy dared to step a little closer. "I swear, I knew nothing about this."

Bridget took on a defiant stance by folding her arms. "Why are you here, then?"

"My brother is about to have a baby, so he sent me here in his place. He was really vague about the details."

"And you expect me to believe that?"

"It's the truth, Bridget. I swear, I knew nothing about this meeting. I assumed I was here to meet with a real estate agent or something since..." Kennedy put a hand over her mouth to stop her lip from quivering.

"Since what?" Bridget snapped back.

"Since my dad can't come up here anymore. He has dementia. It's gotten bad enough that we had to put him in a home that has twenty-four-hour care."

"A fact which I totally would have sympathized with had you bothered to tell me. But that doesn't change the fact that he's been trying to destroy our business for years, and now, even if he doesn't know it, he finally succeeded, didn't he?"

Kennedy couldn't dispute her assertion. Even though she didn't know all the details, there was certainly enough evidence of her father's, and now Michael's, callousness. "I'm going to call my brother," she said. "I'll convince him that there are other options. In the meantime, please don't shut me out."

"I have to," Bridget said. "It was a mistake to ever let you in."

It was all back. The angry indignant expression. The hostile tone in her voice. The fast clip to get as far away from Kennedy as she possibly could. Bridget, Jerry's Version, was back. Only it was worse this time around because Kennedy had gotten a glimpse of the real Bridget Berg. She'd experienced that version with all her senses on full tilt and her heart wide open to the possibility of having something real. Not temporary. Not a fling on Elk Mountain, only to go back home and forget it ever happened.

Life would never be the same now that she'd met Bridget. There would always be the "before time" when life was good and prosperous due to a lot of hard work. But now, there would be the "after time" when life would still be prosperous due to a lot of hard work but also lacking in something. There would also be that question that would nag at her while she drank her morning cup of coffee—could it have worked? Could they have made something real and lasting together?

Of course, every time she drank a cup of coffee, it would remind her of how she had to bribe Seth, and then there would be a snowball of memories that would roll through her mind that she'd probably try to snuff out by having shallow sex. Not just shallow but also very unfulfilling because even though she hadn't yet had sex with Bridget, she was sure no woman would be good enough to make her forget what might have been.

Damnit, why did it all have to end this way? And why did the woman of her dreams have to live on top of a mountain?

❖

It wasn't Bridget's proudest moment when she texted Harriet to let her know she'd be in the storage closet on the top floor if anyone needed her. *Like, hey, I own this place, but I'm gonna go hide out for a while the way I did when I was a sulky little kid.* But that was exactly how she felt. Sulky, hurt, angry, humiliated. She'd been duped. Conned. Seduced. And God, did she feel foolish. She should've listened to Harriet, not to mention all the voices in her own head telling her to be careful, beware, don't get too close, don't believe a word that comes out of that beautiful mouth.

Kissing that beautiful mouth was as far as she'd gotten with Kennedy. On second thought, when they'd kissed on the snowmobile, she had slid her hands down Kennedy's back and for the briefest of moments, had them on a very nice ass. If she was honest with herself, Bridget would admit that a part of her wished they'd had one night together in bed before finding out the truth. The attraction had seemed so strong between them that she was sure it would've been amazing.

At first, the way Kennedy had taken the time to appreciatively gaze over Bridget had pissed her off. So did the clever little comebacks and snarky sense of humor. Everything about Kennedy had pissed Bridget off at first, but that had changed after the snowplow incident. In Kennedy's vulnerable, almost broken state, Bridget had been able to see the whole person, not just the last name, and all the things that had irritated her because of who Kennedy was became desirable. Especially, the way Kennedy had looked at her. She'd wanted those beautiful brown eyes to roam her body when she had nothing on, and that might've happened had Lola not insisted Kennedy stay at that bed and breakfast. Had Bridget brought her back up the mountain, she was sure they would've shared a bed.

Given Kennedy's fractured toe, they might have only cuddled, but also given the strong attraction between them, cuddles might have turned into kisses, and with kisses, hands might have slipped under pajama tops. Bridget smiled because in reality, her speculations were all wrong. She had no doubt that Kennedy wouldn't have let a sore toe keep her from having exactly what she wanted, which brought Bridget back to those roaming eyes. Kennedy wanted her, and it felt good to be wanted that way again. At least, it had before that goddamned meeting yesterday.

In her youth, Bridget had liked the storage closet because it had a small window with a great view. That meant she could hide but not feel shut off from the world. There used to be a stool that she had to stand on to see out the window. Now, it was the perfect height for her to put her elbows on the sill and rest her cheeks in her hands and wonder why the world was so cruel, just as she'd done years before.

A knock on the door caused her to whip around and lean against the wall all casual, as if hanging out in a storage closet was anything normal. "Come in, Harriet."

Lola opened the door. "It's me. She told me I might find you up here."

"Of course she did. Wow, that woman is about to get on my last nerve."

"Seems like you have a few women getting on your last nerve right now."

"When I told her where I'd be, it didn't mean I wanted her to send people up here. Close the door behind you." She turned and leaned a shoulder against the wall with her arms folded.

Lola stood next to her and peered out the small window. "What are we looking at?"

Not wanting to fully admit that she was hiding from the world, Bridget said, "This room has the best view of both the Fleming cabin and the access trail."

"You're not planning to hire a sniper, are you?"

"If I was, I wouldn't tell the local sheriff."

Lola smiled. "I've taught you well."

"It wasn't you," Bridget said. "I watch too many of those true crime shows. Rarely does murder-for-hire go unpunished."

"That's probably true. Also, you'd be suspect number one, and do you know what their first question would be?"

"Yep. And if this is your way of trying to find out where my relationship with the potential victim stands, then color me surprised that Harriet hasn't already filled you in. Not that I told her, but somehow, she seems to know everything, and when it comes to my personal life, I find that incredibly intrusive."

Lola raised an eyebrow. "Um…I was talking about your financial motivation."

"Oh."

"Well, shit. Now I'm talking about your romantic motivation." Lola took off her work coat and set it on one of the shelves next to a stack of toilet paper. Even though her closet hideout had been invaded, Bridget was relieved it was Lola who'd invaded it. She needed her calming presence and rational sensibility, and unlike Harriet, she wouldn't invoke the "I told you so" tone of voice. "How bad is it?" she asked.

Bridget turned from the window and leaned her head against the wall. "Financial clusterfuck is currently tied with romantic shitshow for disaster of the year."

"That bad, huh?"

"It's pretty dire on both counts. Turns out, my dad didn't actually own the access trail, and now, the Flemings want me to pay them a million dollars for it, or they'll fence it off. No lender is going to give me a million-dollar mortgage for a tiny strip of land. Or frankly, any land at all. Oh, and I was this close to sleeping with the victim. Enemy. Whatever. You know who I mean. Her." She gestured with her thumb at the cabin. "We actually had a date scheduled, and then, boom, the Fleming meteor hit."

"We'll get to *her* in a second," Lola said. "What if you could take out a mortgage on the lodge?"

"I thought about that," Bridget said. "But say I do, and we have a bad snow year. How will I cover the property taxes and a mortgage payment? It almost seems smarter to sell the place now rather than lose it in foreclosure."

"Maybe, but the real estate market is soft right now. I'm not sure you'd get what you'd want for it. Especially if you lose your ski-in-ski-out status. Well, definitely then. Sorry, Bridge. I don't mean to make it sound worse than it is."

Bridget sighed. "You're not. It really is that bad. And it's not a matter of if we lose our status. They priced it so high to ensure that we would. They ambushed me *and* my lawyer in that meeting. Neither of us knew what was coming." Bridget turned back to the window. "This whole thing stinks of premeditation, and I, like an idiot, really bought into it when Kennedy had me believing she was here to sell Jerry's cabin. And even worse, I thought our connection was real. God, I'm such an idiot."

Lola put her hands on Bridget's shoulders and said, "Hey. I'm not going to let you beat yourself up over this. You've had a lot on your plate this last year, and you've shown a level of strength that a lot of people don't have. Besides, Jerry's daughter is surprisingly attractive, and honestly, she seems pretty cool."

Bridget huffed. "I might as well have been kissing Jerry because that's about how much I trust her now."

"Gross." Lola grabbed her coat and took Bridget by the arm. "And because I know you so well, I know that you don't want to admit how much it hurts. You'd rather hole up here in this closet and have an unemotional conversation with me, even though I know your heart is breaking a little—"

"Or a lot," Bridget added. "But at least they haven't blocked off the trail yet."

"And I'd put money on you having not cried or yelled or gotten drunk, even though you feel like your world is falling apart." Lola opened the closet door. "I can't help you with the first two, but I can certainly day drink with you."

Bridget looked at her watch. "It'll be dark soon." She took a few steps and stopped. "You won't tell anyone about my closet, right?"

Lola closed the door behind them and patted Bridget's back. "Trust me. There is no one who would find it interesting."

❖

So many people were talking. Not talking, yelling. No. Not yelling. Cackling. Cackling? Bridget's eyes flew open. She sat up and froze so she could hear what was going on outside the bedroom door. "Mom?"

Lola grumbled. "Oh, God. Does she have a key to the penthouse? She can't see us like this. She'll think we slept together."

"I'm pretty sure my mom knows the difference between a raging hangover and you know, afterglow." She threw a pillow over Lola's head. "Shut up. You're not here. This didn't happen."

Lola rolled onto her back and pushed the pillow out of the way. "You're right, it didn't. Because I wasn't as drunk as you were."

"Oh, please. You're still slurring, and you smell like a drunk Christmas tree."

Lola crinkled her nose. "You're right, I do. Blame Lawrence and his wicked wassail." She grabbed the pillow and put it over her face. "Just pretend I'm not here."

"That's the plan, genius." Bridget jumped out of bed in just her bra and underwear, but it was too late. Her mom threw open the door and stood there with her fists on her hips like a winter superhero in stiletto boots and a wool cape. And was that Harriet hiding behind her?

"Hello, my beautiful, unclothed daughter. I thought I'd surprise you for Christmas." She glanced at the clothes on the floor. "But it would seem I've interrupted your policewoman fantasy."

With her face still covered, Lola raised her arm. "Hi, Ingrid. Long time, no see."

Her mom chuckled. "I knew it was you, Lola, but isn't Bridget a little old for you now?"

Lola sat up and ran her fingers through her hair. "I finally grew up and changed my ways." She flashed a grin. "You're looking lovely as ever. Still life-coaching the wolves of Wall Street?"

"It was one wolf, and I learned my lesson. I only take clients who work above Midtown now."

"Watch out, Mom," Bridget said. "Lola likes to date older women now. Do you happen to know Iris at the Corner Cottage? She must be nearing seventy." She stuck her tongue out at Lola and grabbed a robe off the chair.

"Iris happens to make fantastic strawberry jam, that she slathers on this incredible cornbread," Lola said. "And I may or may not have been seduced by it."

Harriet finally came out of hiding. The look on her face had Bridget concerned. "Harriet, are you okay? You look like you just saw a ghost."

"I'm not sure which thing to feel most uncomfortable about," she said. "But I think I'll go with Lola having food sex with my ex-sister-in-law."

Bridget gasped. "Iris was married to your brother?"

Lola pulled the sheet over her head and plopped back down on the pillow. "It wasn't food sex."

Her mom let out a gleeful sigh. "I see the drama still runs high in the small lesbian community of Elk Mountain. Can't wait to catch up."

❖

It'd been years since Bridget had seen her mom sitting in her favorite spot in the penthouse suite. Before the divorce, she'd often find her there by the window, basking in the morning sun with a steaming cup of ginger tea. Bridget would climb up in the comfy leather chair and cuddle with her until it was time to get ready for school.

They couldn't both fit in the chair anymore, but that didn't stop Bridget from trying. The truth was, her mom had arrived at the perfect time. Cramped together, she took her mom's arm and wrapped it around her shoulder the way she'd done hundreds of times before. She intertwined their fingers, and just like before, Bridget knew she didn't have to talk unless she wanted to.

Their fingers were so similar and linked together so well, but something felt different. There was a hardness to her mom's hands. They'd become bony and arthritic, same as her grandmother's. The realization that her mom was starting to show her age caused her to hang on a little bit tighter. "Harriet called you, didn't she?"

Her mom leaned in and kissed her forehead. "Don't be mad, but since Boden's death, I asked her to keep me informed since my daughter insists on acting like everything is fine all of the time. A trait she clearly inherited from her father."

"I just don't want you to worry or feel like you have to come and rescue me. I know you don't love it here."

"You know, baby, it's been a long time. For the first time in forever, good memories are the ones that keep coming back." She pointed to a spot by the coffee table. "Just now, I thought about how you took your first steps right over there."

"Really? I didn't know that."

"When you first found your feet, you'd hang on to the coffee table and reach your chubby little arm out for whatever it was you had your eye on. And then, one day, Boden had fallen asleep on the floor near you, and you took two steps so you could give him a kiss. That was when I knew you were a daddy's girl." She kissed her forehead again. "I know you miss him, honey. It won't hurt my feelings or make me mad if you talk about him, okay?"

Bridget snuggled in even closer. She got her height and her red hair from her mom, although these days, her mom's was a salt and pepper gray that she wore in a short cut. A woman who for years had kept long, thick red hair had barely an inch of hair all over her head now. It looked very chic and showed off her strong jaw. Bridget looked her in the eye and said, "Everything's not fine, Mom."

She tapped Bridget's nose and said, "Good girl. Now, hear me when I say that I won't leave until it is."

And she wouldn't. Bridget knew that. Now that her mom was there, she'd support Bridget in whatever way she could. "Mom, if I promise to tell you the truth, will you stop getting your information from Harriet? She means well, but I think I need a little bit of separation when it comes to my personal life."

"Absolutely. I'd much rather hear it from you anyway."

"I know you would. Do you want the long version or just the highlights?"

Her mom gave her a sly grin. "I want every sordid detail."

Chapter Ten

Out of the corner of her eye, Kennedy could see a small crowd at the top of the access trail. They all probably thought she was there to oversee the raising of Michael's stupid fence. It was a bad look for her, but it didn't seem right to shout the truth at them. All she could do was wait patiently until it was time to attach the no trespassing sign Michael had insisted upon.

Her relationship with her brother was over. She'd never get to be godmother to his child or watch her grow up. But that was on Michael, not her. He and his stubborn greed were to blame for all of this.

Since her dad had given Michael sole power of attorney, Kennedy had no leverage, nothing she could negotiate with. That left her powerless to stop what was about to happen, but she could alter a few small details. Like the gate, for instance. Michael hadn't said anything about putting a gate on the fence, but he hadn't said not to, either.

The fence reminded her of a horse corral. Not that she knew much about horse corrals, but she'd watched that Montana ranch show with Kevin Costner in it, so she had a picture in her head. Five rows of round pipe painted John Deere Green went from a rocky outcropping on the right over to the first in a line of large rocks that separated the lodge land from her dad's. The rocks were big enough to keep skiers from accessing the trail and had probably cost her dad a pretty penny to have placed there. The asinine part was that those rocks weren't protecting anything. They had one job, and that was to keep people from skiing from the lodge to the slopes.

She realized that the yellow tape they'd wrapped around the property when she'd first arrived was to keep guests from climbing on those rocks or straying onto the Fleming property anywhere along the border. Obviously out of fear that her dad would cause a ruckus if it happened.

It was all so ugly and foreign to her, she found herself wondering what she'd say to her dad the next time she saw him. Or if she even wanted to.

The fence guy handed her a pair of keys. "This is for the padlock. And if your brother asks—"

"I'll leave out the part about me bribing you to add a gate. But he's not going to ask. He's too preoccupied with his new baby girl. Plus, no one said there couldn't be a gate. Maybe I'd like this space to be accessible for my own purposes."

The guy smiled. "I have a newborn too. What did they name her?"

Kennedy was embarrassed to say she had no idea because all she'd done with her brother was argue on the phone. "They haven't picked a name yet. Hey, how sturdy is this fence?"

"It's temporary, so don't go swinging on that gate you paid extra for. We'll put in something more permanent when the snow is gone. Have a good one."

"Yeah. You too." She waited until he was out of earshot before she yelled up the trail, "Someone get me Bridget." She hoped it wasn't true that yelling caused avalanches.

In the meantime, she opened the big shopping bag she'd brought with her and pulled out a white snowmobile suit. She'd wanted a black one for its badass aspect, but white was all they had in her size. She also bought matching boots, gloves, a hat, and even a helmet with a mirrored visor that would keep her head warm if the wind kicked up. So basically, she looked like she was ready to ride a rocket into space. In other words, she looked like a slimmed down version of the Pillsbury Doughboy, but it was a price worth paying.

The last thing to come out of the bag was a folding stool that she set against the gate. All that was left was the no trespassing sign her brother had asked her to put on the gateless fence. She'd only agreed so she could fuck with him. She had a normal-size one that she taped on temporarily so she could take a photo of it. Then she ripped it off and replaced it with one that was so small, it was barely readable. "Perfect," she said.

"What are you doing?"

Kennedy whipped around. The look on Bridget's face reminded her of the good old days when Kennedy had privately referred to her as the Norse goddess of something or other. And by good old days, she meant less than a week ago. It felt like longer. It seemed like it took ages to gain Bridget's trust and only a split second to lose it.

The Viking queen stood there at the top of the trail just like she'd done before. Legs spread wider than necessary and arms folded across her chest. All she needed was some sort of headdress, an animal skin cloak, and an army of grimy, bloodthirsty men lined up behind her, and Kennedy would drop to one knee and bow her head the way any good peasant would. And then the queen would command one of those nasty men to bring the peasant to her lair where she'd have a servant bathe her and then present her at the queen's throne to become her sex slave. At least, that was what everyone would think, but secretly, they'd fall madly in love and reign over the north country together.

Instead of falling to both knees and begging for mercy, Kennedy tried for a casual tone and said, "Oh hey, Bridget. I've worked it out. Tell your guests that they're welcome to use the trail. They just have to know the secret password."

Bridget didn't flinch. "I'll ask again. What are you doing?"

"Oh, right. You probably don't know what to make of my outfit. It's for snowmobiling."

"You don't say."

"Yeah, let me show you." She put the helmet on her head before she realized Bridget's tone was full of sarcasm. "Right. I guess you know a snowmobile suit when you see one." She spotted a skier behind Bridget and rushed to open the gate. "Right this way," she shouted.

He stopped and gave her a once over. "What's this?"

"Oh, don't you worry about a thing. As long as you know the secret password, which I'm about to tell you, this gate will magically open for you every time."

He seemed skeptical. "Magically?"

She held up a gloved hand. "Actually, I'll open it. So it's not magic so much as me just standing up." She motioned for him to come closer and whispered in his ear.

He raised an eyebrow and chuckled. "You really want me to say that?"

"No, I want you to whisper it next time. Remember, it's a secret." Kennedy opened the gate for him, closed it again, and sat on her little stool. Bridget still stood there and glared at her, so she closed the visor and tried to clasp her hands together, but her gloves were too thick, so she rested them on her knees. That didn't feel right, so she folded her arms, which felt perfect. It matched Bridget's defiant stance, minus the long, sexy, powerful skier's legs that were currently backlit by the sun, making Bridget nothing but a shadow of herself. Not in a bad way. In the best, sexiest way that really needed to be saved for posterity. Kennedy ripped off her gloves and pulled her phone out of her pocket. Surprisingly, Bridget didn't move until she'd taken the shot. Or was it video she'd gotten? Stupid new phone.

"Dammit." Kennedy wanted a photo, not a video. That was, until she realized that she had Bridget throwing her arms in the air and marching off. "You'll be back," Kennedy whispered. "I hope."

❖

Bridget grumbled under her breath, "She's insane." She marched past her mom, Lola, and Harriet, then stopped and turned. "What does she think she's going to do, man that gate all day in her silly little astronaut outfit?"

"It's a snowmobile suit."

"I know that, Lola, but she looks ridiculous."

Lola put her hands up. "Hey, I think she's smart to wear it, astronaut or not."

"Of course you would. Can you take that gun out of its holster and shoot me now, please?"

The three of them gave each other a concerned glance, as if she really meant it. "Honey, I think you need to take a breath."

"Mom, it's a figure of speech. I don't actually mean it, and I'm pretty sure Lola won't shoot me. Apparently, I need to work on expressing my feelings better." She turned around before issuing an eyeroll and marched back up to the lodge. She needed to call her lawyer.

It wasn't long before her mom was at her office door. "May I come in?"

"Suit yourself." She didn't want a lecture. Especially, a mom lecture about how to treat people.

Her mom closed the door behind her and sat. "I'm so sorry this is a battle you're still fighting. Your dad tried for years to buy that stupid little piece of land, but Jerry had his heels dug in."

"Why, Mom? Why does that man, and now his children, hate us so much? What did we ever do to them? And why did Jerry's note on the lease say they were best friends. I mean, what the hell?"

"There's a history that I'm sure you're not aware of, but honestly, honey, as long as Boden took Jerry's nonsense in stride, it never got out of hand."

"That's not true. Dad didn't take any of it in stride. He seemed stressed about it all the time. Especially in the last few years. It's probably what killed him."

"Your father lived a full life, honey. He enjoyed his bourbon and steaks and whatever other vices came his way. Jerry may have stressed him out, but it's wrong to think that was the only thing. Where is Jerry, anyway?"

"Apparently, he's in a home somewhere. It sounds like he has dementia or Alzheimer's or something. Kennedy said he doesn't even know who she is anymore."

Her mom seemed to tense up. "I see." She put on a smile that seemed forced. "Tell me about Kennedy."

There was so much to tell, but Lola had been right. She wasn't ready to reveal how truly hurt she was. It'd be easier if Kennedy would just go away. Get off their mountain and go back to her fancy Miami life and yappy dog that she supposedly carried around in her purse. Instead, she chose to torture Bridget a little more by making herself the center of attention in that silly snowsuit that screamed, hey, look at me. Aren't I adorable?

It wasn't adorable. It was obnoxious. And even though she'd promised to tell her mom the truth, she chose to lie one more time. "There's nothing to tell."

"Not according to—"

"Stop!" Bridget had had just about enough of Harriet and her meddling. She took a deep breath. "Mom, I'm so glad you're here. I want you here. I'm just not sure I'm okay with why you're here. Harriet has butted into my personal life one too many times."

"I already told you, you can't blame Harriet. I'm here for you. Because of you."

"Then help me understand, Mom. Did you know Jerry back in the day?"

"Of course I did." She averted her gaze. "He was here before Boden was." She'd barely said the words before she clapped her hands on her knees and stood. "I'll let you get back to your work, but tell me, do you still have all of Boden's old photo albums? I'd love to go through them and maybe take a few of your baby pictures for my apartment in New York."

There were plenty of baby pictures in her mom's apartment, but Bridget wasn't surprised she wanted more. She loved collecting memories. "Yeah. They're probably in those boxes in my room."

"I didn't see any boxes in the penthouse."

"I've been staying in a standard room," Bridget said. "We've remodeled a bit. The plan is to eventually rent out the penthouse."

Her mom seemed surprised. "I thought you'd renovated it for yourself. It's your home, sweetie, not an Airbnb."

"My home is a world-class ski lodge, and I don't need that much space. Besides, after this season, I might not have a home or a business."

Her mom sat back down. "Honey, you can't live in a tiny room. And more importantly, you are Boden's daughter and an Olympian in your own right."

"Qualifying for the team and actually skiing for a medal are two different things."

"You were injured. Bridget, look at me. You have to make this place your own now. Keep the name and your father's legacy, but get your picture over that fireplace in the lobby right next to Boden's. And for God's sake, take that nametag off your chest."

"Harriet had it made for me. You don't think I should wear it?"

"Did you ever once see Boden wear a nametag? No, you didn't. Because his face is everywhere in this lodge, and yours should be too." She stood again. "One more reason for me to go through old photos. We'll need some of the two of you together."

Bridget handed the keycard to her. "Good luck finding them in that stack of boxes."

Her mom paused at the door. "This whole thing with the Flemings is just a bump in the road. Every other year, Boden thought he'd lose the lodge, and every other year, he found a way to keep it. You'll figure this one out too."

Bridget wasn't her dad. She would never have that "thing" that kept people coming back to the lodge year in and year out. She should've sold it right after her dad passed away. Then again, a smart buyer would've figured out that the access trail belonged to someone else and backed out of the sale. "I wish I had your faith, Mom."

"And I wish I still had your youth. Don't squander it, honey."

❖

"She's been out there for three days."

Bridget's heart leapt into her throat. "Damnit, Harriet. Don't sneak up on me like that."

Harriet closed the storage closet door behind her. "Why are you so jumpy today? Is it because your mom's prying into your business? I can relate. My mom and sister just got into town, and they're already organizing my cupboards and accusing me of regifting because they can't find the dish towels they gave me for Christmas last year. But that's how it is with family and the holidays. They might drive you crazy, but you can't imagine spending Christmas without them. It's kind of a happy hell, I guess."

Bridget chose not to mention the fact that nosiness must run in Harriet's family. "Just out of curiosity, did you regift them?"

"I know it seems passive-aggressive, but they had roosters on them, and both of them know I was bitten by a rooster when I was young. Makes me think they're playing head games."

Bridget laughed. "Or maybe they were on sale, and everyone in the family got a set that year."

"I hadn't thought of that. See what family does to a person? They make us read into every little thing so we're constantly on alert for the next veiled insult or not-so-subtle hint that we should style our hair differently."

"Yeah, I get it. Mom is going through our old photo albums. She wants to put up more pictures of me and Dad together."

"She told me. It's a great idea." Harriet put a hand on Bridget's shoulder to steady herself and stood on her tiptoes so she could look out the small window. "Can you believe this nonsense with the silly helmet and the secret password she's supposedly making everyone use? Thank God I don't need to go through that gate because I'd probably smack her in the face as I went by."

Bridget had similar feelings, but smacking Kennedy in the face hadn't occurred to her. "That's a little harsh, isn't it?"

"You're going a little easy on her, aren't you?" Harriet's retort came fast. "It's a stunt. A cry for attention. I keep telling the employees to stop taking snacks and coffee out to her, but they insist on feeding the animals."

That comment had Bridget thinking that maybe Seth hadn't told Harriet about the almost-kiss he'd witnessed. It'd be a pretty callous thing to say if she did know. And for the life of her, Bridget didn't know why she had the urge to defend Kennedy. "If it weren't for her, we'd be shuttling guests down to the next access trail, which is certainly not why they booked a ski-in/ski-out lodge. They're probably just showing their gratitude. Maybe we all should."

Harriet scoffed. "The hell I will. That girl could open the gate in the morning and close it back up at night. She doesn't need to escort every damn guest through."

Bridget rolled her eyes. "Wow, Harriet. Why not tell me how you really feel?"

"I could say the same to you, honey. You haven't shown a bit of emotion about this whole thing. It worries me."

"I can't afford to. Whatever happens, I have to stay strong. It's what my dad would do."

On second thought, maybe Seth had told Harriet what he'd seen since she sure seemed to want to see Bridget cry. She wished that she trusted Harriet that much, but more than likely, she'd get that I-told-you-so, silly child look that would result in Bridget actually wanting to smack someone in the face.

She took one last look out the window just in time to see one of her guests give the astronaut a hug. She rolled her eyes and put the key to the storage closet in Harriet's hand. "Take this, and don't give it back to me until she's gone."

❖

"I met your friend, the snow astronaut, today. We had a pleasant conversation. Oh, look at this one. I got so chubby when I was pregnant."

Bridget took the old photo and gasped. "Oh my God, Mom. How did you survive giving birth to me when I took up that much room in your stomach?"

"It wasn't that you were too big around, it was your length. The doctor kept pulling and pulling, and I said, is she out yet? And he said, give me a minute. This girl is all legs." Her mom kept a straight face for about three seconds before she rolled onto her back in a fit of laughter. "That's a true story. I swear."

"You're only saying that because Dad's not here to contradict you."

Her mom's smile faded. She rolled onto her side and reached for Bridget's hand. "I hate to tell you this, honey, but Boden and I had a pact when it came to you. I would back up his lies, and he would back up mine."

Bridget gasped. "You lied to me? When?"

"Oh, parents lie all the time. We have to in order to keep our sanity. To get you to do what we want. To raise little anarchists guided by morals who don't quite know the ways of the world yet. Trust me, that takes a lot of lying. But the doctor really did say that your legs were very long for your age. Which was zero-years-old at the time."

"Mom, are you buzzed?"

"Lawrence served this wonderful Christmas punch in the bar tonight. I may have had two or three servings. Oh, here's another one of you and your dad right after you were born. Boden was such a proud, happy father. He wanted to show you off to everyone on the mountain, and this was before social media, so we bought one of the original Baby Bjorn carriers, and he wore you on his chest whenever he could. Sometimes, people would ask him if something had happened to me. I guess back in 1988, people weren't used to seeing men father their children in such a hands-on way, but Boden loved it."

Bittersweet emotions rose up in Bridget's chest. While she loved reminiscing with her mom, she missed her dad so much that it almost hurt to see him looking so young and energetic. He was in the prime of his life, starting a family, building a business, and loving every minute of it.

She stared at the old photo and wished so much that she could ask for his advice. He'd had a calm, steady way about him that had grounded her when she was upset. And he'd always seemed to have the right solution. So what would he have done about the trail? About the lodge? About Kennedy?

He'd like her spunk. Her spirit. Her undeniable magnetism, a word he'd sometimes used to describe guests he really liked. But would he have warned Bridget against getting involved with her? Surely he would have, given the situation with Jerry.

Bridget blinked back tears. "I wish Dad would miraculously jump out of this photo and tell me exactly what to do because all I want to do right now is run away from it all." Her phone rang. "Seth? Why didn't you call me on the radio?"

"Uh, hey, boss. I didn't think you'd want me saying it over the radio."

Bridget sat up. "What's wrong?"

"Maybe nothing. Maybe something. It's just that I haven't seen Kennedy move in a while. She's just kinda sitting there letting skiers go by. Anyway, you said we can't go near her, and since you and she—"

"Stop right there, Seth." Bridget glanced at her mom, hoping she didn't hear. "I'll be right down." She stood and put her phone in her pocket. "Something's come up."

"Something always does. Go." Her mom shooed her away.

Bridget took the stairs down to the lobby at a normal pace. She smiled at a few guests along the way and tried to convince herself that Seth had overreacted while also trying to control the sense of panic rising in her chest. There were several guests by the door so she darted to the right and went out a side door. A biting gust of wind hit her in the face, blinding her for a few seconds. She didn't have her goggles, but she had a beanie in her vest pocket. She used it to block the wind from her eyes as she ran like hell down to the access trail.

She could see that Kennedy wasn't moving. She had her back up against the fence, her legs splayed out, and her arms hanging at her sides. Bridget dropped to her knees and shook her shoulder. "Kennedy?"

Kennedy's arms and legs flew in the air. She shouted something, but her helmet muffled it. She lifted her visor and said, "I think I fell asleep. Haven't been getting much of that lately. Sorry if I kicked you."

Bridget couldn't seem to catch her breath. She stood and took a few steps but dropped to her knees again. She gasped for air, and each shallow breath was accompanied by a whimper, and then a sob, and then a sound came out of her she didn't recognize. It was loud and guttural, but it seemed to help her breathe, so she sat back on her feet and really let it rip.

It became an uncontrollable release of emotion. She didn't have a million dollars. She couldn't trust the woman she'd fallen so hard for, and soon, she'd lose her home and her livelihood. And to make it all a little bit worse, she'd broken down in public.

Someone wrapped a coat around her shoulders and dropped in the snow next to her. When she realized it was her mom, she buried her face in her shoulder, and together, they walked back to the lodge.

❖

A knock on the door brought Kennedy out of her depressed stupor. She'd been sitting on the edge of the bathtub long enough that the weight of the wet towel wrapped around her head had put an ache in her neck.

After Bridget's collapse, her mom had come running and put up a hand, making it clear that she didn't want Kennedy to go anywhere near her daughter. So she was left to stand there, helpless and not even sure what had just happened. It was gut-wrenching, heartbreaking, soul-crushing to know that she was probably the cause of those emotions that seemed to spill out of Bridget uncontrollably.

Unfortunately, shedding her own tears while sitting in the tub until the water became too cold hadn't helped. She took the towel from her head and used it to dab her eyes. Another loud knock caused her to yell, "All right, already."

It wasn't Bridget. Not that she knew Bridget's knock by heart. But it wasn't her. Kennedy found out that the only reason she'd gone to the trail was because of Seth. At the door, she tightened her bathrobe and shouted, "Who is it?"

"It's Ingrid, Bridget's mother. May I speak to you for a moment?"

Seth had introduced the two of them when she'd accompanied him on a coffee-run to the gate for the sole purpose of checking Kennedy out, she assumed. At the time, she'd taken it as a positive sign that Bridget had mentioned her name once or twice. Now, not so much.

She opened the door and said, "Unless you have a murder weapon hidden under that cape, please come in."

Ingrid neither confirmed nor denied. She stepped into the cabin, ambled into the living room and then the kitchen. Eventually, she took a seat at the kitchen table without any prompting. Kennedy's first impression of Bridget's mom was that she dressed like a woman who had a special wardrobe tucked into the back of her closet reserved for trips to the mountains. The gray wool cape with red trim and fancy silver buckles could've been purchased yesterday or thirty years ago in Switzerland or Aspen or even Milan. Kennedy wondered if she'd ever been featured on the cover of *Town & Country—The Ski Resort* edition. She would have been standing between some snow-dwelling celebrity and the royal skiers of Monaco.

It felt intrusive that Ingrid had made herself so at home. Even so, Kennedy appreciated that the conversation where she'd be warned against ever seeing Bridget again, followed by a veiled threat of violence or ruin, wouldn't take place at the open door. She'd forgotten to put slippers on, and her feet were cold.

"Can I get you something to drink? I have coffee, hot chocolate, and the best tasting tap water this side of…everywhere." It surprised Kennedy when Ingrid smiled. Maybe she wasn't there to rip her a new one after all.

"I always loved the water here too," Ingrid said. "But I'm not thirsty. Not for water, anyway."

Scratch that. She was definitely there to do some sort of damage. "Well, if you're thirsty for the blood of a not-so-young, not-so-virginal lesbian, then you came to the right place."

Ingrid tilted her head. "You have an interesting sense of humor."

Kennedy motioned with her finger. "It's the cape that's throwing me off. I mean, you could hide just about anything under there. Like a really long knife or a hunting rifle or even an ax."

Ingrid winced. "Ew, not the ax. Way too bloody."

"Right. So no blood. Let's go with the rifle. Quick shot to the head seems like a good choice for both of us."

Ingrid unbuckled her cape and spread it open. "See? No weapons. Besides, if I wanted to kill you, I'd just have Seth do it since there seems to be no limit to what he'd do for money."

Kennedy froze. "Wait. You don't think that I told him to do that, do you? I had just fallen asleep on the job, and when she woke me up, it scared me, and I might have said a swear word, but I didn't swear at her."

Ingrid put up a hand. "Okay, I believe you. But you need to understand that Bridget's under a lot of pressure. Boden's sudden death last season was a hard blow for everyone, but for Bridget, her world fell apart in an instant. She didn't even have time to grieve. She had to step into his shoes and finish out the season. In fact, I'm wondering if that wasn't the first time she really let the pain out."

Kennedy had seen some of the guests gather to see what was going on. Bridget no doubt felt embarrassed about that. Anyone would. "She must be furious at Seth," she said under her breath.

"I think she's feeling all kinds of things. I wouldn't be surprised if fury is one of them." Ingrid got up and went to a kitchen cupboard. She grabbed a drinking glass and turned to Kennedy. "Sorry, I changed my mind about the water, but I should've asked first. Can I get one for you too?"

Kennedy shook her head and took a few steps closer. "Can I see Bridget?"

"She's lost her voice. Screaming into an arctic wind will do that, but regular doses of warm tea should help." Ingrid turned on the faucet and filled her glass. She took a sip and held the glass up to the light. "Ice cold straight out of the tap and crystal clear. It's almost a miracle."

"I could do all the talking," Kennedy said. "I just really need to see her."

Ingrid set the glass on the counter and turned. "I guess it depends on what you would say to my daughter."

"So many things." Not sure how honest she should be, Kennedy paused for a moment. She didn't see any ire in Ingrid's eyes. A mother's concern mixed with a little bit of curiosity? Yes, she definitely saw that. So she decided to be straight with her. "Bridget and I have had a rough start, but I know there's something good here between us. Something real. That's why I need her to know that I had nothing to do with what my brother did. Honestly, I didn't even remember that this place existed until he asked me to come up here at the last minute. And from the moment I stepped off the helicopter, I've felt like I was dropped in to this unknown, cold place without a map or details or knowing ahead of time that everyone I met would hate me because I'm Jerry Fleming's daughter."

Ingrid went to the table and pulled a chair out. "Will you join me at this table? I'd like to tell you a story, but I'll need you to promise me something."

"Of course." Kennedy rushed over. She'd promise just about anything if it meant she'd have a chance to speak with Bridget.

"What I'm about to tell you, I'll also have to tell Bridget at some point. I just need a little more time. She has a lot on her plate at the moment. Can you allow me that time?"

"She's not really talking to me right now, so I think you're good."

Ingrid sat in the opposite chair and clasped her hands on the table. "A very long time ago, your father inherited a piece of property from his father. Your grandfather passed away in his early fifties, so you never met him."

"You're right, but how do you know—"

Ingrid raised a hand. "Just listen, and then I'll answer any questions you may have. You see, Jerry was in his twenties and didn't know anything about the property, so he took a trip to see if it was something he could sell and maybe make a few bucks for college. Much to his surprise, he fell in love with Elk Mountain. So he hung on to the land and did some camping and fishing here in the summer months. He grew to love it so much, he came out one year for Thanksgiving. On that trip, he woke up in his tent one morning to find a foot of snow had fallen overnight. That's when he fell in love all over again."

"That's very sweet, but I still don't understand how—"

"You will," Ingrid said with a laugh. "Your generation is so impatient. You want everything streaming on-demand. There was no instant real-time anything back then. Jerry woke up to a foot of snow and fell in love in a whole new way. That's when he decided to build a small cabin on the land so he could learn how to ski and snowmobile. The very cabin we're sitting in, minus the helipad and the weird outcropping on the roof."

Kennedy shook her head in disbelief. "I should know this story. I'm his daughter. I mean, why keep this place a secret? Why take your family on ski trips to Whistler when you have a cabin right on the slopes in Utah?"

"I can't answer that question, but if it's okay with you, I would like to finish my story."

Kennedy leaned back and folded her arms. "I can't believe I'm saying this, but please do. I'd really like to know more about my own father."

"One day, a very famous skier knocked on Jerry's door. He was looking for property because he wanted to build a ski lodge. Jerry thought he was crazy because the ski resort was a long way down the mountain, but he liked the guy and thought it might be nice to have a neighbor, especially one who knew how to ski. So he sold him half of the property and gained what he thought at the time would be a lifelong friend."

"Boden...Berg?" Kennedy said the name with hesitation. This story was about to go south, and she wasn't sure she wanted to hear more awful things about her dad. "Please don't tell me they were secret lovers," she half joked. "I know I said I'd like to know more about my dad, but I don't think I can handle another *Brokeback Mountain* story. The first one was sad enough."

Ingrid laughed. "You have no idea how ridiculous that statement is."

Kennedy wiped her brow. "Whew. I can cross jilted lover off my list of possible reasons everyone hates my dad."

"Not so fast," Ingrid said. "This is the part that won't be easy for me to tell Bridget. Or you, for that matter."

Kennedy's mouth gaped open. "Wait. It was you?"

Ingrid took in a deep breath. "Okay, here goes. Before I was Boden's wife and Bridget's mother, I was Ingrid Fleming for a time."

"I don't understand. Are you saying—"

"I was married to your father, Kennedy. Untenably so, and it was short-lived, but there was a time when I loved him."

Kennedy couldn't find any words. Was her entire life a lie? "My mom was my dad's only wife. Crystal Fleming." She stated it as if it was fact, but she had to question everything now. Including her own lineage because if her parents could lie about this, they could lie about anything. She needed to put a little more space between them. She needed room to move and throw her arms around and yell profanities because what the hell was true anymore?

"You're limping," Ingrid said. "What's wrong with your foot?"

Kennedy jabbed a finger at her. "Don't change the subject when you so casually just blew up my life."

"I'm still a mom who recognizes when a foot looks like it could use some ice."

"It's had plenty of ice. I just forgot to put that boot back on because the door rang and—"

"I'll get it. Sit back down, please."

Of course Ingrid knew right where the bathroom was. This revelation also explained how she knew which cupboard the water glasses were in. Kennedy needed to stay civil, but a part of her wanted to get up, march over to the lodge, and tell Bridget that their parents were liars. Ingrid came back with socks and the boot. She looked like she was about to bend down and help, so Kennedy grabbed them out of her hand. "I can do it myself."

Ingrid gave her a smile. "Of course you can. What was I thinking?"

Kennedy eyed her while she put the socks and boot on. "So… eventually, you and Boden ended up together and had Bridget. Is it safe to assume that has something to do with this feud?"

"It is. It's not easy to admit, but I was the one who fell in love first. Boden tried his hardest not to betray his friend. It was only when he could see that my marriage to Jerry would soon be over anyway that he revealed his own feelings to me. And after that, we were inseparable."

The wistful expression on Ingrid's face pissed Kennedy off. "Are you seriously going to wax nostalgic at a time like this? The lodge is in danger. Bridget and I are a disaster. I'm not talking to my brother and will probably never meet my new niece because of this mess." Kennedy froze. "Wait. Michael isn't yours, is he? I mean, if ever there was a time for him to be someone else's problem, but still."

Ingrid laughed. "I promise you, cross my heart, on your grandfather's grave, in memory of my mother, this story has no secret babies. None."

"Well, thank God for that. But, Ingrid, Bridget should know this. Everyone should know this because right now, they think my dad is a batshit crazy man who harassed them for no reason when really, he had his heart broken by you and Boden. My God, this makes me angry for him."

"You have every right to feel angry," Ingrid said. "And given the situation, I guess I have no right to demand that you not tell Bridget. She's going to find out eventually."

"It's not that I want to tell her. It just doesn't seem fair that my dad is seen as this gigantic asshole while Boden is this exalted, beloved person with his picture hanging above the fireplace."

"Maybe not. Or maybe, at least on this mountain, their legacies are right on point." Ingrid paused for a moment. "Kennedy, can I give you some advice?"

Advice from a cheater? This should be interesting, Kennedy thought. She motioned for Ingrid to continue and said, "Have at it."

"The only thing we can control in this life is our own actions."

Kennedy raised an eyebrow. "That's not advice. That's something you needlepoint onto a pillow."

Ingrid seemed amused by the comment. She scrutinized Kennedy for a few seconds before she said, "I like you, Kennedy. You're nothing like your father. Bridget, however, got all of Boden's best qualities, and I think you already know that, or you wouldn't be out there every day making sure her guests have the wonderful holiday experience they paid a lot of money for."

"I do know that," Kennedy said. "She's amazing. I mean, I practically fell for her the second I laid eyes on her tall, hot, redheaded self." She slapped a hand over her eyes. "I shouldn't have said that."

Ingrid laughed. "It was the same way for me with Boden. Unfortunately, I've never loved anyone like that since. It was a once in a lifetime kind of love, and although our marriage didn't last, I will always cherish every moment I shared with him."

"Just curious. How can it be both? I mean, if you loved each other so much, why didn't it last?"

"Unfortunately, love doesn't conquer everything."

"Wow. That's both vague and also pillow-worthy."

"Maybe you could start a reality-based pillow line with quotes and sayings that you're not sure how to feel about," Ingrid quipped.

Kennedy gasped. "That's a brilliant idea. The tagline could be, confusing the emotions of people everywhere."

"Seems like it could also be the theme of the week on Elk Mountain."

"Right? I so badly want to hate you right now, but I kinda dig you, Ingrid. So tell me, how do I fix things with Bridget?"

Ingrid stood and buckled up her cape. "It's a great thing you're doing out there at the gate. That's all she needs from you right now."

"I can't do it forever. My brother will put a stop to it eventually."

Ingrid put her hand on Kennedy's shoulder. "At least you will have done all you could for the woman you claim to love." She turned and sauntered to the door.

Kennedy got up and followed. "Did I say that I love her? I mean, I do, it's just that I shouldn't blurt those words out all willy-nilly."

Ingrid stopped at the door and smiled. "You didn't have to say a word. It's written all over your face. Keep icing that toe." She pulled the hood on her cape over her head. "And dress warmly. There's another storm on the way."

Chapter Eleven

Donny was up early. And he had company. His usual ETA at the gate was sometime after ten because he didn't like to have breakfast during the early morning rush. Also, because he was a fabulous diva who needed his beauty sleep.

His ski outfit was different too. Yesterday, he looked like he'd gone back to the 1960s in his tight black ski pants and thigh-length red jacket that buckled at the waist. Today, Kennedy praised the lord almighty because who didn't love a white man over sixty in a yellow Lycra one-piece ski suit with a red scarf, hat, and gloves? If Ronald McDonald went on a ski holiday…

Kennedy squealed with glee. "Oh, my God, Donny, you just made my day."

"*The Spy Who Loved Me*, 1977." He spread his arms, poles in hand and shouted, "James Bond ain't got nothin on me!"

James Bond? Oh God. Kennedy swallowed the words, Ronald McDonald. She pushed them right back down her throat and gave him a thumbs up. "Killin' it, Donny. What brings you out so early?"

The woman next to him raised her goggles. "Lola," Kennedy exclaimed. "I mean, Sheriff…oh God, I forgot your last name."

"How could you forget her last name?" Donny asked. "She's an Olympian. A champion skier. And today, Lola Johns is all mine."

"For three hours," Lola clarified.

Donny unzipped his suit and pulled out a small brown bag. "This is from Chef Lawrence. He said it'd warm you right up.

Also, after I told him how handsome he was, he said he'd send someone out later with a grilled cheese sandwich."

"Aw, he's so sweet. Will you thank him for me?"

"Given the opportunity, I'll do more than that," he said with a wink. "Oh, and Bridget looked as gorgeous as ever this morning. Sometimes, all we need is a good cry, right, Lola?"

Lola gave him a hesitant nod. "Right, Donny. Now, do you want to give Kennedy the secret password so we can get going?"

Donny leaned in and lowered his voice. "Time is a tickin, and if I'm going to score myself some hot male skier action, I need Lola to help me up my schuss-bada-boom game."

"I don't know what that means, but I think your outfit is going to do all the work for you."

Donny made the sign of the cross. "From your lips to God's ears. Oh. The password." He leaned in and whispered, "I have it on very good authority that Bridget watches you from a window on the top floor, but don't tell anyone it came from me." He zipped his lips and lowered his goggles.

It wasn't the password, but it was extremely valuable information. Kennedy opened the gate. "Enjoy your day."

Donny went first. Lola stopped next to Kennedy and adjusted her gloves. It seemed like a stall tactic, so Kennedy broke the silence. "What does it cost to ski with you for three hours?"

"This is just a trial thing that Harriet set up. We'll see how it goes."

"But how much?"

Lola squinted. "I'm embarrassed to say what she's charging folks. Anyway, I should get going."

Kennedy reached for her arm. "Is there something you wanted to say to me? Something along the lines of, wish me luck with Ronald McDonald?"

Lola snickered. "I almost said that out loud when I saw him."

Kennedy gasped. "Me too."

"But, hey. At least I won't lose him on the trail."

"That's a good point. And good luck with the shushy-boom thing."

"Thanks. I have a feeling I'm going to need it."

She pushed off down the trail, and Kennedy shouted, "Whatever you charge, I'm sure it's worth it."

She peeked in the bag and took a whiff of the delicious aroma. "Mmm...chocolate croissants are my fave." She took a bite and casually scanned the top floor of the lodge. She couldn't see anyone, but a part of her wanted to march up there and take Bridget by the hand and drag her to the penthouse so they could fight it out and then make up with cuddles and sweet kisses, followed by hot, passionate sex.

Two things stopped her. One, she didn't dare leave the gate in someone else's hands. Not even Seth. And two, Ingrid's words from the night before had stuck with her. She hoped it was true that this was all Bridget needed from her right now because in reality, she had nothing else to give. She couldn't offer any reassurances that everything would turn out okay. She had no control over anything except the gate. So she'd stay there until Michael or their lawyer showed up and forced her to stop.

She sat on her little stool and took another bite of the croissant, then closed her visor so no one would notice her staring at the windows on the top floor. She stopped chewing when she heard a helicopter.

❖

Kennedy stepped into the cabin and stamped her feet on the rug. "Welcome to Elk Mountain, secret land of the crazies and home of the even crazier."

Michael turned from the window and tucked his hands in his pockets. "Oh my God. It's even worse up close."

Kennedy glanced around. "Huh. And here I thought I'd warmed the place up with my spunky personality and knack for making good coffee."

"I was talking about my sister, the abominable snow astronaut. Even the helicopter pilot had a good chuckle. Oh, and we both know you spend five hundred dollars a month at Starbucks."

She set her helmet on a chair and slid out of her boots. Clearly, Michael wasn't there to do anything but belittle her and make her feel even worse than she already did, but it was in her best interest to stay calm so they could have a reasonable conversation. "Maybe it's the water up here that makes coffee taste better," she said. "And what's so wrong with my outfit? It's perfect for the current weather conditions."

"For one thing, you look ridiculous. And for another, I know what you're doing, Ken."

She pursed her lips and resisted the urge to kick him in the nuts. Besides, it would hurt too much, given her bad toe. "How long are you staying?"

"Does that mean you're planning to stay longer? Ken, you haven't even asked me if I'm a father yet or how Josie is doing. You're so wrapped up in your little fling with Boden's daughter, you've forgotten you have a family who needs you."

"I'm only here because you sent me here. The fact that it hasn't gone as perfectly as you'd planned is your fault. Maybe next time, don't send your sister to do your dirty work." She unzipped her snowsuit and stepped out, then hung it on a hook by the door. Yes, she wanted details about the baby, but first, she needed to have a few family questions of her own answered. She also needed to warm up with a hot cup of tea, so she filled the kettle and put it on the stove.

"You're limping," Michael said.

"Yeah, that's the least of my worries." She pointed at the table. "How about we sit down, and you tell me if the name Ingrid Berg rings a bell." She took a seat, but Michael hesitated. "So you do know about her and Dad. God, Michael. You really thought it would be okay to send me up here not knowing a goddamned thing about all of the shit that's been going down for years?"

Michael finally sat. "Honestly, I thought you'd cozy up by the fire all weekend and read those gay romances you love so much." He glanced around the cabin. "It was all very different in my head."

"Yeah. Mine too."

When the kettle whistled, Michael stood. "I'll get it."

Kennedy pulled her feet off the floor and wrapped her arms around her legs. "You'd like her, Michael. Bridget, I mean. She's not like anyone I've ever dated."

"So you're dating now?" He set a cup in front of her and sat back down.

"No, not exactly. I mean, I'd like to have the chance to date her."

"But you live in Miami, Ken." He reached for her hand. "Your family, including your goddaughter, lives in Miami."

The tears of joy came quickly and so did the need to give her brother a hug. Kennedy stood and opened her arms. "I'm so happy for you, bro. Truly, I am."

He wrapped his arms around her waist, lifted her into the air and swung her around. "She's beautiful, Ken. I can't wait for you to meet her."

Kennedy giggled. "Put me down and show me a picture."

He set her down gently and pulled his phone out of his pocket. "She's why I can't stay. I have to get back to Josie and my little angel."

Kennedy put her hands over her mouth and gasped when she saw her niece for the first time. She took the phone from him and sat. "She's gorgeous. Absolutely gorgeous."

Michael knelt next to her. "Come home for Christmas, Ken. I want you with me when we introduce her to Dad."

It was the right thing to do. Their past might have been all fucked-up, but their future was this little one with the big pink bow on her head. And really, what else was she going to do, other than spend Christmas Day at that gate while Bridget glared at her from some window on the top floor of the lodge? She'd rather be where she was wanted. And loved. Because as much as she liked to think otherwise, Bridget had made it clear that she didn't need or want Kennedy in her life. She wrapped an arm around Michael's shoulder. Too emotional to say the words, she gave him a nod. It was time to go home where she belonged.

❖

It hadn't taken much convincing for Michael to agree that leaving the gate open on the access trail until after the new year was the decent thing to do. He still had dollar signs in his eyes, but that conversation could wait until they were back home.

It was important to Kennedy that the no trespassing sign, small as it was, didn't hinder anyone from using the gate. If she could've removed the entire fence, she would have. Instead, she found a piece of rope in the garage and trudged up the slope to the trail one last time to put the sign off to the side.

It was early enough that most of the guests would still be in the lodge having breakfast. That was a good thing since she had no desire to see anyone. Unfortunately, tying a secure knot in anything other than her own shoelaces wasn't as easy as she'd thought it would be. Was it right over left or left over right? She gave it a good yank, which only seemed to loosen the knot, but maybe if she wrapped the ends all the way around the poles and tucked them in nicely, it would hold. Especially if she didn't yank on it.

Just as she was about to walk away, she heard the now familiar sound of skis swooshing through the snow. Since it had been bitter cold on the mountain, everyone skied bundled up in hats, scarves, goggles, and some of them wore full face coverings that made them look like burglars on skis. She'd learned to identify the guests by their parkas because that seemed to be the one thing that didn't change, probably due to the high cost and how much room multiple parkas would take up in a suitcase.

The person skiing toward her wasn't wearing a parka she recognized, so she turned away and fiddled with the rope in hope that they'd ski right on by. As they sped past, a feeling of anger welled up inside her. Had she still been manning the gate, the new guest would've stopped, and she would've had to explain that there was a secret password and blah, blah, blah. It all seemed so juvenile and stupid and meaningless that she wanted to scream, but someone else had stopped behind her.

"Where's the astronaut suit? I mean…sorry. I didn't mean to call it that."

It was Lola, so Kennedy turned. "You can call it that. Everyone else does."

Lola lifted her goggles and furrowed her brow. "You look like you're going somewhere."

"So do you." It was a terse reply, but what did it matter now? She wouldn't be missed by Lola. Or Bridget, for that matter. Maybe a few of the guests would miss seeing her at the gate, but they'd be gone soon anyway. She did find a slight bit of satisfaction in knowing that the last time she'd be seen by anyone on Elk Mountain, she looked normal. She wasn't wearing her dad's old clothes or an unflattering snowsuit. Nor was her hair doing its own crazy thing on top of her head. She'd finally made use of the clothes and toiletries she'd purchased right before everything went to shit for the flight home. But who was she kidding? Aside from a few nice moments with Bridget, her entire time on Elk Mountain had been one gigantic shitshow. And even though her tight jeans and even tighter ski sweater were meant for Bridget's enjoyment, she'd take what little bit of pride she could in knowing that Lola could at least report that she'd gone out looking pretty damn good.

One of the guests skied up to them and said, "Wowza." He took his goggles off and gave Kennedy a slow whistle. "Had I known there was an extremely hot woman under that puffy suit, I would've spent a little more time whispering that password into her helmet."

There it was again. The stupid password Kennedy had been making people use for days. She felt like such a fool now; she could barely look at them. The easier thing to do would be to turn around and pretend she was still working on that knot.

Lola sidestepped over and lowered her voice. "Can I fix that for you?" She untied the rope, and with a few quick flicks of her wrists, she tied it into a much better knot and yanked on it. "There you go. All secure now."

"Great," Kennedy said. "I think my job here is done."

She headed back down the trail, eager to get away, but Lola skied along next to her. "Are you leaving the mountain?"

"Yep." She pointed to the helicopter where Michael was waiting for her. "That's my ride out."

Lola stopped, but Kennedy kept going. There was nothing left to say. Not out loud, anyway. Under her breath was another matter. "*Hasta la vista*, motherfuckers."

By the time she got to the helipad, her anger had turned into sadness. She was angry-sad, if that was a thing. But she didn't dare let Michael see any of it. She couldn't risk him believing that Bridget *wasn't* worthy of the kindness and consideration that Kennedy hoped to convince him of.

He offered his hand and helped her into the helicopter. "Everything good?"

She gave him a smile. "All good, bro."

As they lifted into the air, she kept her eyes on the balcony where she'd first seen the redheaded stranger who'd turned her world upside down. Unsurprisingly, Bridget had seemingly chosen not to watch Kennedy's departure. Once the balcony was out of view, she turned to Michael and said, "Show me that picture of my goddaughter again."

❖

There was a new ornament on the Christmas tree in the lobby. Bridget didn't need to get closer to know what it was, but she did anyway because—and this was something she hadn't known about herself until recently—she was into self-torture. It was a paper cutout one of the kids had made. In fact, there were several different versions of the same image hanging on the tree. One had drawn the astronaut on skis. On another, the astronaut was riding their bronze elk statue like a bucking bronco. That one made her giggle. High on the tree, another astronaut was giving a little boy a hug.

Low on the tree, another astronaut hung, but on this one, the kid had drawn a little arrow on the bottom right corner of their ornament, indicating that it should be turned over. And that was when the self-torture thing really kicked in because like an idiot, Bridget bent and flipped the ornament around. Written in crayon it said, *Kendy loves Brijet*. Of course, their names were misspelled, but what kid would know how to spell a hard name like Kennedy? And it made total sense that Bridget would be spelled with a J instead of a D and G.

"Such sweet gestures," her mom said, stepping next to her. "Merry Christmas Eve, sweetheart."

Bridget took the cup of wassail and clinked it against her mom's. "Merry Christmas Eve, Mom." She took a sip of the warm deliciousness and then another. She could do without the holiday eggnog they served in the lobby every year, but the spiced apple cider and orange drink had always been a favorite. It didn't hurt that her mom had given her the rum version, either. Maybe it would take the edge off of how badly she felt about everything.

"You're thinking about her, aren't you?" Her mom asked.

"How could I not when she's all over this tree?"

"I think it's safe to say, she's everywhere you look but nowhere to be found. That's how it works when you miss someone you love. You search for memories of them that make you smile, but it doesn't take away the ache in your heart. The longing to touch them. Feel their skin and take in their unique scent. It's all very visceral for us humans. And we don't always get to choose who we end up loving so deeply. Sometimes, the universe chooses for us, and I can't help but wonder why a Boden and a Fleming are in this situation again. Why is Jerry's daughter so clearly in love with my daughter?"

Her mom looked at Bridget as if waiting for an answer. Bridget turned back to the tree and took another sip. "She's not in love with me. If she was, she wouldn't have left without saying good-bye, don't you think?"

"Under that logic, you couldn't possibly love her, given the way you ignored her while she was out at that gate. Even after I told you about my history with Jerry, you still didn't go out there and sort it all out."

Ire rose in Bridget's chest. She couldn't shout at her mom. Not in a lobby full of people on Christmas Eve. So she turned to her and calmly said, "I'm not Dad, Mom. He took all the abuse Jerry dished out because he felt guilty. Well, I don't have that guilt. I didn't break up a marriage. And I shouldn't have to fight Jerry's kids to keep what's mine." She punctuated it with a wide-eyed look that was code for, this conversation is over, and turned back to the tree.

"I wonder what Christmas is like in Miami," her mom said.

Bridget threw a hand in the air and then downed the rest of her wassail in one gulp. "I'm going to need another if you plan on keeping this up."

Her mom took the cup. "I guess it's understandable that you'd want to get drunk tonight. Hell, even Harriet thinks you blew it big time."

She gave Bridget a wink and walked away, leaving her to wonder who else her mom had discussed it with. Lola? Chef Lawrence? Maybe she'd sidled up to the bar and hashed it out with Kevin while he made her a dirty martini. Her face went hot while thinking about the possibilities. She decided she should find someplace more private to stew, but when she turned around, Harriet was right there. "I have to get home to my mother and sister before they think I've abandoned them on Christmas and decide to drive home in a snowstorm just to prove a point."

"Of course," Bridget said. "I didn't even know you were still here."

Harriet shrugged. "I'm not surprised. You've been in your own world lately. Oh, and there's a call on line two I'd like you to handle. See you in a couple of days."

Bridget hadn't noticed it earlier, but Harriet seemed down. She followed her to the door. "Harriet, you're right. I haven't been myself lately. I hope you and your family have a wonderful Christmas."

Harriet gave her a pat on the arm. "Don't worry, honey. You'll make it up to me with some paid time off in the spring. And don't forget to answer line two. Merry Christmas."

Bridget watched until Harriet was safely down the steps and then went to the front desk and picked up the phone. "This is Bridget. How can I help you?"

"Um...you called me."

"I'm sorry?" Bridget's heart dropped into her stomach. "Kennedy?"

"Why do you sound surprised? Harriet called and said you wanted to talk to me. Look, I need to get back to my family."

"No! No, wait," Bridget said. "Just wait." It was a shock to hear Kennedy's voice again, but in a good way that had Bridget smiling, even though she could hardly breathe. "Kennedy, stay on the line while I change phones, okay? Don't hang up."

She didn't wait for a reply. She rushed into her office and shut the door, then picked up the phone. "Okay, hi. I'm alone now. I mean, it's quiet in here. We can talk. Kennedy?"

"I'm here."

"This was Harriet's doing. She told me I had a call on line two, but I had no idea it was you. Not that I'm upset it's you, just... surprised."

"Harriet did this? I find that hard to believe since she seemed to hate me."

Bridget sat behind her desk. "Wait. You believe me, don't you?"

"You know, I remember saying something along those same lines to you. In fact, I begged you to believe me, but you just walked away."

"I did," Bridget admitted. "And I regret that and so much more. Kennedy, I..." Bridget put a hand over her mouth to stop it from quivering. She took a breath and said, "Not even five minutes ago, my mom was telling me that sometimes, we don't get to choose who we love, it just happens. And while it's really inconvenient for me to have fallen for a Fleming, it's my current reality."

After an achingly long pause, Kennedy said, "You're in love with my brother?"

Bridget laughed. And the realization hit her that she hadn't really laughed since the night she and Kennedy were in that dumb little room in the bed and breakfast. She could've held it in, but she continued to laugh until she heard Kennedy giggling too. "You're such a smartass," she said. "But you're also my hero. And I miss you, Kennedy. I really miss you."

"Does that mean I can get your phone number? I mean, I think I've worked hard enough for it, don't you?"

"Yeah," Bridget whispered. "I do."

"Good. Because you need to see pictures of my niece. She's gorgeous and has the chubbiest little cheeks. Oh, and Bridget, leave my brother to me. We'll work this whole land thing out, okay? One way or another, I'll make sure you don't lose what's rightfully yours."

Bridget grinned. "You really are my hero, Kennedy Fleming."

"Okay, but there isn't any kind of weird rule where you don't sleep with your heroes, right?"

Bridget cleared her throat. "Actually, I think it's a requirement. You know, so we can confirm that the hero aspect applies to the bedroom as well."

"Oh, you are in so much trouble, Bridget Berg. You should probably get in better shape. Work on your cardio or something."

Just the thought of the two of them in bed together sent a jolt of electricity through Bridget's body. "Will do, hero. Will do."

❖

Three Months Later

There was no need for a helicopter this time around. The roads were clear, the sun was shining, and according to Bridget, some people were even skiing in shorts and T-shirts. Kennedy couldn't picture it. Not after the harsh weather she'd experienced the last time she was there. Also, she didn't trust that the good weather would hold once she was on the mountain. It didn't matter if she got stranded due to a freak springtime storm this time around, but she was determined to be ready for it, which was why she might have shopped every winter clearance sale on the internet and managed to pack all her purchases into two large suitcases. She might have sent a few last-minute items directly to the lodge as well, and yes, it was overkill, or as she liked to think of it, over-survival.

"Doing okay back there, ma'am? The road is pretty windy from here to the top."

"Fine, thanks," Kennedy said. She took the complimentary water bottle from its holder and took a sip. It reminded her of the crystal-clear tap water in her dad's cabin, which then reminded her of Ingrid. Sweet Ingrid, who'd secretly traveled to Florida to visit Kennedy's dad in the nursing home but was caught red-handed when Kennedy showed up at the same time. She'd said she felt the need to apologize and wish him well into the next life. It was more than he probably deserved but kind nonetheless.

The higher they climbed, the more snow and ice was still on the road. Not enough to ski on if one were so inclined, but enough to remind Kennedy of that awful day when she'd tried. It was all a very bittersweet memory now. More sweet than bitter because of who she was about to wrap her arms around. The truth was, she didn't linger on any of the painful memories, not when there was so much to look forward to.

The car pulled up to the lodge, and standing on the top step was Kennedy's Viking Queen, Goddess of the North, soon-to-be sex slave. Okay, maybe not the last one, but a girl could dream. She unrolled her window so she could get a better look. Grinning from ear to ear, Bridget bounded down the steps and opened the car door. Since it was an SUV, they were eye to eye, but it seemed like Bridget's eyes were everywhere, taking in all of Kennedy. When their eyes finally locked, she said, "We have seventy-two hours and twenty-six minutes, and we're not wasting a single second of it." She took a breath and paused as she touched Kennedy's cheek. "Maybe just a few while I try to remember why I ever let you leave."

Kennedy took her hand and kissed it, then held it against her cheek. "Promise me we won't go backward unless it's to laugh about the ridiculousness of it all."

With a straight face, Bridget reached behind her and put her radio up to her mouth. "Hungry Hippo is on the premises. I repeat. Hungry Hippo is on the premises." She lowered the radio and said, "You mean, like that?"

Kennedy snickered. "That wasn't exactly what I had in mind."

"Well, maybe you meant something more like this." Bridget moved out of the way, and standing on the top step were Seth and Harriet, both dressed in white snowmobile suits with matching helmets.

Kennedy leaned out of the car and shouted, "Oh, very funny, guys." She shrieked with laughter when they faced each other and proceeded to do what looked like the moonwalk. Seth wasn't half-bad, but Harriet's version was more of a backward jog. A car horn blared behind them several times. Bridget put her hands on her hips and shouted, "You're too late."

Lola rushed up to the car holding a beautifully wrapped bouquet of flowers. "It's never too late for irises." She gave them to Bridget and in a loud whisper, said, "I filled in the card for you. It says, I dare you to love me." She winked at Kennedy and backed away.

Bridget placed them on Kennedy's lap. "It's not really a dare, per se. More like, a shameless plea."

Kennedy leaned forward and took Bridget's face in her hands. "Okay, fine. I'll love you, but only if you moonwalk me to your bedroom."

❖

Months of imagining, fantasizing, and yes, a little bit of sexting, hadn't prepared Bridget for how amazing it would feel to have Kennedy up against a wall, their fingers intertwined above her head. She couldn't say all the things she'd longed to say and also have that velvet tongue tease her with little licks. Words would have to wait because she needed to devour that tongue. Make it hers. Marry it. Adopt little babies with it.

She took it into her mouth and caused a shared, low moan to reverberate through their lips. Kennedy's hot, bated breath, her hips jutting forward, the tiny whimpers, and her fingers gripping Kennedy's for dear life—all of it had caused some sort of brain malfunction.

She had a desperate need to show Kennedy how much she'd longed for this moment. How much she'd thought about where her hands would go first. What words she'd whisper in her ear. How many kisses it would take to get from her breast to her belly button. She'd contemplated all of it. Made love to her over and over in her head.

It was all a blur now. Her entire life was a blur. All she wanted to see or hear or touch or taste was…Kennedy. But her emotions had risen so far up into her chest, she had to pull away from the kiss to catch her breath.

With their bodies still pressed against each other, she could feel the rapid contraction and expansion of Kennedy's lungs. "I'm sorry," she whispered. Because she knew she wasn't the only one who was on fire. And she shouldn't have stopped.

Kennedy cupped her cheeks and whispered, "Talk to me."

Hard as she tried, Bridget couldn't keep the tears at bay. "Sorry. The weight of this seems to be hitting me all at once."

"You mean the part where we almost lost each other? Or the part where months of pining for each other has led to this moment, and it's even better than we thought it would be? Or maybe—"

Bridget covered Kennedy's mouth with her hand. "All of that. And maybe a little bit of fear."

Kennedy took that hand and circled a finger with her tongue. "I'm just going to make out with your finger while you process your insecurities."

Bridget laughed under her breath. "You always could make me laugh. Even when I didn't want to, I was laughing on the inside."

"I knew it," Kennedy exclaimed. She took Bridget's hand and led her down the hall to the bedroom. "I'm in this," she said. "You know that, right?"

"Define, this."

"Up to my neck in all things Bridget Berg." She let go of Bridget's hand and sauntered into the room like Sharon Stone would have if she was staying in the penthouse suite.

Still standing in the doorway, Bridget cleared her throat and said, "You have a very sexy walk when you're not limping."

Why did everything about Kennedy seem twice as sexy now? She was still herself. Funny. Cheeky. But she had an air of confidence about her now. Or maybe she'd had it all along, but it had been tempered with baggy clothes and a helplessness that certainly wasn't there now.

Bridget remembered when she'd opened Lola's car door and found Kennedy looking like an abandoned dog, dirty snow melting on her face, her expression so forlorn Bridget couldn't possibly have turned her away, and she realized that she'd only seen glimpses of Kennedy until now.

The person standing before her was whole. And a sight to behold. She stood at the end of the bed and folded her arms. "Do you have any idea how much I've thought about this moment?" she asked.

Bridget gave her a nod. "Yeah. I think I do."

"Then, what can I say to make you believe in us? Because I've heard it in your voice lately. You're wondering how we'll make this work."

"It's kind of up in the air, don't you think?"

Kennedy shook her head. "Nothing about you is up in the air for me."

She looked so gorgeous standing there with one leg to the side like a badass. Bridget wasn't sure she had any badass left inside her. Not enough to keep a woman like Kennedy Fleming happy. Her doubts seemed to suck all the air out of the room, along with the fire they'd ignited by the front door. "I want you," she said. "But I don't know how to keep you."

Kennedy sauntered back to her. "Then let me be the one to keep you."

Had she gotten prettier? Bridget had always thought she was beautiful, but now, standing in front of her and staring with those big brown eyes, she seemed so far out of Bridget's league, it scared her. Because for Bridget, what about her life wasn't up in the air? They'd had a stellar few months, due to a record-breaking amount of snowfall, and thanks to Kennedy, the access trail remained open to their guests, but the ownership issue had yet to be resolved. Everything felt precarious, but she couldn't leave Kennedy hanging, so she took her hand and said, "I'm so sorry. I just have so many thoughts running through my head right now."

Kennedy stepped even closer. "It's just us here. Just you and me. Kennedy loves Bridget, remember?"

"I remember."

"Good. And we don't have to do anything if you need some time. But you should probably know that when you kissed me just now, it did things to me." Kennedy let go of her hand and sat on the bed. She leaned back on her arms, her legs crossed.

Bridget's throat went dry. "What kind of things?"

"Hot, wet things." She uncrossed and then crossed her legs again. "What I'm telling you is, if talking is all you want right now, then it should probably be dirty talk."

"You're just trying to get me out of my own way. How wet?"

"I can hear us fucking in my head. So, yeah. Pretty wet. Is it working?"

Bridget took a few steps closer. "Yeah, it's working. I haven't told you this, but I've thought about your breasts a lot. What they look like. What they feel like. How they'll feel against my tongue."

Kennedy leaned forward. "They'll feel rock hard against your tongue. I know that because they're rock hard right now. And you're doing a stellar job with the dirty talk."

A wave of relief that she hadn't ruined the moment washed over Bridget. "About that wetness you mentioned? I want you to spread your legs for me so I can see all of you, and taste all of you, go inside you and..." She paused and bit her bottom lip.

Kennedy's eyes widened. "Oh, don't you dare stop now."

Bridget urged Kennedy back onto the bed and climbed on top of her. Whatever fears she had dissipated when she saw the mix of passion and adoration in Kennedy's eyes. She leaned down and whispered, "It won't be the last time you say that tonight."

Their lips locked in a passionate kiss, Kennedy pulled Bridget's blouse up and over her head. Bridget got on her knees and took it the rest of the way off. Kennedy's eyes grazed over her upper body. She reached out and said, "Pull me up, you fucking gorgeous goddess of the north."

Bridget giggled and offered her hands. "Where did that nickname come from?"

"It was my first thought when I saw you on that balcony. Can I?"

She'd slid her fingers under Bridget's bra strap, ready to slide it off her shoulder. Bridget took that soft, slender hand and held it against her cheek, then placed it on her breast and whispered, "Mine are hard too."

Kennedy massaged through the bra and then slid the strap down, followed by the other strap, revealing Bridget's breasts. She stared with a look of awe and then met Bridget's gaze. "You're so beautiful, you take my breath away."

Bridget had long ago stopped feeling self-conscious about her smaller breasts. With age and wisdom, she'd realized they were the perfect size for her tall, lanky body. She'd also learned what a turn-on it was to play with them in front of a lover.

When Kennedy reached up to touch her, she swatted her hand away. "Me first."

Kennedy leaned back on her elbows and said, "By all means."

Bridget took her time getting her finger wet on her tongue and then circling her hard nipple with it. She rolled both nipples between her fingers and massaged them until she threw her head back, satisfied that she'd sufficiently reignited that white-hot fire burning between them.

Kennedy's hands slid up her sides, thumbs grazing her nipples. She opened her eyes just in time to see Kennedy's tongue flick one nipple and then the other. It was a tease. She wanted Bridget to ask for more. Not ask, beg. Bridget knew this because Kennedy's eyes were locked on hers, waiting.

Bridget took her head with both hands and pressed into her until she felt a nibble and then a suck that made her gasp and whisper, "Oh my God, yes."

Kennedy's fingernails scraped down Bridget's back while she sucked and nibbled on both breasts. Bridget rocked against her, but she couldn't get much friction through her pants. She needed more contact. She needed both of them naked. And she needed Kennedy on top of her.

She rolled onto her back so she could unzip her pants but Kennedy swatted her hands away. "Me first," she said.

"Okay, but I need to see you."

Kennedy got up and kicked her boots off. "Which part of me do you want to see first?"

Bridget had never been given the choice before, but she didn't hesitate with her answer. "Your pussy."

Kennedy gave her a sly grin and unzipped her jeans. She slid them over her hips, let them drop to the floor, and stepped out of them. Bridget sat up and waved her over. "Let me do the rest."

The black panties were hi-cut and lacy. Bridget put her hands on Kennedy's hips and took a moment to fully appreciate her beauty. She rested her forehead on her tummy and slid her hands under the panties and squeezed her backside. She massaged her ass and inhaled deeply, taking in her scent.

Kennedy ran her fingers into Bridget's hair and urged her head up so they were eye to eye. "Can we take a moment to appreciate that your hands are on my ass?"

"I've thought about it so much."

"Does it measure up?"

"Off the charts sexy." Bridget spread her fingers and palmed both cheeks, pulling them apart slightly.

Kennedy tightened the grip she had on Bridget's hair and said, "God, you turn me on."

It was time to remove those sexy black panties so Bridget moved her hands back to Kennedy's hips. She pushed her sweater up enough so she could lean in and kiss her left hip, and then her right. She circled her belly button with her tongue while sliding the panties down a bit.

She didn't want to take them off in one quick motion; she wanted to go slow. She wanted to tease until it turned into delicious torture for both of them. She peppered her stomach with wet, firm kisses until she felt the edge of her panties, and then she pulled back and glanced upward. Kennedy had thrown her head back, so Bridget slid the panties lower but still didn't let them drop to the floor.

Bridget whimpered at the sight before her. With her thumbs, she spread Kennedy open just enough so she could blow air directly on her clit. Kennedy moaned in response, so Bridget got closer and did it again, but this time, she followed it up with a flick of her tongue, and then a longer, deeper, swipe.

Bridget desperately wanted to let go, but the desire for sweet torture was even greater. Kennedy had other ideas, though. And she didn't seem to care for the way her sexy panties prevented her from spreading her legs.

She took a step back and removed them herself. "I can only take so much," she said. Then she straddled Bridget and whispered, "Fuck me."

Bridget moaned. She was so turned on she thought she might spontaneously combust. Not all women enjoyed penetration, which was a damn shame since she had long, talented fingers. She wrapped an arm around Kennedy's hips and slid the tip of her thumb over her clit. "Tell me again what you need," she said.

Kennedy's entire body flinched at the touch, followed by light thrusting of her pelvis. She pulled Bridget's head back by her hair and whispered into her mouth, "I need you to fuck me."

When she entered her, Bridget also wanted to be kissing her, so she offered her tongue and Kennedy took it into her mouth. They kissed until Kennedy threw her head back and cried out in pleasure from Bridget's first thrust.

The second thrust made her grab Bridget's shoulders to brace herself as her hips bucked. Their eyes locked for a moment, but Bridget didn't stop. She drove in harder and deeper with every heavy breath that Kennedy took until Kennedy grabbed Bridget's head and pulled it to her chest. Bridget slowed down, but she stayed inside. "Will you take off your sweater?"

Kennedy pulled it over her head and pushed her bra down around her waist. Bridget took a hardened nipple into her mouth and rolled it around with her tongue. Again, Kennedy held on to her head, adding pressure as she sucked and licked.

Bridget wanted to stay right where she was, worshipping Kennedy's gorgeous body. She let go of her hips so she could hold a soft breast while also moving her fingers around inside her. She hit a spot that made Kennedy gasp and beg for more with her eyes. Bridget obliged by tapping the same spot and rubbing her clit with her thumb. Kennedy gave her a nod and closed her eyes. This would be the first orgasm of many that she hoped to give Kennedy. The first in a lifetime of orgasms if wishes came true.

Kennedy's hip thrusts became more forceful. Her breaths, shallow. The grip she had on Bridget's shoulders tightened almost to the point of causing pain, and then for a second, there was stillness and silence, followed by every swear word Kennedy could seemingly come up with as she came hard against Bridget's thumb.

❖

Kennedy needed water and more air in her lungs. But more than either of those things, she needed Bridget to be completely naked. The only problem was, she really liked the feel of Bridget's hands on her ass. And her fingers. God, those fingers felt magical inside her. She felt safe and loved. And she really couldn't think of a better post-sex combination. It had all the elements of what she'd longed for and finally found.

She raised her head off Bridget's shoulder and cupped her cheeks. Those blue eyes looked bright and happy. Her face seemed to glow, even though she wasn't the one who'd just orgasmed. "Are you happy?" Kennedy asked, believing she already knew the answer.

Bridget grinned. "My hands are on your ass. How could I possibly be anything but?"

"Good. But I'm not so happy."

Her smile faded, and her grip on Kennedy's ass loosened. "You're not?"

"No. Because I showed you my pussy, but you haven't shown me yours." Kennedy rolled off her and lay sideways on the bed.

Bridget stood but didn't turn. "Did you know that skiing gives you a great ass?" She glanced over her shoulder and waited for an answer.

Kennedy bit her lip. "I kinda figured that out already. You know, from all the staring at it I did the last time I was here."

"Right. I remember catching you a few times." She pushed her pants down and let them drop to the floor. "So far so good?"

It was perfect. Muscular. Round. Kennedy reached out and squeezed the air. "I can't be sure until I touch it, but I can't quite reach."

Bridget turned around. "You'll get your chance." She pushed her pink panties down and crawled onto the bed.

Kennedy urged her onto her back and lay on top of her. "You didn't give me very long to admire the freckles on your thighs.

Is there any chance you'd let me play connect the dots while I'm down there?"

"Oh, I think you'll have plenty to do. And don't you dare write on me with a ball point pen."

Kennedy laughed. "I was teasing." She gently nudged Bridget's knees. "Open your legs more."

Bridget complied, and Kennedy settled between her legs, pressing their bodies together. She scanned Bridget's face and ran her index finger over her bottom lip. "You really are happy, aren't you?"

"The happiest I've felt in a long time."

"If back in December, someone told you that I'd be lying naked on top of you in late March, would you have believed it?"

"I find so much of this whole thing unbelievable and yet so exactly right because it brought us to this moment where you're lying on top of me naked in late March." She spread her legs even farther apart and wrapped them around Kennedy's hips. "Can we stay in bed all weekend?"

"You read my mind." Kennedy raised up on her hands so she could more easily create some friction between them. She pressed down on Bridget and was met with upward pressure. It was a slow rhythm that allowed for intense eye contact. Kennedy would've given anything to read Bridget's mind in that moment. Was she repeating the same three words in her head that Kennedy was?

Bridget cupped Kennedy's breasts. She massaged the nipples with her thumbs. Wetness had built up between their legs. It was time for Kennedy to move lower. She slid down a bit and took a nipple between her teeth. Bridget's hand wrapped around her head. She kissed her way lower, moaning when she felt how wet Bridget was, and plunged her tongue inside her as far as she could.

Bridget rocked her hips. "Yes," she cried out. "God, yes."

Kennedy entered her again, this time with two fingers and the tip of her tongue flicking over her clit. Bridget cried out again, this time something unintelligible but with just as much feeling. After a few thrusts, Kennedy removed her fingers and wrapped both hands around Bridget's thighs so she could focus on her swollen clit.

She wanted the build-up to last so the pressure was light. Bridget shouted, "Fuck," and bucked her hips even harder. She seemed to want more, but Kennedy didn't give it to her. Bridget reached for her hand, and she intertwined their fingers.

She wanted to see it. She wanted to watch Bridget come, so she kept her eyes open. Bridget's head was flat against the pillow, her neck red from straining. Her breasts swayed with every buck of her hips. And their hands were gripped so tightly, they'd turned white around the knuckles. It was a beautiful sight. One forever etched in her memory.

Bridget came hard. She squeezed Kennedy's head between her legs and raised up, then fell back onto the bed. Her breathing slowed, and she sat up and urged Kennedy up too. Bridget took her face in her hands and kissed her lips, then her cheeks, then her lips again.

Kennedy pushed her back down and lay on top of her again, her head resting on her chest. "What have you done to me? I can't even muster the strength to hold you," Bridget said.

"That's okay. I'm holding you."

"I know," Bridget whispered. "I can feel it."

❖

The breakfast crowd bustled around them, but all Bridget wanted to focus on was the woman sitting across from her. Kennedy's hair had grown long enough to part on the side and have bangs swoop across her forehead. Her eyes were bright. Her coy smile, sexy. She picked up her coffee and took a sip, then left it in front of her mouth. Her eyes crinkled, so Bridget knew she was grinning. "What," she asked.

"I was just remembering our first kiss on the snowmobile. I was so hot for you. Also crazy about you but definitely turned on by you."

Bridget reached for her hand. "I liked how tightly you held me."

Kennedy put her cup down and leaned in. "If only you could've told me that at the time."

Bridget shook her head. "There was too much at stake for me. I had too much to lose."

"And now?"

Bridget started to answer, but Kennedy's phone went off. She picked it up and said, "Crap. I thought I'd have more time to explain."

"Explain?" Bridget's heart sank. Was this bad news? She couldn't handle any more bad news, especially if it meant Kennedy had to leave early.

Kennedy stood and offered her hand. "Walk with me? I have something to show you."

Bridget followed her through the lobby and out the front door. Neither of them had coats, but it was a beautiful, sunny morning. Once they were down the steps, Kennedy reached for her hand and grinned. "Where are we going?" Bridget asked.

"I have to let someone into the cabin."

Kennedy looked so cute in her fur-lined snow boots and ski sweater that Bridget had a sudden urge to grab her. Kennedy melted in her arms, and right there in front of the lodge, they shared a kiss that sent Bridget's heart into overdrive. "What if I can't let you go back home on Sunday?" she asked.

Kennedy's phone went off again. She took Bridget by the hand. "C'mon. We need to get down there."

"Okay, but you didn't answer."

"What are you going to do, tie me to a chair?"

Bridget shrugged. "If you're into that, sure. I mean, whatever it takes." She stopped short. "Who's that?"

"Oh, that? I just had some things shipped here. It's no big deal, really."

"Ken, that's a moving truck."

"Is it? Yeah, I guess it is." She turned to Bridget. "The thing is, I really hate the furniture in my dad's cabin, and since I sold my condo in Miami and used it to pay off Michael—"

Bridget grabbed her by the shoulders. "What are you saying?"

Kennedy put her hands on Bridget's cheeks. "What do you hope I'm saying? Because whatever it is, you're probably right."

"It sounds like you're saying I won't lose the lodge, which is amazing, but it also sounds like I won't have to tie you to a chair."

"Yes. And no. I mean, no, you aren't going to lose the lodge because I will officially own that strip of land soon. And no, you won't have to tie me to a chair because the love of my life is here on this crazy big mountain."

Bridget wrapped her arms around Kennedy's shoulders and held her close. "Don't mess with me right now. My emotions are way too high for that, and you specifically said you were only here for the weekend."

"True. I guess I was giving myself an out if things didn't seem the same between us. And if that was the case, I was still ready to give you that land so you wouldn't ever feel like you were being held hostage by a Fleming again."

Bridget pulled back and held on to Kennedy's face. "You'd do that for me?"

"I would."

Bridget kissed her and pulled her close again. "Thank God the sex was hot."

Kennedy laughed. "I had no doubts about that."

Bridget kept her arm firmly wrapped around Kennedy as they walked down the hill to her driveway. "So are we talking Miami chic? Like, lots of flamingos and palm trees?"

"That's not Miami chic, that's Miami kitsch. And just so you know, what I've done isn't completely free of charge."

"It isn't?"

"Well, I had to give Michael his half of what he would've gotten for the land, and then I convinced him to throw in the cabin. But I'm going to need a job so I can keep the lights and heat on."

"Oh," Bridget said. "We have an opening in the kitchen. Our dishwasher just quit."

Kennedy gave her a side-eye. "Uh. Huh. I was hoping for something in upper management. Something where I can ogle the boss most of the day. Oh, and when all the snow is gone, I'll need to hire someone to remove that ugly outcropping on the roof so we can stand on the balcony of the lodge and gaze at the pretty lights in the canyon."

Bridget stopped at the driveway while Kennedy went ahead to talk to the truck driver. It had seemed impossible to overcome all that had happened between their families before they'd met. Impossible to reconcile the past with having some sort of future together. But Bridget had underestimated the incredible woman standing before her. She wouldn't ever make that mistake again.

She watched Kennedy intently, knowing that one day, she'd probably choose a special place to propose. A place that meant something to both of them. Maybe it would be where they'd had their first kiss, or even their second kiss in that silly little pantry. Maybe it would be on the trail that had almost torn them apart. Or maybe it would be a place they'd never been before.

Wherever it happened didn't matter. All that mattered was that it happened sooner rather than later. Because Bridget had found the love of her life. And she was never letting her go.

About the Author

Elle Spencer is the author of several best-selling lesbian romances, including *Casting Lacey*, a Goldie finalist. She is a hopeless romantic and firm believer in true love, although she knows the path to happily ever after is rarely an easy one—not for her and not for her characters.

When she's not writing, Elle is getting vaccinated, working on home improvement projects, dining in fancy restaurants (well, she used to anyway, pre-Covid). She loves to entertain family and friends, but they never visit anymore because COVID. She also loves football, gambling on football, and drinking while gambling on football. She used to love Christmas, but that shit's lonely as hell now. Does anyone ever read these bios? Didn't think so. Anyway, none of that is true, or maybe all of it is. You decide ;)

Elle grew up in Denver, and she and her wife now live in Southern California.

Books Available from Bold Strokes Books

A Long Way to Fall by Elle Spencer. A ski lodge, two strong-willed women, and a family feud that brings them together, but will it also tear them apart? (978-1-63679-005-3)

Barnabas Bopwright Saves the City by J. Marshall Freeman. When he uncovers a terror plot to destroy the city he loves, 15-year-old Barnabas Bopwright realizes it's up to him to save his home and bring deadly secrets into the light before it's too late. (978-1-63679-152-4)

Forever by Kris Bryant. When Savannah Edwards is invited to be the next bachelorette on the dating show When Sparks Fly, she'll show the world that finding true love on television can happen. (978-1-63679-029-9)

Ice on Wheels by Aurora Rey. All's fair in love and roller derby. That's Riley Fauchet's motto, until a new job lands her at the same company—and on the same team—as her rival Brooke Landry, the frosty jammer for the Big Easy Bruisers. (978-1-63679-179-1)

Inherit the Lightning by Bud Gundy. Darcy O'Brien and his sisters learn they are about to inherit an immense fortune, but a family mystery about to unravel after seventy years threatens to destroy everything. (978-1-63679-199-9)

Perfect Rivalry by Radclyffe. Two women set out to win the same career-making goal, but it's love that may turn out to be the final prize. (978-1-63679-216-3)

Something to Talk About by Ronica Black. Can quiet ranch owner Corey Durand give up her peaceful life and allow her feisty new neighbor into her heart? Or will past loss, present suitors, and town gossip ruin a long-awaited chance at love? (978-1-63679-114-2)

With a Minor in Murder by Karis Walsh. In the world of academia, police officer Clare Sawyer and professor Libby Hart team up to solve a murder. (978-1-63679-186-9)

Writer's Block by Ali Vali. Wyatt and Hayley might be made for each other if only they can get through noisy neighbors, the historic society, at-odds future plans, and all the secrets hidden in Wyatt's walls. (978-1-63679-021-3)

Cold Blood by Genevieve McCluer. Maybe together, Kalila and Dorenia have a chance of taking down the vampires who have eluded them all these years. And maybe, in each other, they can find a love worth living for. (978-1-63679-195-1)

Greener Pastures by Aurora Rey. When city girl and CPA Audrey Adams finds herself tending her aunt's farm, will Rowan Marshall—the charming cider maker next door—turn out to be her saving grace or the bane of her existence? (978-1-63679-116-6)

Grounded by Amanda Radley. For a second chance, Olivia and Emily will need to accept their mistakes, learn to communicate properly, and with a little help from five-year-old Henry, fall madly in love all over again. Sequel to Flight SQA016. (978-1-63679-241-5)

Journey's End by Amanda Radley. In this heartwarming conclusion to the Flight series, Olivia and Emily must finally decide what they want, what they need, and how to follow the dreams of their hearts. (978-1-63679-233-0)

Pursued: Lillian's Story by Felice Picano. Fleeing a disastrous marriage to the Lord Exchequer of England, Lillian of Ravenglass reveals an incident-filled, often bizarre, tale of great wealth and power, perfidy, and betrayal. (978-1-63679-197-5)

Secret Agent by Michelle Larkin. CIA agent Peyton North embarks on a global chase to apprehend rogue agent Zoey Blackwood, but her commitment to the mission is tested as the sparks between them ignite and their sizzling attraction approaches a point of no return. (978-1-63555-753-4)

Something Between Us by Krystina Rivers. A decade after her heart was broken under Don't Ask, Don't Tell, Kirby runs into her first love and has to decide if what's still between them is enough to heal her broken heart. (978-1-63679-135-7)

Sugar Girl by Emma L McGeown. Having traded in traditional romance for the perks of Sugar Dating, Ciara Reilly not only enjoys the no-strings-attached arrangement, she's also a hit with her clients. That is until she meets the beautiful entrepreneur Charlie Keller who makes her want to go sugar-free. (978-1-63679-156-2)

The Business of Pleasure by Ronica Black. Editor in chief Valerie Raffield is quickly becoming smitten by Lennox, the graphic artist she's hired to work remotely. But when Lennox doesn't show for their first face-to-face meeting, Valerie's heart and her business may be in jeopardy. (978-1-63679-134-0)

The Hummingbird Sanctuary by Erin Zak. The Hummingbird Sanctuary, Colorado's hottest resort destination: Come for the mountains, stay for the charm, and enjoy the drama as Olive, Eleanor, and Harriet figure out the meaning of true friendship. (978-1-63679-163-0)

The Witch Queen's Mate by Jennifer Karter. Barra and Silvi must overcome their ingrained hatred and prejudice to use Barra's magic and save both their peoples, not just from slavery, but destruction. (978-1-63679-202-6)

With a Twist by Georgia Beers. Starting over isn't easy for Amelia Martini. When the irritatingly cheerful Kirby Dupress comes into her life will Amelia be brave enough to go after the love she really wants? (978-1-63555-987-3)

Business of the Heart by Claire Forsythe. When a hopeless romantic meets a tough-as-nails cynic, they'll need to overcome the wounds of the past to discover that their hearts are the most important business of all. (978-1-63679-167-8)

Dying for You by Jenny Frame. Can Victorija Dred keep an age-old vow and fight the need to take blood from Daisy Macdougall? (978-1-63679-073-2)

Exclusive by Melissa Brayden. Skylar Ruiz lands the TV reporting job of a lifetime, but is she willing to sacrifice it all for the love of her longtime crush, anchorwoman Carolyn McNamara? (978-1-63679-112-8)

Her Duchess to Desire by Jane Walsh. An up-and-coming interior designer seeks to create a happily ever after with an intriguing duchess, proving that love never goes out of fashion. (978-1-63679-065-7)

Murder on Monte Vista by David S. Pederson. Private Detective Mason Adler's angst at turning fifty is forgotten when his "birthday present," the handsome, young Henry Bowtrickle, turns up dead, and it's up to Mason to figure out who did it, and why. (978-1-63679-124-1)

Take Her Down by Lauren Emily Whalen. Stakes are cutthroat, scheming is creative, and loyalty is ever-changing in this queer, female-driven YA retelling of Shakespeare's Julius Caesar. (978-1-63679-089-3)

The Game by Jan Gayle. Ryan Gibbs is a talented golfer, but her guilt means she may never leave her small town, even if Katherine Reese tempts her with competition and passion. (978-1-63679-126-5)

Whereabouts Unknown by Meredith Doench. While homicide detective Theodora Madsen recovers from a potentially career-ending injury, she scrambles to solve the cases of two missing sixteen-year-old girls from Ohio. (978-1-63555-647-6)

Boy at the Window by Lauren Melissa Ellzey. Daniel Kim struggles to hold onto reality while haunted by both his very-present past and his never-present parents. Jiwon Yoon may be the only one who can break Daniel free. (978-1-63679-092-3)

Deadly Secrets by VK Powell. Corporate criminals want whistleblower Jana Elliott permanently silenced, but Rafe Silva will risk everything to keep the woman she loves safe. (978-1-63679-087-9)

Enchanted Autumn by Ursula Klein. When Elizabeth comes to Salem, Massachusetts, to study the witch trials, she never expects to find love—or an actual witch…and Hazel might just turn out to be both. (978-1-63679-104-3)

Escorted by Renee Roman. When fantasy meets reality, will escort Ryan Lewis be able to walk away from a chance at forever with her new client Dani? (978-1-63679-039-8)

Her Heart's Desire by Anne Shade. Two women. One choice. Will Eve and Lynette be able to overcome their doubts and fears to embrace their deepest desire? (978-1-63679-102-9)

My Secret Valentine by Julie Cannon, Erin Dutton, & Anne Shade. Winning the heart of your secret Valentine? These award-winning authors agree, there is no better way to fall in love. (978-1-63679-071-8)

Perilous Obsession by Carsen Taite. When reporter Macy Moran becomes consumed with solving a cold case, will her quest for the truth bring her closer to Detective Beck Ramsey or will her obsession with finding a murderer rob her of a chance at true love? (978-1-63679-009-1)

Reading Her by Amanda Radley. Lauren and Allegra learn love and happiness are right where they least expect it. There's just one problem: Lauren has a secret she cannot tell anyone, and Allegra knows she's hiding something. (978-1-63679-075-6)

The Willing by Lyn Hemphill. Kitty Wilson doesn't know how, but she can bring people back from the dead as long as someone is willing to take their place and keep the universe in balance. (978-1-63679-083-1)

Three Left Turns to Nowhere by Nathan Burgoine, J. Marshall Freeman, & Jeffrey Ricker. Three strangers heading to a convention in Toronto are stranded in rural Ontario, where a small town with a subtle kind of magic leads each to discover what he's been searching for. (978-1-63679-050-3)

Watching Over Her by Ronica Black. As they face the snowstorm of the century, and the looming threat of a stalker, Riley and Zoey just might find love in the most unexpected of places. (978-1-63679-100-5)

#shedeservedit by Greg Herren. When his gay best friend, and high school football star, is murdered, Alex Wheeler is a suspect and must find the truth to clear himself. (978-1-63555-996-5)

Always by Kris Bryant. When a pushy American private investigator shows up demanding to meet the woman in Camila's artwork, instead of introducing her to her great-grandmother, Camila decides to lead her on a wild goose chase all over Italy. (978-1-63679-027-5)

Exes and O's by Joy Argento. Ali and Madison really only have one thing in common. The girl who broke their heart may be the only one who can put it back together. (978-1-63679-017-6)

One Verse Multi by Sander Santiago. Life was good: promotion, friends, falling in love, discovering that the multi-verse is on a fast track to collision—wait, what? Good thing Martin King works for a company that can fix the problem, right…um…right? (978-1-63679-069-5)

Paris Rules by Jaime Maddox. Carly Becker has been searching for the perfect woman all her life, but no one ever seems to be just right until Paige Waterford checks all her boxes, except the most important one—she's married. (978-1-63679-077-0)

Shadow Dancers by Suzie Clarke. In this third and final book in the Moon Shadow series, Rachel must find a way to become the hunter and not the hunted, and this time she will meet Ehsee Yumiko head-on. (978-1-63555-829-6)

The Kiss by C.A. Popovich. When her wife refuses their divorce and begins to stalk her, threatening her life, Kate realizes to protect her new love, Leslie, she has to let her go, even if it breaks her heart. (978-1-63679-079-4)

The Wedding Setup by Charlotte Greene. When Ryann, a big-time New York executive, goes to Colorado to help out with her best friend's wedding, she never expects to fall for the maid of honor. (978-1-63679-033-6)

Velocity by Gun Brooke. Holly and Claire work toward an uncertain future preparing for an alien space mission, and only one thing is for certain, they will have to risk their lives, and their hearts, to discover the truth. (978-1-63555-983-5)

Wildflower Words by Sam Ledel. Lida Jones treks West with her father in search of a better life on the rapidly developing American frontier, but finds home when she meets Hazel Thompson. (978-1-63679-055-8)